TIMBERHILL

DIVERSIONBOOKS

Also by Samantha Harte

Cactus Heart
Autumn Blaze
The Snows of Craggmoor
Angel
Hurricane Sweep
Sweet Whispers
Kiss of Gold
Vanity Blade
Summersea

Diversion Books
A Division of Diversion Publishing Corp.
443 Park Avenue South, Suite 1008
New York, New York 10016
www.DiversionBooks.com

Copyright © 1988 by Samantha Harte
All rights reserved, including the right to reproduce this book or portions thereof
in any form whatsoever.

This is a work of fiction. Names, characters, places and incidents either are the
product of the author's imagination or are used fictitiously. Any resemblance to
actual persons, living or dead, events or locales is entirely coincidental.

For more information, email info@diversionbooks.com

First Diversion Books edition March 2015.
Print ISBN: 978-1-68230-093-0
eBook ISBN: 978-1-62681-662-6

Give of yourself
The whole of your heart.
The day
Is but a breath
And then 'tis gone.
Memory
Made sweet by loss
Is but a shadow.
Dreams
Of tomorrow's promise
Can seduce the soul.
This day is your gift
Unto your love.
Give of your self
The whole of your heart.

One

1793

As the horse-drawn chaise reached the top of Washington Street Hill, Dr. Forrest Clure drew to a stop. Beside him sat his young wife. Spread out before them was the dark silhouette of Philadelphia.

In the distance came the sound of a lone cannon boom. A gloomy cloud of acrid smoke drifted just above the deserted city streets and the smell of camphor and vinegar was in the air. And cutting through the fumes was the putrid scent of disease and death.

Carolyn Clure edged closer to her husband. Her eyes were wide with fear as she stared down the dark street.

"It's much too quiet," she whispered.

"Everyone must be dead," her husband replied, his voice betraying defeat and despair. Carolyn reached out to touch his arm, seeing a trace of tears in his eyes.

How much older than thirty-seven he looked, Carolyn thought, how tired and worn. There were dark circles beneath his eyes, and his face was drawn. He looked quite unkempt. The garters just below his knees had come loose, and his scuffed white cotton stockings hung limply at his ankles.

Forrest removed his high-crowned felt hat and wiped his brow. "Forty more dead at the hospital today," he muttered, letting the horse's reins slip from his trembling hands.

Carolyn patted his arm, longing to lend him strength. "But you saved five. Remember that and be glad."

A smile flickered on his thin lips. "Forgive me for resisting your entreaties to help. You've been a godsend these past days, Carolyn."

Looking away quickly, she brushed away grateful tears. He so seldom praised her, so seldom showed any feeling for her at all...

Forrest raised his head, eyes narrowed. "But I must insist that you go on without me, Carolyn. You need rest. I'll go back to the hospital and work through the night—I'd feel better if I did," he insisted. "I'm not as weary as I appear and I don't feel that I'm fulfilling my duty by repairing to a soft bed when so many hundreds are still in need of my care."

Alarmed, she clutched his thin arm. "I won't hear of it!" He would be of no use to anyone, living or dying, if he grew too weak. "Last night you slept only two hours, Forrest. Our esteemed Dr. Winston can carry on without you for a while. Most likely he snored away the afternoon in some secluded closet. He should not have summoned you so early this morning. He knew you were beyond exhaustion."

Forrest rubbed his eyes. "I'll be quite all right. The epidemic must soon be over."

Momentarily refreshed, he was about to urge the horse forward when an eerie wind swept in from the shadows. Shaking his wild mane, the bay pranced and snorted, jostling the black chaise and its passengers.

Not far off down the road, a mule cart heaped with white shrouded bodies emerged from an alley, crossed the narrow street, and disappeared into an opposite alley.

At the sight, Forrest's shoulders sagged. Carolyn felt helpless to comfort him—as helpless as he felt attempting to save scores dying of dreaded Barbadoes Distemper.

"At least I can say with assurance that I haven't murdered as many patients with my less-educated doctoring as the esteemed Dr. Winston with all his diplomas from Padua. What imbecile can go on believing in the ancient cures of bleeding and purging?"

Carolyn nodded. "You can be proud, Forrest."

The wind teased brittle brown leaves from the gutter. Like

demon spirits they soared and swirled around the nervous horse.

A dagger of silver lightning slashed through low black clouds on the horizon. Carolyn shielded her eyes. In seconds, ominous rumbles could be heard in the distant mountains.

Uneasily, Forrest eyed the flashes of lightning. "I must get you home."

Though her husband shunned familiarities, Carolyn gently kissed his cheek. "I'll make mutton stew and put the warming pan in the bed. You'll have a fine sleep. Please come home to rest, Forrest."

Another bolt of lightning split the black sky and a crack of thunder sounded like an explosion. The bay reared, wrenching the reins from Forrest's weary grasp.

Suddenly, the chaise plunged down the hill at a terrible speed. Past rows of deserted brick houses, all displaying the dreaded yellow flag, it raced. Past smoky, deserted lanes, iron gateways and mammoth black oaks, the horse dragged them as if devils nipped at his hocks.

Carolyn clutched her husband's threadbare sleeve. "Can't you stop him?" she cried.

Careening after the horse, the chaise threw them about like jackstraws. Except for one night buried in Carolyn's memory when she actually had been pursued by something terrifying and incomprehensible, she had never felt a chaise go so fast!

As if alive, the reins whipped about in the wind inches from Forrest's grasping hands. "It's useless!" he shouted, coughing at dust stirred up by the horse's pounding hooves.

"We'll have to let him run!"

Forrest braced himself, clutching at his black leather instrument satchel bouncing around his feet. When his hat blew off, his long graying hair streamed across his face. Teeth clenched, eyes wild, he looked as if he were grimly welcoming the threat of death.

Carolyn grabbed for handholds as the chaise lurched on over jagged potholes. Hurtling by rows of houses, leaving the murky streets behind, the terrified horse dragged them on. Pounding hooves mimicked Carolyn's pounding heart. Ahead of them on the road, an overloaded death cart was turning in to St. Anthony's cemetery gate.

"Forrest! Forrest, look out!" Carolyn screamed.

It was too late to stop the dreadful collision. Suddenly the horse reared, and the chaise hurtled into the animal with a terrible crash. Together, horse, chaise and passengers were thrown into the air. Wheels spun wildly. Screams filled the silent night. And then, just as suddenly, all was deathly quiet.

A tall black man emerged from the shadows of the cemetery. Behind him lay a freshly dug trench, soon to be filled with victims of the fever. Crooning softly to his old mule, Chester Gibbons urged the beast to stand fast against the fearsome stench of death in the air.

A tall freed black, he held himself with cautious dignity. His cropped grizzled hair and mustache grew thick. Long ago he had accepted the world's frailties, and now gazed from gentle dark eyes with thoughtful watchfulness.

Securing the lines, he climbed down from the cart and raised his pierced tin lantern. Feeble patterns of smoke rose from the mauled earth and he picked his way over deep wheel ruts, which were beginning to run muddy in the rain.

At the cemetery gate, he gazed sorrowfully at the toppled chaise. One wheel still spun crookedly. The bay lay on its side, grunting, its forelegs broken.

With a sorrowful sigh, Chester circled the overturned chaise. "Mercy Lord, look at this mess." He stared at the driver sprawled beneath the wreck. The dead man's glazed eyes stared up in surprise into the rain.

Chester's breath caught. He shook his head sadly. "Mercy Lord, I shook hands with Doc Clure just a few hours ago. By the looks of that neck, sir, you're past recall." He leaned over and eased the doctor's eyelids closed.

Didn't seem right, he thought, as he pulled a kerchief from his oversized coat and mopped the rain from his face. Forrest Clure was the only doctor who could cure fever, not like some butchering physicks, he thought with disgust.

Moments later, lightning struck twice like blinding fists. Cringing, Chester swung his lantern about, looking for the other person he'd seen in the chaise. He saw no one.

The pale light of the lantern spilled across tangled weeds, a gaping satchel, a lone tree standing apart from the woods beyond the road. Finally, the light fell across the ghost-white tombstones of the cemetery.

"Poor Miz Clure's going to be mighty sorry to hear 'bout this," Chester muttered. "Good woman, Miz Clure is. Saved my Lizza from the fever. Can't reckon on how the good Lord decides what folks to take to heaven. Don't make sense to me, that's sure."

He went back to his heavily burdened cart and unhitched the mule. Clearing his throat, he turned to the shrouded bodies. "I reckon you folks can wait another hour to begin your eternal mouldering," he murmured.

Rich and poor heaped together…it was a fitting end, he thought. After a lifetime of acting high and mighty, dead folks were still just plain dead in the end.

He tipped his hat to them. Most folks couldn't understand why he wasn't afraid to tend victims of yellow fever. They didn't know how well the town paid to be rid of them!

"Yellow Jack's no special death." Chester delivered the observation to the arching black branches of the trees overhead. He turned pridefully on his worn boot heel. "It's the Lord's justice in a wicked world."

Leaving his lantern to mark the accident, Chester pulled himself atop the soaked shaggy mule and plodded back to town to report the accident.

• • •

Darkness surrounded her. She felt lost and frightened. So small and alone, she was running, running, running! She ran through the woods, her tiny hand clutching her mother's. She ran until her lungs burned, until her feet were raw and bleeding, but she seemed to get nowhere!

The night air was moist against her cheeks. Scratching branches snapped at her, tearing her arms. The grass was slippery and cold beneath her bare feet. She was so young, so bereft, so afraid!

Her mother kept pausing to catch her breath. Because her mother couldn't breathe, Carolyn couldn't breathe! Her throat was raw and sore. People were chasing them—nameless, angry people. Somewhere in the darkness beyond the trees, Papa waited with a wagon. They must get to him, or else...

She was running, running!

Then her mother fell.

"We must keep going, Mama!" Carolyn cried, her ragged voice swallowed by darkness.

"Find Papa," her mother whispered frantically. "Go on without me. Find Papa!"

Running. No breath. Carolyn knew she couldn't cry out for Papa. She had to go on, afraid and alone!

The people had sticks and rocks. They called her Papa names which she didn't understand. As they shouted, spit flew from their mouths. They surrounded her father's house in the night, carrying torches! They set fire to the surgery. They were going to kill him, Carolyn, and her frail, beautiful mother!

Running! Running! Mama began to cough blood. Through bare tree branches ahead, the pale moon appeared suddenly, round and cold. She couldn't find Papa! She was going to die! All around was coughing. Running! Torches!

With a terrified scream, Carolyn woke. Panting, she lifted a trembling hand to wipe her sweat-soaked forehead. She tried to look around her but could see nothing. Dark, unsettling shadows renewed her alarm.

She still heard coughing! Forcing herself upright, she realized she was not at home in bed but in a strangely chilled room. Across from where she lay was a long wall of large windows. Outside, turbulent black clouds were racing across the sky. Alongside her was a row of cots, and beside her lay a woman whose face was a haunting yellow.

The coughing grew insistent. In horror, Carolyn cupped her hand over her mouth. The smell of vinegar stung her nose and suddenly she realized where she was—in Liberty Hospital!

Fighting panic, she tried to call out, but her voice was little more than a whisper. "I don't have the fever! Take me from this place! Please, someone!"

She heard not a sound except coughing. She fell back, overcome by the reek of fever and death. She tried to get up, but a shock of pain shot through her body. "Someone, help me!" she gasped.

A night attendant, wearing the customary black gown, appeared between the double doors at the far end of the ward. The heavyset woman paused, dipping her fingers into a basin of vinegar by the door. Taking up her oil lamp and holding it high, she crept along the narrow aisle, patting her face with her vinegared hand. "Who calls?"

Carolyn fought oblivion. The attendant ventured past her, going farther into the dark ward.

"What has happened to me?" Carolyn whispered, reaching toward the light.

The woman spun around, swinging the lamp high. Garish light was thrown across her face, making her broad features monstrous. "I can do nothing for you now," she croaked. "The physick, he'll see to you come morning!"

Carolyn felt herself sinking, drowning, yet she tried to hold on to consciousness. "Don't you know me? Please…please help me!"

The woman hurried away, taking the precious light with her.

Hours later, Carolyn heard a coach rattle by outside the window. A man, carrying a limp child, hurried into the ward toward a vacant cot in the corner.

"Don't leave your child here," Carolyn whispered desperately in the dark. "Dr. Winston will kill him." But, as in her nightmare, her voice was too weak to be heard.

Falling back against her pillow, she succumbed to nightmares of another time, when fear and the smell of death lay close at hand.

Two

The coming of dawn brought pale gold light to the sick ward. A slight breeze from the open windows brought a sigh of relief from the patients. At the desk in the near-deserted vestibule, the matron held herself erect, hoping she wouldn't faint again today. "You, there!" she snapped at a tall black man loitering near the stairs. "Be off with you! Haven't you any sense? You'll catch fever!"

The grizzled man grinned, quickly taking off his shapeless gray hat and holding it in his gnarled hands. "Just here to see how Miz Clure's doing, please, ma'am."

"Mrs. Clure only works here at her husband's indulgence. I don't expect her this morning, so be off with you! The dead wait in the cellar."

"Beg pardon, please, ma'am. I carried Miz Clure in myself last night. Terrible accident, there was!" Drawing a breath, he drew closer to the desk. "I was just turning into the cemetery, and here comes this chaise racing like a bat straight from hell…"

Carolyn forced weary eyelids open. Waves of pain throbbed in her right leg. She rolled over on her side and pressed her cheek against the mattress, trying to ignore the agonizing ache.

Moments later, a ragged black man and the matron entered the capacious ward.

Slapping her hand over her mouth, the matron exclaimed, "My Lord, I do see Mrs. Clure!" With black skirt rustling, the woman hurried out, her right hand raised as if hailing someone.

Chester approached Carolyn's cot. The presence of a man with such compassionate eyes did much to relieve her anxiety, and she mustered a feeble smile.

The man shook his head with gentle amusement. "Can you feature it? That old crone didn't know you was here! I told her I carried in Miz Clure myself an hour after midnight. Would've brought you in sooner, but didn't see you at first. After that, I went back to St. Anthony's, but I was too late. Weren't nothing I could do but recollect the spot so I could tell you 'bout it now."

Confused by his words, Carolyn gathered her strength and tried to lift herself up. "Be so good as to fetch my husband, please, Mr. Gibbons. I must be released immediately. I don't belong here, that I'm sure of. If you could find him for me, please…"

"You was half dead last night, Miz, and you don't look much better now. I was afraid I'd be laying you out tonight at St. Anthony's. Do you remember the accident, Miz?"

The pain of her leg momentarily forgotten, Carolyn turned frightened eyes on the man. Clamping her teeth, she braced herself. "My husband, Mr. Gibbons, what of him?"

The old man shook his head, his large black eyes filled with sorrow. "His neck snapped, Miz Clure, I'm sorry to say. It just don't seem right, happening to such a good man. He was always decent to folks. I'm real sorry for you."

Horrified, Carolyn stared at him, silently pleading with him to take back his words. But he only watched her with pitying eyes and said no more.

Sagging against the ungiving mattress, she found her strength ebbing. Struggling to keep her voice calm, she whispered, "So he is dead, Mr. Gibbons?" She closed her weary eyes. "Then I suppose I must attend to his funeral."

"Ain't no use bothering about that, Miz Clure. The good doctor got buried last night with my last load. I tried telling the constable that Doc wasn't dead of fever, but folks are mighty frightful. He said you had fever, and they sent me to the hospital with you. They threw the doc in the ditch, quick as you please. Some no-account grave digger was shoveling in dirt when I got back. Now, got no truck with robbing the dead, but they had already taken Doc Clure's pocket watch. I had to act like it was commonplace for me to haggle over pickings from the dead. I bought this watch off the gravedigger, 'cause I seen the good doctor take it from his waistcoat pocket many a time. And here it is, Miz. I hoped it might be a comfort to you."

The heavy gold chain she had last seen dangling across the worn front of Forrest's narrow waistcoat appeared in the man's mud-encrusted fingers. The gold cross was missing, but the watch and winding key looked unharmed.

She was overcome. "I must repay you somehow, Mr. Gibbons. I am truly grateful that you thought to do this for me."

"No need for repaying, Miz," the old man said kindly.

Carolyn's heart ached, and she thought of what a terrible waste of human life her husband's death was. In truth, she could not say that she had felt an undying love for him—never had passion arisen in their marriage. And yet, they had been friends, and she felt a terrible loss now that he was gone.

"If they's anything I can do," Chester offered, breaking into her thoughts.

Carolyn seized his frayed sleeve. "If you would, take me from this place!"

Chester was nodding when the matron returned, pushing him out of her path. "Away, filthy vulture! Here, Dr. Winston. It surely is Mrs. Clure. My dear child!" She bent over Carolyn, clucking with concern. "How are you feeling?"

Scarcely aware of the woman she had often assisted, Carolyn stiffened in alarm at the doctor's approach.

Ignoring the attendant's rude dismissal, Chester Gibbons frowned. "Excuse me, ma'am, but I'd kinda like to see that Miz Clure leaves this place o' death soon as possible. If you'd be good enough to let her leave with me, we won't be no bother—"

The matron snorted with disgust. "Keep your death-hands away from this poor woman! Off with you, or I'll have you arrested!" She brushed past the man, leaving him to back away in defeat. "There's nothing you can do for Mrs. Clure, so I insist that you leave this instant!"

From behind the matron appeared the learned Dr. Winston.

Dressed in a high-collared black tailcoat and neckcloth, slouching knee breeches and stockings, he swept off his hat and peered at Carolyn through a pince-nez. "My, my, if it isn't our dear Mrs. Clure. What *have* you done to yourself?"

He made a great show of mopping his furrowed brow with a rumpled handkerchief. His dark, glinting eyes stared at her unfeelingly and his thin lips were set in a grim line as unbending as his mind.

Carolyn recoiled. "I was injured last night in an accident that—"

"Silence, if you please, madam."

He proceeded to examine Carolyn from head to foot, concentrating at last on the excruciatingly tender break in her right leg. Clearing his throat, he peeled off her knitted kersey stocking. He made curious noises, as if her injury were most unusual and required an excessive amount of prodding. Carolyn twisted in agony under his touch.

"I wish to be discharged at once! Doctor, please, I do believe you've located the source of my pain!"

"If you will kindly refrain from making such noise so that I can concentrate," the doctor insisted. His chilled hands closed around Carolyn's ankle. Without warning, he yanked.

An involuntary scream tore from her throat.

"Now, my dear young woman, I did ask that you remain silent. Such a shame to be crippled in your prime. My deepest regrets on your loss. Though a fine colleague, your husband was filled with untried medical notions which surely did put his every patient at risk of life and limb."

Carolyn dragged herself from an abyss of pain. "Notions, Dr. Winston? Notions like using tincture of opium, or rum, to make this bone-setting more bearable? If you will take a moment to examine my leg again..." She shivered. "It's not yet properly set!"

Upon further examination, he nodded. "You're well aware that such substances as you mentioned are useful only during amputation surgery." He stressed the last two words.

He jerked, resetting the bone correctly. Carolyn reeled in a haze of agony.

"You're a credit to your sex, my dear, and a healthy, attractive young woman. It's a shame you'll be utterly dependent from this moment on. Perhaps you should have stayed with me when you had the chance. I would have taken good care of you after your mother's death."

Carolyn knew he wanted only to frighten her. He and Forrest had clashed for years. She'd be walking with a crutch in a matter of days, and completely healed by November.

As Dr. Winston positioned two halves of a stiff, leg-shaped leather splint around her calf and laced the leather straps around it, Carolyn's mind spun and sank into a river of black watery unconsciousness.

During Carolyn's second night in Liberty Hospital, Dr. Winston scarcely had a moment for her, proclaiming he could attend to only so many patients, and no more.

A blessing that was, Carolyn thought, her leg throbbing. His usual treatments with blood-sucking leeches and horrible purgatives reduced patients to bloodless shells. Those same treatments on victims of yellow fever offered no relief and, in fact, hastened death. At least Forrest had taught his attendants to give bland food, clean cool water and soothing sponge baths. These were his modern "notions."

On the afternoon of the third day, welcome rain again fell against the windows. Unable to move from the cot, and given no crutch, Carolyn had nearly abandoned hope of escaping the hospital. When she heard her name shouted out, her heart leaped with hope.

Her husband's attorney, Evan Burck, stood at the doors to the ward. He shook rain from his black greatcoat.

"Evan!" she gasped, ashamed of her intense joy at seeing him. She feared she was only dreaming! "Evan!" She bit her lips to hold back words that threatened to gush forth unbidden, words that she, as a new widow, dared not utter. Certainly she had never dared utter them in the years that she'd known—and secretly admired—Evan.

He strode into the ward, his head high. He shook back the wet dark hair that curled on his forehead. Stopping at the foot of her cot, he let his eyes travel over her scarcely concealed body outlined beneath the threadbare bed linen. His expression grew unreadable, intense.

He wore a marvelous double-breasted tail coat of finely woven moss green worsted over snugly tailored sable breeches that were tucked into gleaming black top boots. He possessed an admirable figure, with shoulders too broad and masculine for the fussy fashions of the day. He preferred riding horses to coaches. When he was not away on business in distant cities, he rode the six miles to his estate east of town both ways.

Carolyn shrank from his frank appraisal, feeling uncommonly aware of herself as a woman. She resisted matching his stare lest he mistake—or rather detect—her wayward thoughts.

"Carolyn, I came as soon as I got your message!" His handsome face revealed his concern. "I had no idea Forrest had been killed. What agony for you!" He searched her face, again letting his summer-blue eyes sweep down her body. "It seems that once again I've been out of town at the very moment you most needed…a friend." He cleared his throat. Then his eyes caught sight of the ungainly shape of her splinted leg. "What's this? A new treatment for fever?"

Her thoughts were an impassioned jumble. She felt so safe suddenly, and yet guilty for the feelings long kept hidden in her heart. She had yearned for Evan almost as much as she had once yearned for her father's first medical apprentice, John Rasner. Now, to have Evan near electrified her with awareness.

Feeling foolishly helpless, Carolyn reached up to touch him. "You can't know how glad I am you've come! These witlings! My leg was broken, and I lay all night with no treatment. Please, Evan, get me out of this place!" Ashamed to be seen in such an unkempt state, she clutched the ragged bed linen beneath her chin.

Evan's eyes grew dark and tender. He edged close, as if about to take her in his arms. It was as if he, too, realized at this very moment that she was now alone and unfettered. Boldly, his shining eyes caressed her face. He crouched and took her hand in his. "Of course I'll take you from here!"

His hand was so gentle, so large over her own, so masculine and arousing. Carolyn's breath began coming in gasps.

She couldn't remember when they had ever dared touch. She found herself thinking scandalous thoughts, wondering what it would feel like to be in his arms...

She forced breath into her lungs. His strong hand, with its sure, steady caress, ignited her long repressed imagination—and terrified her!

He pushed back thick, curling brown hair from his forehead. As wonderful as his gaze was, Carolyn thought, she was suddenly more afraid to be near him than by herself.

Did this virile, self-possessed object of her secret fantasies see her now as only a helpless cripple? Was the softness in his eyes merely pity?

Carefully, she withdrew her hand. "Evan, will you notify Forrest's brother, or shall I?" She hated even to bring up the matter of the will.

Evan straightened. "Of course I'll notify Silas. Don't trouble yourself. Think only of getting well."

"I'm not sick, only broken!" she said, a plaintive tone in her voice.

Evan's eyes softened still more. He bent close, as she had dreamed so often that he might, and pressed his trembling lips to her smooth forehead. "I don't know what I would have done if you had died, my dearest."

The nearness of him undid her. Unbidden, her composure fled. Oh, such scandal if someone were to see them like this! "You mustn't talk so!" she whispered raggedly, frightened that the matron would overhear him. She felt unprepared to deal with her passionate response. She was a widow of mere days! "If you could just see to a marker for Forrest. Ask Mr. Gibbons to tell you the location. Evan, please tell me, will Silas come for the reading of Forrest's will?"

He smiled reassuringly. "It's too far for Silas to come. You mustn't worry! It's been ten years since I helped Forrest draw up his will, but…" Evan paused, searching his memory. Unable to recall any details, his blue eyes clouded. Quickly he masked a flicker of concern. "Forrest provided generously for you, I'm sure. I would have seen to it. I doubt very much that I would have allowed Forrest to bequeath his goods to his brother. After all, I thought of myself as your…friend, even then." His expression showed his long-repressed feelings for Carolyn.

If only she had known at the time that Evan cared, she thought with a sigh. Ten years before, she'd been a frightened fool to marry a man she didn't love. "I won't be an invalid. In time, I'll find employment. I'll be grateful if Forrest provided for me, but I don't expect much. When Forrest drew up the will he was far closer to Silas than myself. Did Forrest ever have call to revise his will? He was not a man to think of dying." He had not had much time for living, either, she thought sadly.

Evan smiled, eager to reassure her. "I'll look into the matter immediately. Your welfare is my greatest concern, Carolyn."

"Our chaise was lost, our horse shot. Our last two servants died of fever last month. Evan…"

Her voice broke. She couldn't stop herself from wanting, for the briefest moment, to cling to his strong shoulders. How many times in the past, when he came to call, had she longed merely to touch him?

"You're the only friend I have left!" Foolishly she began weeping her first tears since learning of Forrest's death. "I'm too proud to throw myself on the charity of some hapless individual who might be saddled with my care…however short that care may be! I must look after myself!"

At her words, Evan stooped suddenly and kissed her lips. "Nonsense! You have me. You've always had me!"

Instantly she was drowning in sensations she had only dreamed of feeling. His lips were so warm and stirring. She found herself wanting to yield to him, and felt suffused with a spreading heat of arousal more astonishing than her unbidden thoughts!

"You mustn't!" she gasped, twisting away from temptation. "My husband's hardly cold!"

"Forgive me," Evan whispered, looking far from contrite. "You needn't be alone just now. Wouldn't your brother-in-law's wife look after you?"

"They've never had a kind word for me," Carolyn said softly.

"Surely you exaggerate?"

"Forrest and Silas were never on good terms. Tell me plainly, Evans, will Silas inherit?" It was wicked to ask so bluntly, she thought, but she had to know. "I ask for nothing that belonged to Forrest, nor for anything that should rightly go to Silas and his family. But I do feel those things that I brought to the marriage should remain mine. Silas couldn't want my father's medical instruments or his journals. Surely I'm entitled to those things so precious to me!"

"Of course," Evan said, holding her hand protectively.

"When my father died, he left our family estate to me. When Forrest and I married, of course the estate became Forrest's. Is there any hope now that it might revert to me?"

Evan's expression darkened. "Was Forrest aware of the property?"

"We didn't speak of it. I—I found it distressing."

She wasn't sure if Evan had ever been told that she and her parents had been forced to flee from the isolated estate. "The place was called Timberhill," she said absently, recalling the terrifying autumn night she and her mother fled to her waiting father and the wagon. Vaguely she remembered a mob and a fire, but for years she'd been convinced that the memory was merely a childhood nightmare.

"If Silas inherits," she went on, "he'll get our house here in town. I don't begrudge him the place, for he has a growing family, but he wouldn't need Timberhill as well. I've always wanted to go back there, but Forrest wouldn't hear of it. He had no time for holidays or trips. My childhood home pulls at me like a—Evan, why do you look at me so strangely?"

"You needn't go away, Carolyn. I'll care for you. I would

consider it an honor!" He was unable to keep his feelings to himself, though he knew he ought not to be saying such things at this time.

Carolyn's heart sprang with joy, yet even as Evan clasped her hand, she felt a bewildering panic. She had been a mere girl when circumstance forced her to marry Forrest in such regrettable haste. Instinctively now, she resisted letting circumstance rob her once again of her long-buried desire to return home and lay to rest the unanswered questions of the past.

Struggling to make Evan understand, she saw by his suddenly dark eyes that he was confused and hurt. "I—I care for you, Evan." Her words sounded so lame, so lacking in emotion when in truth she felt far more for him than that.

"Then *why*?"

Would Evan try to control her as Forrest had, she wondered? For the moment she was free to do what she chose. Could she risk giving that up in haste?

"All my life I have been under the care of a man, first my dear father and then my respected husband. It must seem odd to you that a woman should want to look after herself, but can you imagine being nearly twenty-nine and…" she searched for the right words "…like a helpless, ignorant child? I'm not ignorant! I know much of medicine and I could learn so much more. But, as a woman, I'm fit for nothing better than emptying bedpans and changing linens— and at my husband's discretion! As deeply as I regret Forrest's death, I cannot help but think this is my chance to gain command over my life!"

"This is your chance to have what we both have wanted, and have had to keep hidden for years," Evan whispered, taking her hand.

"If you take care of me, Evan, I'll never know if I could be anything more than a helpless woman-child!"

Evan frowned. At length he drew back, shaking his head grimly. "Very well, Carolyn. I'll bring Forrest's will to you the moment you're home."

Trembling, she kissed his cheek. "Thank you, Evan. You have the kindest, most welcome face in Philadelphia."

He cocked his head but didn't smile. For a long moment, he let his eyes roam her body. Then he gazed steadily into her eyes, stealing away her breath. And suddenly, before she could utter word, he murmured good day, and strode out of the sick ward.

She had angered him, she thought. Why? For years she had loved Evan from afar. She had known that he loved her. Now that they could be together, why was she hesitating? Were the feelings she had had for him all these years real? Perhaps she had only dreamed of Evan to fill the emptiness in her heart.

Thinking then of her brother-in-law, Carolyn wondered if Silas would inherit all that had belonged to Forrest, as was the prevailing law of the time. Before the war, Forrest and Silas had been very close. When Forrest drew up his will ten years before, it was quite likely that he expected Silas to accept his choice in a wife eventually, and care for her in the event of his death.

Oh, how Carolyn wished she could believe that Forrest had revised his will, leaving at least *something* to her. She couldn't turn to Silas. If she was left without means, she might be forced to depend on Evan.

Evan didn't want her to return to Timberhill. He didn't understand the haunting need she felt to learn why she and her parents had run from there.

Carolyn didn't want to feel trapped again by circumstances. She wanted to return home to Timberhill to lay the past to rest. And then she wanted to be certain that when she turned to Evan as her new husband it was because she loved him completely, not because she had nowhere else to go.

Three

"And how are you fairing today?" Dr. Winston asked on the seventh day of Carolyn's virtual imprisonment in the hospital.

"I'm going home if I have to crawl."

"Come, come." He lifted her leg slightly to see if the splint was tight. "Mending nicely. In another week I'll take you home, and Mrs. Winston will care for you."

Giving the appearance of being subdued, Carolyn watched from beneath downcast lashes as Dr. Winston nodded good day and continued on his rounds, ordering a purge here, a bloodletting there. He indicated to a nurse that one poor man must be filled with extract of Jesuit's bark. Carolyn knew quinine had no effect on yellow fever whatsoever, but the patients seemed relieved that something was being done to help them, no matter how unpleasant.

She would not go with Dr. Winston, she vowed, casting him daggered looks as he left the ward. Nor would she put herself in Silas Clure's debt.

If Silas inherited Timberhill, then so be it. After seeing her childhood home one last time, she would go away somewhere to study medicine. Then she would open a school of nursing where male physicks with useless diplomas didn't reign supreme over all, especially over female underlings.

There she would do what her father, the highly respected, self-taught surgeon Orion Adams, had inspired her to do, and what she had learned at Forrest's side: She would cure the sick.

She could not cure the sick, however, if she died of flux in Dr. Winston's care.

After the doctor had left the hospital for the day, Carolyn hailed the ward matron. "I have written yet another note to be delivered to Mr. Burck," she said. "Please insist that the messenger wait for a reply this time."

With narrowed eyes, the matron accepted the folded note. She nodded at Carolyn's promise of a generous remuneration and edged away.

Carolyn sank back, telling herself that soon she'd be home and safe. When the epidemic yielded, those who had fled the town would return. After a while, life would settle back to the way it was before.

Or almost. Now Forrest was gone. And Carolyn felt abandoned by Evan, couldn't understand why he had failed to send help after all her notes. Mopping her forehead, she opened weary eyes.

At that moment, Carolyn spotted the ward matron. Standing at her desk, she held Carolyn's note to the oil lamp's flame. When the paper caught on fire, the spiteful woman dropped it to the floor.

Carolyn's eyes narrowed. So! Evan was not receiving her messages! Had Dr. Winston ordered the matron to burn her notes?

That night the cannons were silent. Smudge pots all across town remained unlit. The acrid pall of smoke, thought to ward off yellow fever, no longer drifted dreamlike over the hushed streets.

Making certain that no one would be suspicious, Carolyn asked the night attendant to find Chester Gibbons. "I must know if he has placed the marker over my poor husband's grave," she explained sorrowfully.

By eleven o'clock that night, clouds had covered the yellow moon and lightning flickered high in the dark sky. At last, a shadowed man loomed in the lamplit doorway of the ward.

"Thank God you've come, Mr. Gibbons!" Carolyn cried. "I need you to help me get out of this hospital!"

Shaking his head, the old man backed away. "But please, ma'am, where should I take you?"

"Anywhere! To my home on Dewberry Lane, if you can."

"All I got is my cart, Miz."

"It'll have to do."

Forcing herself upright, Carolyn loosened the splint. She knew she was jeopardizing the proper healing of the bone, but a limp was preferable to another night in this terrible place.

At the far end of the ward, Chester wrapped in a sheet the child who had died that evening and carried it away. When he returned, Carolyn was ready.

Drawing the linen over her like a shroud, Chester slipped his arms beneath Carolyn's knees and back. She felt the break in her leg give, and the next moment she was oblivious to all discomfort.

"Another one?" the night matron asked, sounding surprised when Chester tiptoed toward the stairs with another wrapped body.

"Yes'm."

He skirted past a scrawny girl scrubbing the stairs and hurried down the dark cellar corridor, which led to the rear exit. Very gently, he placed Carolyn in the crowded cart. With a worried backward glance, he went inside to fetch the rest of his load. In half an hour, he had finished. Carolyn was still unconscious.

"You there!" called a medical student loitering by the door. "I'll have the law on you for stealing jewelry."

Indignant, Chester whirled around to face the young man. He knew it was common practice among the students to rob the dead. "I was just covering this poor soul's face."

The student sauntered closer, wrinkling his nose. "You wait too long to collect the dead, old man. This load stinks," he said, trying to intimidate Chester. He poked at the wrapped bodies. "It's a shame to waste linens on such trash. Linen costs money."

Lips tight, Chester climbed onto the cart's seat. He would remember that intolerable fool when *he* lay black-faced and dead. He snapped the lines. "Git up, mule!" Glancing back, he saw that Miz Clure's arm had fallen from beneath the covering, her ring finger now bare. "I see who's robbing the dead!"

Quickly, lest he be attacked and beaten by the thieving white men, Chester urged the mule to a trot. He headed across the dark service yard and turned onto the street.

Hunching his shoulders against the encompassing darkness, he hummed a hymn, feeling grateful despite himself for the summer and the heat that brought him so much work. He would be able to feed his sprawling family for a year on this autumn's earnings.

When he arrived at his shack, his sixteen-year-old daughter Lizza peered out from the low candlelit doorway. "You're early, Pappy!" she called quietly, scampering toward the pale light of his lantern. Tall and barefooted, she wore a loose linsey-woolsey smock and had a pretty, animated face.

Chester leaped down, rounded his sagging cart and snatched the linen from Miz Clure's face. "Child, get a drap of that rum I keep hid."

Her eyes wide, Lizza peeked around the edge of the wagon. "What've you done, bringin' these haunts here? No rum this side of paradise's going to help them!"

"Any damn fool could see this lady ain't dead. Wake up, child, and help me with her! You're comin' with me."

A ripe, rank smell in the wagon brought Carolyn violently upright. Her unsplinted leg throbbed. Forcing herself to remain still, she whispered, "Chester, are you there? Where am I?"

"Shhh!" he hissed from the seat. "We're almost at your house. I got my daughter here. Remember, you sat up with her three nights when she had fever? Now she's goin' to take care of you."

The cart slowed to a stop.

"Dewberry Lane looks mighty dark tonight, Miz. They's a big slouching coach standing in front of your house, Miz. It looks to be the saw-bones, ol' Doc Winston. I guess he knows you got out of the hospital—the fool."

A sinister rumble rolled across the sky. In moments Carolyn's rumpled gown was rain-soaked. "If you were ever Forrest's friend, Mr. Gibbons, don't let Dr. Winston take me back to the hospital! How could he have gotten here so soon?"

Chester made a satisfied noise in his throat. "No'm. He's going off now. Hold on."

Moments later Chester turned the cart into the curving coachway. To see the red brick house looming to the right made Carolyn feel a rush of homesickness and grief.

She had been almost seventeen when her father proudly brought her to Dewberry Lane. The nightmare existence that followed their flight from Timberhill had finally seemed at an end.

When they had first arrived in Philadelphia, four years before, Carolyn's father had expected to find his displaced family a comfortable residence where they could forget what had driven them from their home in the northern Pennsylvania woods.

But the war had just begun, and physicks were needed by General Washington's army. He was impressed into service, taken away so quickly he could make no provision for Carolyn and her sick mother.

Alone in the city, possessing only what they had managed to carry away from Timberhill, Carolyn and her mother tried to make ends meet. Eventually, they were reduced to living in cellars. Carolyn's father was unable to send them much money, and then, as the war went on, he could send nothing. There was no money to pay soldiers.

Carolyn's mother worsened, and Carolyn could not afford to buy food, much less the medicine her father had been giving her mother for years.

Carolyn got work scrubbing floors at Liberty Hospital for a pittance, but in the end her mother died. Dr. Winston took Carolyn in, but she couldn't abide his advances and decided that scrubbing floors was far preferable to his unwanted attentions.

By the time her father was wounded and released from service, Carolyn had been living alone for over a year. Her father was accompanied home by Evan Burck, who was also recovering from a slight wound. The two men found Carolyn working on her knees in the hospital—scrawny, mistrustful and desperately frightened.

Carolyn was too traumatized to notice Evan's keen interest in her then. She knew only that at last her father had come home, that they had a house to live in and food to eat.

In time, her father took on Forrest Clure as his medical apprentice. Those two years on Dewberry Lane seemed like an answer to a prayer. Then suddenly her father died, his war wound never having healed and she was left alone once again, this time with Forrest living in the back room off the surgery.

Living unchaperoned with a young, rather attractive man, she became terribly afraid that everyone would gossip about them—about her.

"You needn't weep so despairingly, Carolyn," Forrest had said to her a few nights after the funeral. "If the opinion of meddling strangers upsets you so, then I'll marry you. We'll look after one another."

They had married a few days later. Their relationship was cordial, but in time Carolyn realized she had married a man whose dedication to medicine was complete, almost religious. They had lived out their marriage in the house on Dewberry Lane as friends until this epidemic and the tragic accident which once again left Carolyn utterly alone.

Now, as Chester carried her inside, she was assailed by memories of her father and husband. If only Chester were carrying her into the rambling old house called Timberhill instead. That was where she had had a happy childhood. That was where she wanted to be!

Lizza hurried from room to room opening shutters to let fresh air into the stuffy house. "Sakes alive, Pappy! There's a mouldering mouse on the windowsill!" Then she let out a shriek. "There's bones standing in there!" she wailed, catching sight of the surgery room across from the parlor. "And wicked pictures of folks with all their flesh stripped off! I ain't workin' here, Pappy! There's no way you can make me stay."

Chester brusquely pulled his daughter aside and whispered harshly in her ear. A moment later Lizza bobbed a tearful curtsey before Carolyn. "I'm sorry, ma'am. I'd be proud to work for you. And I aim to clean up this house first thing. I'll do that for you!"

• • •

Evan Burck scowled at the parson sitting across from him at his desk in the law office. The preacher scowled back. He certainly looked impatient. Just the thought of Carolyn's being forced to seek refuge—even temporarily—with this hard-hearted, selfish man made Evan's temper flare.

Why hadn't she sent for his coach? he wondered irritably. Surely she was ready by now to leave that wretched hospital, and yet he'd heard nothing from her. And he was wary of visiting her again.

The Reverend Silas Clure rapped his stiff hat on the edge of Evan's desk. "Please, good sir. Just tell me if I inherit, or if my brother has chosen to insult me from the grave."

Evan met the man's steely gray eyes. "As my messenger told you, I'll read Dr. Clure's last will and testament only after Mrs. Clure is discharged from the hospital. I feel she must be present when it is read."

"Look here, I've come a long way, and, I might add, on a parishoner's borrowed horse!" Silas jabbed his blunt finger in the air. "You needn't worry about Carolyn's welfare. A woman will always remarry. Someone will provide for her. I, however, have a growing family. I need whatever Forrest had."

Evan's secretary opened the office door a crack. The young man's serious face reflected his reluctance to disturb his employer. "Begging your pardon, Mr. Burck. There's a servant girl insisting she must see you."

Before Evan could order the servant to wait outside, the determined black girl forced her way into his office.

"I've come all this way to give you a message, sir. I've been kept waiting a long while."

Seeing Carolyn's stationery in the girl's outstretched hand, Evan heaved a sigh of relief. Eagerly he reached for the paper. "Excuse the intrusion, parson. This is a note from Carol—Mrs. Clure." Heart hammering, he took the note, shook it open and read quickly.

Dumbfounded, he sank into his chair. "She's already home?"

He glared at the cocky serving girl. Why had Carolyn not sent for him? Had he misread her feelings?

The note crumpled in his fist. "Excuse the interruption, Parson," Evan said at length.

He signaled his secretary to give the girl a token of his thanks. Then he hastily scribbled a reply and dripped black wax onto the paper's fold to seal it. "I've indicated in my note that we shall meet at her house to read the will tomorrow afternoon at four. Until then, sir..." He rose, towering over the pale-faced parson.

The Reverend Clure stood, and clapped his parson's black hat on his graying head. "I'll be there, you may count on it!" he said, storming out.

The serving girl left after him, and the secretary closed the door. Alone at last, Evan heaved a weary sigh.

As always, propriety was keeping Carolyn at a distance. He understood her feelings, and yet from the moment he had heard of her husband's death—and it had been a blow to lose such a good friend—he had been unable to prevent himself from thinking of Carolyn, at last, as his future wife!

He had fallen in love with her years before, almost on sight when she was still a rail-thin waif scrubbing floors in the hospital. She had blossomed so beautifully in her father's company, but even so she had been shy and withdrawn, traumatized by the terribly lean war years and her mother's tragic death.

He had vowed to wait patiently before beginning a careful courtship of the young girl. He was a lawyer, after all, a man schooled to self-control and thoughtful consideration. He had assumed that she was like all young ladies, not prone to rapid decisions—certainly not where marriage was concerned. He had thought he would have plenty of time to woo her.

But Carolyn was like no other woman. She did not sit back and wait for life to move her along. She preferred to be *doing* something, taking charge of her own life rather than waiting for others to take control of it for her.

How he did admire that! Unfortunately, though, he had been in

New York on business when her father died. Before he could dash back to assist her, the little fool had married Forrest, an apprentice of mere months.

"Of course I don't love him," she had told him when he asked. Then, as now, his heart ached. "I married him only to…to keep curious people from my door, to silence their whispers, to make them all go away."

Only the passage of several years with Forrest had eased her unreasonable fear of scandal. Even now, Evan did not know what made her so afraid of gossip and speculation.

Still, despite her fear of scandal, she had a streak of rashness, he knew. At times she didn't think clearly. How could she? Women weren't allowed to think. She had such a fine, inquiring mind. If he might be allowed to cultivate her intelligence, to help her blossom once again, he would realize one of his fondest dreams.

But now that she was free, was she perhaps less entranced by him? He'd always believed that when she gazed at him in that fulsome, yearning way, she secretly loved him as he loved her. Would he ever move swiftly enough to win her heart?

Balling his fist, Evan stared at the will lying on his desk. What earthly difference could it make to Carolyn if the property once in her family passed to the greedy parson? She hadn't been to Timberhill in sixteen years. Surely, if no one else was living there now, it must be in ruin.

Why must she see it? Why, when she dashed ahead with what he considered unimportant pursuits, must she delay committing her heart to him? If she was concerned about having a place to live, he could easily convert one of his many properties into her name.

Tempted to break the seal and satisfy his curiosity, he decided against the unethical deed. He tucked the will into his breast pocket and prayed that it contained the words necessary to guide Carolyn gently—and swiftly—into his waiting, loving arms.

• • •

Wearing only a sheer white chemise, Carolyn sat on a wooden stool in the kitchen of her house on Dewberry Lane. Before her was an oaken tub of heated water.

Cleansed, at last, of the hospital's horrid stench, she worried a moment about her aching leg. Her incapacity made her feel so like a helpless child that she wanted to scream with frustration.

When a knock sounded at the front door, she twisted toward the servant's stairs, moaning as her splinted leg shifted. "See who it is, Lizza. Look out the window before unlatching the door."

The girl scampered down the staircase, dropped her armload of wrinkled muslin petticoats into Carolyn's lap and dashed along the hall. Carolyn struggled to get the first petticoat over her head and tied about her uncinched waist. Some of the hem fell into the tub.

"Mercy Lord, it's a preacher, Miz! Should I let him in, or is this somebody I ought to shoot?" Lizza called, remembering Carolyn's grumblings the day before that she would rather shoot "Butcher" Winston than see him again.

Carolyn muttered a curse. "No, no!" Her fingers grew clumsy with haste. "Show him into the parlor." She threw the heavy woolen skirt over her head, causing her knotted dark curls to come undone. "Lizza, come help me with the bodice hooks! Oh, my shoes, my stays…*Why* must he be early?"

Moments later, dressed and presentable, Carolyn sighed anxiously. "How does my brother-in-law look?" she asked Lizza. "Is he truly the ogre I remember?"

The young girl pursued her lips. "Sour as pickles, Miz." Then she giggled.

Inclined to agree, Carolyn braced herself. Leaning on Lizza's sturdy arm, and using a crutch for support, she made her way toward the sparsely furnished parlor. Her heart was pounding wildly.

"Parson Clure, how good of you to come so far in my hour of need," Carolyn said when she entered the room, hearing a false ring to her words. She had met the man only once before, following her marriage to Forrest. The meeting had been strained, to say the least.

The large man rose and bowed as gravely as an undertaker.

His dour face indeed reminded Carolyn of an ogre's, so pale and unsmiling.

"Carolyn," he said without warming his expression. "We can dispense with formalities. You know how I have always felt about you. I daresay that you cannot find me much to your liking, either. I will soon possess all that you surely assume should become yours."

"I assume nothing!" Carolyn said sharply, relieved that she did not have to pretend cordiality. His honesty made her no less tense, however.

"I saw your attorney yesterday," he said, taking his seat again. "Have you known him long?"

"He met my father during the war—at Valley Forge, in fact. They were wounded at Germantown. After returning to Philadelphia, they became close friends until Papa died two years later. Evan was Forrest's close friend as well. I have always found him trustworthy."

"I hope he is indeed," Silas said, looking around the spacious parlor with obvious envy. His cool eyes settled on her bare left hand. "I see you have already removed your wedding band."

Carolyn lowered her head sadly. "It was stolen while I was unconscious in the hospital, along with Forrest's watch, which I'd been able to save."

Silas's gaze dropped to Carolyn's splinted leg. Lizza was helping her arrange herself with the leg raised on the settle. Then the girl covered Carolyn's lap with a fringed blanket.

An awkward silence followed.

When again the front door shook with a knock, Carolyn flinched. "That doesn't sound like Evan," she gasped, wishing that this miserable day was over.

Silas lowered his head, regarding her suspiciously. She had called her husband's attorney by his Christian name.

Lizza had run to see who it was, and she called from the entry. "Mercy Lord, it's the doctor!"

Stiffening with alarm, Carolyn forced a trembling smile. "I—I'm safe receiving the esteemed Dr. Winston so long as my brother-in-law is here to protect me." Leaning forward, she looked at Silas imploringly. "I'm certain he is here to chastise me for leaving his hospital. Please, Parson Clure, this man opposed all that Forrest believed in. Regardless of how you viewed Forrest's profession, he was the finest doctor in Philadelphia. Dr. Winston would like to humiliate me now that Forrest is not here to defend me."

Silas straightened, lifting his heavy head as if he were about to deliver a scalding sermon. His scowling brows promised devout protection…of his own interests.

Dr. Winston barrelled in, his neck stock and standing collar high about his jowls. He bore down on her. "You've made me look very bad indeed, with your dramatics, young woman. Tut, tut! You will surely have a limp—"

Carolyn bristled. "I don't believe you've met my brother-in-law, Dr. Winston."

The doctor scowled. "Ah! How unexpected."

The gentlemen shook hands.

"Your servant, Parson."

"Your conscience, Doctor," Silas replied, his nostrils flared.

Dr. Winston cleared his throat and returned his attention to Carolyn. "If you wanted to leave the hospital, I would have discharged you."

It was pointless to argue with the stubborn man, Carolyn thought impatiently.

Yet another knock was heard at the door, and suddenly Evan Burck pushed his way in. He handed his hat and cloak to Lizza, then stood imposingly in the parlor doorway.

Seeing Evan, Carolyn's anger and fear evaporated. "Dr. Winston, you may remember my husband's attorney—"

Evan's expression darkened. "I remember Dr. Winston only too well. We spoke, sir, every day last week. Carolyn seems to have recovered from her fever in remarkable time."

Dr. Winston's eyes narrowed, and he had the good sense to blush. "I may have overestimated the gravity of her case, sir. As my services are no longer needed, good day, Mrs. Clure." He bowed and strode out without another word.

Evan waited for the door to close and then scowled at Silas. "And I met the parson only yesterday. He demanded a private reading of Forrest's will." He took it from his breast pocket. "Shall we dispense with this?"

"Do," Carolyn pleaded, eager to have the messy business over with.

Evan broke the seal and read hastily through the legal wording at the beginning of the will. As he read into the body of the instructions, his voice faltered and a look of concern came over his gentle face.

Dr. Forrest Clure had abided by the custom of the time, bequeathing all his possessions to his brother. As Evan had feared, Forrest never found the time to alter the will in Carolyn's favor.

Carolyn sat in stunned silence, scarcely able to believe what she had heard.

"Everything goes to me?" Silas breathed.

"It would seem so," Evan said, going to Carolyn and taking her chilled hand in his.

She seemed oblivious to his presence.

"Even this fine house?" Silas asked, his eyes widening eagerly.

Tears were spilling down Carolyn's ashen cheeks.

Evan turned his angry gaze on the astonished parson. "You can't inherit what has always belonged to me, good sir."

Alarmed, Carolyn looked up. "What can you mean?"

"When I brought your father home from the war, Carolyn, he had not a coin to his name," Evan explained gently. "He needed a place to practice and a home for you. We arranged for him to buy this property, but he died before payment could begin.

"Forrest felt he must keep the arrangement from you. He tried to buy the house, but on occasion he had to borrow against the amount paid. He had your comfort in mind when he did it. I'm afraid you'll find, however, that I still own eighty-five percent."

"You might have told me you owned this house when I asked that day in the hospital!" Carolyn said, embarrassed and frightened.

"That was not the proper time," Evan said, rubbing warmth into her chilled fingers. He looked as if he was resisting the temptation to kiss them. "I tell you now only to make the parson realize how little his brother had."

He looked deliberately at Silas, wanting the pastor to know his place. Silas turned away, chastised.

Evan then returned his attention to Carolyn. "You're welcome to go on living here as long as you like, my dearest. You have several months' recuperation ahead."

She could scarcely shake her head. "What of my father's house, Timberhill? Shouldn't it be mine?"

Evan's eyes were dark and bleak. "I'm sorry, Carolyn. The will clearly states that *everything*...As I mentioned before, when he drew up the will he may not have known about Timberhill. *I* certainly didn't. But I'm afraid that the property was his at the time of his death. And so it now passes to his brother."

"What property are you speaking of?" Silas asked, standing.

Carolyn waved him silent. "I can't bear to speak of this anymore. Please excuse me. I'd like to be alone."

Her papa's house lost? She shook off the numbing disappointment. How could it be? What would become of her? She had been disinherited, out of neglect. Forrest had thought his brother would look after her—if he had ever truly given the matter sufficient thought.

When she finally looked up, Silas was gone, ushered out by Evan, who stood forlornly at the door.

Evan paused before speaking, as if gathering a barrage of arguments needed to reassure and comfort Carolyn. "If you had inherited, that man would have given you no peace, my dear."

She closed stinging eyes. That threat meant nothing in the face of what Forrest had done to her from the grave. She had been left with nothing to call her own! She felt empty. Desolate.

"You'll never want for anything, Carolyn." Evan whispered, crouching before her. He took her hands and held them tightly.

"You mustn't pity me," she said, trying valiantly to smile. "As soon as I'm whole again, I'll—"

"Don't make any plans until you hear me out."

She opened her eyes to his eager smile. She felt so very tired suddenly that she leaned against Evan for strength.

"I know it's too soon to ask, and I wouldn't dream of dishonoring my friend's memory...but Carolyn, if you could possibly consider me..."

Carolyn's thoughts began racing with her heart. She had often dreamed that such a time as this would come. Now that it had, she could only wish that Evan would remain silent. *She wasn't ready.* She had made a decision like this once before in haste, and had regretted it ever since.

Still, a part of her savored Evan's words.

He drew her chilled fingers to his soft, warm lips. "I want you to marry me...when the proper amount of time has passed, of course. Until then, you're welcome to stay here. You'll want for nothing, Carolyn. I'll even deed you the house if that would make you feel better about the arrangement."

She looked into Evan's tender eyes. Dare she consider his proposal? Since the accident she had known bewildering moments of relief and a heady sense of freedom floating just beyond her grasp.

Evan loved her, and she desired him, but she had unfinished business waiting at Timberhill.

Evan drew back, not understanding Carolyn's hesitation.

"Do forgive me, Evan. This simply comes too soon." She drew his hand to her lips. A spark of desire leapt through her as her lips touched his skin, but she forced herself not to give in to it. He would wait for her.

"You're not saying no?"

She released his trembling hand and smiled sadly. "Dear me, no! I'm only asking that you give me some time."

He seemed to brighten at her words.

"I intend to visit Timberhill. I can't imagine that Silas would want to live there. It must be in ruin. He'll likely sell it, and then I would never see it again!"

His eyes were filled with surprise. "Aren't your memories of the place painful?"

"Not those of my early childhood," she said, staring into the past. "And if I could talk to the people still there—"

Evan's eyes grew wide. "Your father once told me that you three narrowly escaped death. He would say nothing more, no matter how often I asked. But surely it cannot be safe to return there, my dear. If anyone remembers, you might be in danger."

"I'm hoping someone *does* remember!"

He shook his head. "You must put this idea aside, Carolyn. Soon life in Philadelphia will be back to normal. I long to give you all Forrest was never able to."

"Would you deny me this one request, then?"

He paused and considered his words carefully. "I would deny you nothing. The moment you're able to travel in the spring, I'll see to the arrangements."

Suddenly he knelt before her, gathering her gently into his arms. He kissed her, his lips urgent against hers. His desire flowed into her, rendering her helpless, startling her with her own response.

Was the past more important than this? she wondered despairingly. She wrapped her arms around Evan's neck and thought that if she were not so foolishly bent on going back to Timberhill she might have this new love, now!

Electrified by her response, Evan pulled her to him even more tightly. As he did, her leg twisted uncomfortably.

The sharp ache reminded Carolyn of her dependence. Feeling inexplicably trapped, she pulled free. "This leg is such a nuisance!"

"Carolyn, I love you!" Evan whispered, cupping her face and looking earnestly into her eyes. "I have always loved you."

She could only smile and tilt up her face for another dizzying kiss. Oh, yes, he would wait for her!

Evan saw that she was not ready to give in, and for a moment his eyes grew sharp. But finally his impatience gave way to resignation. "I would not bend you to my will, Carolyn. I've waited ten years for you and I'll go on waiting. I can only hope that one day you find what you're looking for."

He straightened abruptly and moved away. A gulf widened between them, and Carolyn sensed his withdrawal. She felt quite chilled, all of a sudden.

"I'll leave you now, Carolyn," he murmured. "I'll call again when you're feeling stronger…or if Silas is any trouble."

Why was it so hard for him to wait? she wondered sadly. Yet she couldn't bring herself to beg his patience again. When he called on her next, he would find her gone.

Four

At dawn two days later, Carolyn and Lizza started their journey north from Philadelphia. Lizza had packed the items they would need to last a month and had loaded them onto a lightweight road wagon that Evan had given Carolyn. He had meant only to replace the chaise destroyed in the accident; never had he imagined that Carolyn would use it to escape the confines of the diseased town without so much as a note of explanation to him.

Spending the better part of four days on the rutted winding pike, Carolyn secretly hoped that Evan would follow. Though she didn't intend to let him bring her back to Philadelphia, she hoped he could be persuaded to go on with her to Timberhill.

But as they drove deeper into the bronze and scarlet wilderness, she feared her flight had destroyed Evan's feelings for her. She felt a twinge of regret, and was more than a little disappointed he hadn't even tried to lure her back.

By night, she and Lizza slept at lonely rustic roadside taverns—the Grouse, the Red Turkey, Millers and Spoon—and marveled at the grandeur of the Delaware River plunging from the Kittatinny Mountains. Lizza spoke endlessly of haunts awaiting them in the gloomy, shadowed woods, but Carolyn felt pure contentment in the beautiful land.

At long last, just outside Eudoxia, where Carolyn's mother had been born and raised, the two stopped to rest by a tiny brook they found hidden among the majestic black birches.

Water fell in an icy veil over a sloping shelf of rock. Lizza wandered among the nearby maples and oaks while Carolyn carefully eased herself to a low boulder and rinsed away the road dust from her hands and face.

Several minutes had passed when Carolyn heard a distant shriek. She looked up to see Lizza hurrying toward her, her face wild with terror. She threw herself into Carolyn's arms. "Lordy, I'm in trouble now! I just peed in a burying ground!"

Chuckling, Carolyn shook the girl back to her senses. "If such a thing would frighten you so, why would you do it?"

"I didn't see the tombstones! They've all fallen over and are covered by weeds. I'm going to die for sure, roasted on a spit in hell!"

"Whatever makes you think that?" Carolyn asked, rising to balance on her left foot and taking the girl's trembling arm. "Show me where you saw the headstones."

"Haunts don't take to such disrespect, Miz! Don't you know anything about such things?"

"No, and I don't care to."

Protesting wildly, Lizza at last helped Carolyn through the dense underbrush. A dark sense of forboding descended upon them as they hobbled up a leafy slope to a gloomy overgrowth of trees. Chill rain should be falling, soaking her bonnet, she thought as she ran her hand over her bare head. With a shiver, she could almost hear rain falling on wooden coffins, and a distant rumble of thunder.

"Do you see any sign of a storm, Lizza?" Carolyn whispered anxiously.

"No'm. But I'd hate to be caught here if one breaks out. Please, let's don't stay!"

In the distance were the desolate, craggy heights of the Pocono Mountains. A gloomy fog gathered in the darkly wooded valleys.

As they made their way, they came to a hillock of tall dry grasses beneath some old elms. Approaching the trees, Lizza stumbled over a fallen black iron fence. Looking closer, Carolyn made out cracked gray marble slabs lying beneath the tangle of tan grasses.

"Brush off the stones, if you will, Lizza," Carolyn said, giving the girl a gentle push when she began protesting.

After some searching in the tall grass, Lizza was able to uncover four lonely tombstones. The first and largest was in reasonable condition.

"Joshua Ebey, loving father, died 1779," Carolyn read with a shiver of recognition. "Why would my best friend's father be buried here, so far from the village? I wonder if we've strayed onto the Ebey estate. Surely they must all have moved away years ago if this plot is so neglected?"

"Who's mouldering under those three other stones, Miz?" Lizza was clutching on to Carolyn's arm for support.

"Clear off the leaves so I can read them. The lettering is nearly eaten away."

As Lizza brushed clean the worn lettering from each of the three smaller headstones, Carolyn went weak and sank to the ground. "My best friend, Katarinia...buried here? And her little sister, Juliannah! Their brother Phillip. They all died in the same year, the year my parents and I...left here. I feel almost as if I must have stood on this very spot the evening they were buried. Until now, I had forgotten." A chill raced down her back.

"All I know, Miz, is that they're haunts," Lizza said, her eyes darting among the shadows. "We got to leave this sorry place!"

Carolyn allowed the girl to help her back to where their wagon stood on the deserted narrow pike. Slowly they continued on toward Eudoxia, while all along Lizza bemoaned her decision to come so far without her pappy. In mournful silence, Carolyn tried to listen to the young girl. But her thoughts were tormented by the awful question: Why could she not remember the death of her best friend?

Her mind was blank. In the remembered mural of her life she found no memories of her friend's death nor of the events that had led to her own family's flight. It was as if the events in her twelfth autumn had been erased...or perhaps locked away.

Fifteen minutes later, they passed a timeworn milestone for Eudoxia. "I remember this turn, Lizza! See the fork ahead? Turn that way."

Beneath the trees curved two leaf-strewn lanes that disappeared into the silent gloom.

"I want to get to civilization again, Miz, not off to the middle of noplace!" Lizza frowned at Carolyn and then looked again at the lonely way ahead.

"Once I see Timberhill, I'll know what we must do."

"Meaning what?" Lizza's dark eyes reflected a dangerous defiance.

"Meaning, Lizza, that I'll decide whether we stay at Timberhill or take the road back to Eudoxia, where my aunt lives."

"And supposing only haunts are at this timber place?" Lizza asked warily. "Then can we go home?"

"I doubt that anyone lives at Timberhill now. If you want to know, I expect to find the house charred rubble."

Lizza regarded Carolyn suspiciously, and her voice became hushed. "Why's that?"

"Because..." Carolyn didn't dare tell her that she feared the house had been burned by that torchbearing mob she sometimes dreamed about. "Because old houses often burn when they've been left untended for a long time."

"I hope it's ashes, then," Lizza muttered.

Deep in the gloomy woods, they found the lane overgrown with weeds so deep they scraped the wagon's underside. When they passed the brick posts marking the entrance to the Ebey estate, Carolyn knew she was now only a mile or so from home.

Unable to ease her anxiety and excitement, she strained to see between the thick stand of trees arching long bare branches over the narrow lane. She remembered traveling this same lane as a child in a fine coach, catching sight of Timberhill's main house, its walls a gray-green fieldstone. Its steeply peaked slate roof was high, the five chimneys reaching up toward heaven.

But after all these years, the way ahead was not as clear and open as Carolyn remembered. And now the sky was beginning to darken and a chilling wind disturbed the dead leaves on the forest floor.

"I don't like this place," Lizza whimpered, huddling close to Carolyn.

For a brief moment Carolyn wondered if she should have come. She had an uneasy feeling that Evan might have been right to think she could be in danger here.

Back in Philadelphia, the idea of danger had seemed preposterous. Even during an epidemic, with death all around her, Carolyn couldn't imagine her own mortality. Here, alone in the woods, amid indefinable memories of sixteen years past, she sensed peril as alive as any lurking, watchful, wild animal.

Suddenly, Carolyn stopped short. "There! Lizza, look!" she cried. "Can you see it? The fence posts, and the rock walls around the old gardens, and the chimneys! It's Timberhill! And it wasn't burned after all!"

In the middle of the overgrown lane, she brought the wagon to an abrupt halt. Just up ahead, stood the house, almost a part of the encroaching forest now. Many of the upper windows, and all of the lower ones, had been shattered. Even now she could hear the glass as it rained to the ground that long-ago night when stones were hurled from the lane.

Startlingly fresh memories, wonderful memories unlike any she had relived in countless nightmares, washed over her. All at once she could picture her small, frail mother standing in the open doorway, wearing her beautiful rose-print polonaise gown. And she could clearly imagine her proud father coming out that same doorway, swinging his long dark cloak about his broad shoulders, clapping a tricorn on his head, and mounting his chestnut mare.

The house had been so beautiful then, so solid and secure among the trees. The virgin forest had once been cleared back and a fine lawn had surrounded the house. Now, however, Timberhill was almost lost amidst the forest of trees. It was so mysterious, so distant, and yet in a peculiar way almost welcoming, Carolyn thought. There was a feeling about the house that gave it a queer kind of warmth, like a beating, passionate heart. She could almost hear voices, soft hushed voices murmuring inside, urging her to come closer, drawing her in.

Clearly Timberhill held no such memories for Lizza. "I'm not goin' in there!" the girl hissed, rearing back on the hard seat.

"It'll look better by morning," Carolyn whispered, patting the girl's icy hand. "I must see the inside. I can't go away now, not after coming so far."

"It won't look better to *me* in the morning, Miz."

"Let's explore before dusk falls," Carolyn insisted, urging the wagon ahead over deep holes and protruding roots.

The coachway was completely overgrown with weeds. Behind, in the meadow where her father's surgery cottage used to stand, was an overgrown cellar pit with several charred beams sticking up through a dense tangle of vines. The single stone chimney still stood, jutting like a finger pointing accusingly at the sky.

She saw no sign of the coach house, stables or gardener's shed, and the flower garden was gone. The simple statuary had long since crumbled into the earth.

Turning the wagon into what remained of the gravel coachway, Carolyn came to an uncertain halt before the scarred front door of Timberhill. Three stone steps led up to it. "Bring the lantern," Carolyn whispered, wondering if she herself had the courage to go inside.

"Have you taken leave of your senses, Miz?" Lizza cried. "I'd be crazy if I go in that place! We won't come out. I got no pleasure becoming a haunt! Can't you feel it? We're being watched."

"Don't be ridiculous, Lizza. The house looks completely deserted. I'm sure it's perfectly safe. Do come inside with me."

"No'm! Not for nothing!"

"Very well, then, but I'd be grateful if you'd kindly help me down. I'll go inside alone and leave you here with the horse."

"You're not leaving me for nothing, Miz!" Lizza exclaimed, flinging herself from the wagon in fright.

After disembarking, the two young women gingerly circled the silent house to assure themselves that it was completely deserted. They found an overgrown flagstone path leading to the back where the windows of the kitchen were still intact. Thick ivy branches twisted up the kitchen chimney, but the leaves had recently fallen, leaving bits of faded red among the weeds at their feet.

As they struggled toward the rear verandah, wild arms of

brambler roses plucked at their skirts. At last, Carolyn sank gratefully to a step by the kitchen entrance. She listened to the still silence of the forest beyond, and wondered if time had stopped.

She felt like a child again, waiting for her papa, listening for her mama. Tears stung her eyes, threatening to overwhelm her with grief.

Across the densely overgrown meadow, three pairs of silvery eyes glowed at them from the shadowed forest. Startled, but quickly composing herself, Carolyn was about to point and laugh when Lizza saw the direction of her gaze.

"Haunts!" the girl gasped.

Lizza bolted, holding her skirts high as she rounded the house with a wail of terror.

"They're only deer!" Exasperated, Carolyn listened to the thud of Lizza's panicked footsteps disappearing down the dark lane. She muttered a curse, helpless to chase after the girl.

An eerie silence settled around her. She sat perfectly still, staring at the blackened beams jutting from the cellar pit. The chimney stood so tall, so alone. At last she knew that the fire she remembered had been no childish nightmare. That torchbearing mob had burned her father's surgery to the foundation!

With renewed resolve, Carolyn struggled to stand. She had to look around. Using the awkward crutch, she clambered onto the sagging verandah.

Stout boards were nailed across the rear door. She tried to pry them off, but the nails were rusted. Discouraged, she struggled down to the weedy path. Her leg throbbing, she hobbled back to the front porch.

The front door opened, though somewhat reluctantly. Clutching the handle of the pierced tin lantern in shaking fingers, Carolyn limped into the cobweb-festooned entry hall.

Childhood memories assailed her. Her own happy shouts lingered in the murky corners. Her father's warm voice beckoned from the shadows. Her mother's adoring replies lilted in the persistent silence.

Once there had been a parlormaid, cook, gardener, nursemaid and so many friends! She recalled parties, dinners, guests and happy times from her earliest days. With a whimper, she realized how much she had forgotten, how much might have been hers if only life had gone on as always at Timberhill.

By the looks of the rotting steps in the staircase, Carolyn dared not venture above to see her old bedchamber. To her left was the parlor. The fine old furniture was all in place, as if no time had passed since she'd seen it last.

To her right was the dining room. The massive mahogany table dominated the shadows, gray with dust. Pewter plates still rested on the table in a setting for four. A broken goblet lay on the floor near an overturned chair. All else stood in perfect silence—the massive sideboard, the buffet, the excess chairs waiting in the corners.

Shaken and growing morose, Carolyn found her way back to the rear hall. In the massive kitchen, the huge stone hearth stood empty and cold, where once it had been the focal point of the house, filling it with sweet fragrances and warmth.

The trestle table still stood amid smashed stools and chairs. A coat hung on a peg beside the door. There was a pie table, an open chest with a white linen board cloth still trailing onto the planked floor. An iron pot lay on the wide stone hearth, filled with leaves. She wondered if she dared lay a fire in the ancient grate. Surely the chimney was clogged with leaves and abandoned birds' nests.

But in spite of the overwhelming ruin, Carolyn felt safe and protected, as if returning after a long holiday to this solid hearth to warm her hands and snitch a bite of freshly baked, crusty bread.

This was her home.

Still favoring her leg, she gathered scattered chair legs, scooped dry leaves into a pile and got a meager fire started from the flame in the lantern. Warming herself, she thought of Lizza running through the dark, unfamiliar woods, and fretted for the frightened girl.

She could do nothing until morning, however, and so went out to unhitch and tend the horse. Stumbling, and now feeling slightly dizzy from the exertion, she dragged bedding to the kitchen and made herself a pallet before the fire.

Before lying down, she took one last look from the shattered front windows. The night was quiet, and there was no sign of life outside the house. Setting the lantern on the parlor sill, Carolyn turned to look at the broken glass strewn on the dusty carpet. Stones that had been hurled from the lane lay as they had fallen.

Awed to think it had all happened just as she dreamed, Carolyn returned to the kitchen. By returning to Timberhill, she was disturbing a memory perhaps best left alone. And yet, something was urging her to stay, and she knew in her heart that she had needed to return to the place of her childhood.

Flickering orange light danced on the beamed ceiling and walls as Carolyn lay down for sleep. She hadn't missed her parents so pointedly in years. Even as she closed her eyes that night, she felt the tears come. Sad as she was for the tragic past, she knew at last she was home.

Lavender light filled the kitchen windows. The hearthfire had gone out. Alert, Carolyn sat up.

A black shadow passed the window. Then another. The boards nailed across the rear door were forcefully wrenched away.

With a terrified gasp, Carolyn looked around for some kind of protection, but could find nothing. Unable to scramble to her feet, she pressed herself into a dusty corner, trembling.

"Miz Clure?" Lizza called, her voice quivering. "Mercy, I know she's dead! Haunts got her for sure!"

Carolyn laughed with relief. "It's all right! Lizza, I'm here!"

The last of the boards fell away and the door was thrown open with a creaking groan of rusted hinges. Lizza appeared in the gauzy morning light flooding the doorway, her gown in tatters. "Lord a mercy, she's not dead!"

Carolyn breathed a sigh of relief. "I'm so very glad you're back! Are you well?" She pressed her hand to her pounding heart.

Stepping into the kitchen, a short, bronze-skinned woman wearing a black woolen cape peered down at Carolyn. "We thought this child had lost her mind, telling us there be someone at the house. What be your business here? You lost?"

Before Carolyn could answer, a stocky, scowling man appeared at the doorway. His jaw was darkly bearded, and his straight brown hair fell loosely about his collar.

He frowned at Carolyn in amazement. His eyes were the color of a dawn sky—haunting, unsettling, fascinating. Perhaps in his thirties, he had an intimidating air about him as he prowled around the littered kitchen. "What are you doing here? Have you been hurt?" he asked, his wary tone hushed as if he were afraid of being overheard.

"No, I'm all right. How good of you to bring Lizza back. I've been so worried about her."

Carolyn's cheeks burned as the man's pale, intense eyes raked over her. Only Evan had ever looked at her so! She struggled stiffly to her feet.

The dark-skinned woman standing by the door leaned closer, peering suspiciously at Carolyn's leg. "Crippled?" Her voice was deep like a man's.

"Why are you traveling in such a condition? Are you fleeing the law?" the man asked, also edging closer.

Lizza protested. "I told you already—"

"It's perfectly all right for them to question me, Lizza. I'm quite capable of speaking for myself. I'm wearing a splint, sir, but no, I'm not fleeing the law."

"You can't be traveling alone," he murmured, his expression betraying interest rather than disapproval. "Where are your menfolk?"

"I'm a widow, sir. My leg was broken in the accident that claimed my husband. I would be grateful if you could help Lizza unload our wagon. It's so much for her to—"

"You can't stay here!" he said, his eyes flashing with anger. "This house has been empty nearly twenty years. It's not safe!"

The woman gazed at Carolyn with fathomless black eyes. "It

be haunted."

Lizza began whimpering. "I knew it. I just knew it!"

"Nonsense, Lizza, hush! I assure you, sir, I have every right to be here." Distracted by his gaze, she almost wished to have back the blush of her youth. Though the years had been kind, Carolyn knew at the moment she looked bedraggled and weary.

"Please allow me to introduce myself," she said. "I'm Carolyn Clure. Adams was my maiden name. If you have lived near here long, you might recall that the family once residing here was called Adams. I once had relatives in Eudoxia."

The man stepped back, his eyes narrowing. For a moment Carolyn thought there was something familiar about him. But the beard gave his face a sinister cast and she knew she'd never met anyone so forbidding. The woman's face reflected disbelief.

Carolyn was about to assure them that she spoke the truth when the woman's skepticism vanished. Suddenly she smiled, though, strangely, the smile failed to reach her disturbing black eyes.

"Little Carolyn...Don't you know me? I'm Ona, your old cooking woman." She frowned and her voice dropped to a whisper. "Why you come back? We thought you were dead."

Too stunned to answer, Carolyn, too, searched her memory. The cook she remembered had smoked a long clay pipe. Her playmates had whispered chilling stories about her.

"Ona Ruby?" Carolyn murmured in amazement. "To think that you would be the first person I would see...I do remember you! You began working here when I was ten."

"It be long ago, that's sure," the dark woman said, shaking her head. "I was a slave in many a house before I find myself here, alone. So cold here, so far from everyplace. No one want Ona to work in their house. Your father, he say I must stay and he would not hold my ignorance against me, that I am better than a beast in the field, that I am surely as human as the next sinner." Her voice had a sinister ring. Her eyes went deathly cold.

Carolyn smiled, nodding eagerly. "My papa was a generous, understanding man. I'm so pleased that you remember him."

The woman's eyes looked fathomless. "Be he coming back soon?"

Carolyn shook her head. "He died some years ago."

"Of a wound that would not close." She nodded. "I know. I see. Your mama coming, then?"

"How could you know my father's wound never healed? And my mother is dead." As briefly as possible, Carolyn filled in the last sixteen years. "I've always wondered, why did we have to leave here? Do you know?"

Ona turned away. "I know nothing. You be a fool to come back."

"Perhaps, but I'm not leaving until I find out what happened. After seeing Timberhill again, I know that the people who burned my father's surgery and drove us into the woods that awful night must have known us."

Without a word, the bearded man suddenly strode out of the house.

Lizza watched Carolyn from the doorway, her eyes round with horror. Carolyn cursed herself for having spoken of the past so freely before the girl, but there was no taking it back now.

Ona turned to Carolyn. "If you knows what be good for you," Ona whispered, her black eyes even yet expressionless, "you'll get right back in that wagon and go back to where you come from."

"I'm ready to go!" Lizza exclaimed, starting for the hall. "I ain't laying my head down in this place, no sir!"

"I understand your concern, Ona, but I intend to stay," Carolyn said firmly. She would not be intimidated by a queer old servant.

"I be warning you. Don't stay here," Ona whispered. "I know what I be saying."

"I couldn't possibly leave without visiting my aunt," Carolyn said, watching the woman's dark, mysterious eyes. What did she know? "But don't worry, Lizza. We'll go back to Philadelphia... in time."

Ona looked around the lonely kitchen. Then she turned her gaze slowly back to Carolyn. "If you can."

Five

During the following two days, Carolyn directed Lizza to tidy the kitchen and clear away all debris. For a time the girl complied, sweeping and setting to rights any usable stools, as well as the table, and sorting through unbroken crockery.

As they had no firewood, the burning of broken furniture kept them warm for a time, but all too soon they had exhausted their supply. Lizza had only to step outside to gather branches fallen from the trees, but the endless chores wore on her already high strung nerves.

By day, weak but welcome sunshine streamed in the filmy back windows. Carolyn's delight at being home burned bright. But by night the kitchen grew close with sombrous shadows. The hearthfire proved meager protection against the cold, damp night that stole in around the windows and doors.

At twilight, the house assumed its true character, and the feeling of neglect, ruin and despair was inescapable. With the advent of another eerie darkfall, and a seemingly endless night of listening to wind howling in the upper chambers, Carolyn grudgingly admitted that staying more than another day at Timberhill was sheer folly.

On the third morning, Carolyn stood in the kitchen doorway, watching Lizza carry in branches. The girl's stormy expression reflected her opinion of such labor.

Sighing, Carolyn closed the door and went inside. She watched Lizza move into the parlor, hearing her complain unhappily under her breath about all the work she must do in "this haunted house."

In spite of the hearthfire, Carolyn felt chilled. By day, the echoes of her past could be shut away. She could revel in the quiet of Timberhill and breathe freely of the fresh air. But by night she knew this place was no refuge. Here she would find the darkest part of her heart, and reckon with it.

"Lizza?" she called softly, starting to doubt the wisdom of remaining in Timberhill. To come to a town where she might not be welcomed…What had she been thinking?

She called again for Lizza and heard no reply. With a start of alarm, she hobbled into the hall and peered into the parlor. Lizza stood frozen amid the dusty furniture, her expression fearful.

Wide-eyed, Lizza let out her breath. "I didn't answer…'cause I thought Death was calling me."

Carolyn sighed. "Your head is filled with utterly useless notions. Leave the sweeping for later, Lizza. We're going into Eudoxia to find my aunt."

The twisting lane led to a rocky ford in Willimahana Creek. The lane started up again on the far side of the creek, winding away into dense trees.

Carolyn guided their wagon across the gurgling water, and on through the rolling farmland. The way opened to small, irregularly shaped fields. Shocks of dry corn and golden hay were stacked in rows.

Scattered across the gently rolling hills were Eudoxia's small frame or stone farmhouses. Clustered in the center was the village diamond where the red brick courthouse, steepled white Presbyterian church, frame Quaker meeting house and a few stores stood.

Eudoxia was scarcely two generations old. The original settler had been Elias Tilbury, Carolyn's maternal grandfather. His wife had given her name to the village. Their daughters, Felicity and Verity, had been considered belles of the township.

Ahead rolled a farmer's wagon, loaded high with round orange pumpkins. Carolyn slowed until he turned off the lane, leaving her to meander through the silent village. She searched her memory for the direction to her aunt's house.

At last she saw it on a rise beyond an elbow of the creek. The stone house, with white door and five windows sporting black shutters, stood solitary and still. It appeared empty.

This was the original Tilbury homestead, a small house of simple design. If Carolyn had continued on the road, she would have wound her way to the riverside timber mill where her Uncle Isaac Harpswell and her grandfather Elias Tilbury had made their living.

The grand house at Timberhill had been built from the Tilbury Mill profits. Elias had removed his family to the secluded estate, and there they had lived comfortably for several years. Because Verity had married first, she and her husband Isaac were given the homestead. Later, Felicity married Carolyn's father, a penniless doctor with no European diplomas—only American ones—and they had remained at Timberhill with her parents.

Carolyn scarcely remembered her grandparents' deaths when she was three. By then, the dispute over which Tilbury sister should occupy Timberhill, the larger of the two family homes, had become a bitter one.

Seeing the homestead again, Carolyn shivered. How clearly she now remembered hearing her aunt complain that, because her husband managed the mill, they should have the larger house. Carolyn's father, she insisted, was a mere indenture, not entitled to an estate.

An indenture! Carolyn hadn't understood the word then, but now she realized why she knew nothing of her father's past. As the blanks in her memory filled, she was saddened to realize her childhood had not been as idyllic as she'd once believed.

Her heart was pounding as she drew to a stop before the old house. Lizza climbed down, rounded the wagon and helped Carolyn alight. Apprehensive but determined, Carolyn made her way to the door. She rapped the knocker three times. Remembering only Death rapped three times, she rapped a fourth and fifth time, then laughed at herself, for her foolishness.

At that moment, a tall young black man with wavy dark hair

came from the rear yard. He had an ax balanced on his wide shoulder, and he was carrying his shoes. He had gentle eyes and a full mouth.

"That's Noah Ruby!" Lizza whispered, her cheeks rounding into the first real grin Carolyn had seen since they'd left Philadelphia. "He's Miz Ruby's boy. I met him after they found me and brung me in from the woods."

"I never realized Ona had a boy." Amused by the girl's exuberance, Carolyn gave her a nod. "Why don't you visit with him while I'm inside. But don't go far. We may not be asked to luncheon."

Lizza darted down the white gravel coachway and then paused. Playing the coquette, she followed the tall, husky youth toward a nearby shed.

Carolyn gathered her resolve, tightened her shawl about her shoulders and knocked at her aunt's door again.

A maid opened the door. She stared curiously at Carolyn.

"Good morning." Carolyn's voice betrayed a nervous quaver. "I've come to see Verity Harpswell, if you please."

From one of the house's four lower chambers came a petulant voice. "Close that door! The draft!"

A woman in black with tidy blond curls appeared in a rear doorway, squinting at Carolyn. Then she approached quietly as if trying not to disturb someone nearby. She was young, perhaps no more than thirty, her eyes a sharp, suspicious blue. She seized her maid's arm and gave her a sharp jerk. "I said close the door!" she hissed.

Cringing, the maid obeyed once Carolyn had had time to limp inside. She hurried away, peering back at them from a rear stairhall.

The blond woman regarded Carolyn's plain traveling bonnet and shawl, and the threadbare quality of her skirt. Her own attire was no less shabby. "Why do you come here?"

"My name is Carolyn Adams Clure," she said uncomfortably, wondering who this stranger was and what she must be thinking. "I once lived at the estate near here known then as Timberhill. I had an aunt and uncle living in the village…here in this house, if I remember correctly."

56

The woman's face flushed with horror. She took a step back, regarding Carolyn as if she had uttered naught but curses. "We heard that someone was at…But we couldn't believe…What are you doing there?" Her acute gaze swept once again over Carolyn, settling with consternation on the crutch.

Longing to be off her feet, Carolyn realized that the woman had no intention of inviting her into the parlor.

"I've come to Eudoxia to see my home one last time. The estate is no longer mine." She mentioned that to determine if this staring woman was acquainted with the old dispute over the house.

The woman gave no sign of recognition and continued to stare at Carolyn quite boldly.

"Timberhill has passed on to my brother-in-law, after the death of my husband. I only expect to stay a few days, just long enough to visit with my relatives…and ask a few questions that I hope won't trouble my aunt too much to answer."

"Questions?" The woman's alarm increased. "About what?"

"Forgive me, but does Verity Harpswell live here?"

Impatiently, the woman looked away as if deciding what to do about Carolyn. "You should probably sit down," she finally muttered, as if greatly vexed. "Come into the parlor. Yes, Verity lives here. I'm her daughter. You must not recognize me. I'm Annatie."

Carolyn attempted a smile, but her cousin was so distracted that she never noticed. Carolyn's only memory of her cousin was of a very unpleasant child who enjoyed pinching. Carolyn's usual childhood playmates had been from surrounding farms.

Annatie Harpswell jerked a bell cord in the corner of the parlor chamber, summoning her apprehensive maid. She hissed instructions for the girl to stoke the meager fire in the grate. Without further explanation, she then hurried out, leaving Carolyn to ponder the Spartan decor—a few ladderback chairs, an unpadded settle by the hearth, an embroidered fire screen, several simple tables.

Carolyn realized that the maid was watching her from the corner of her eye. Carolyn resisted fussing with her wrist frills and began to wonder if she could endure such a cheerless welcome.

At length, a white-haired woman tottered in. Like a whisper of warning, the wind rose outside, brushing unbending branches against the windows.

The woman had small dark eyes lost in feathered folds of powdery white skin. Her chin trembled, and her head tottered slightly, giving her an air of antiquity far beyond her fifty-three years.

Annatie entered behind her, her expression tense, her cheeks reddened. Her mother was ashen, groping for a rocker near the fire even before she fully crossed the chamber. Annatie settled her mother in the chair before making introductions.

Verity remained on the edge of the rocker, peering at Carolyn as if into a ghastly past. There was a disquieting air about her, Carolyn thought, as if beneath her feeble exterior beat a granite heart.

"What are you doing here?" the woman finally asked, her voice raspy, and cold.

Carefully, Carolyn explained how she lost ownership of Timberhill. She expected the women to fly into a rage upon hearing that the estate had passed from the family. But to Carolyn's bewilderment, her aunt and cousin seemed far more concerned about why she should appear before them at this day and hour, and after such a long absence.

She went on to explain Forrest's death, and her injury, concluding with the doubtful possibility that Silas might come to claim the property.

At the mention of Silas, Verity stiffened, her dark old eyes glowing. "A clergyman coming here, to Timberhill?"

"As I said, I don't know that my brother-in-law will come at all. With winter soon upon us, he might not make an appearance until spring. Before I return to Philadelphia, I should like to tidy the house for him." She saw that her feeble explanations for returning to such a hostile place were transparent before these two suspicious women. "Aunt Verity, I've already told Cousin Annatie that I would like to ask you some rather awkward questions. I don't wish to trouble you, but if you feel able to..."

The woman stiffened, looking ready to bolt from the room, if she'd been able.

Annatie soothed her mother with a low whisper and cast Carolyn a look of furious reproach. "Mother isn't well, as you can see."

"If I could give you back the estate in return for answers, I would, but—"

"I wouldn't have that land for anything in the world!" Verity cried, clutching the arms of the rocker. "I wouldn't have that house, nor a stick of the furniture. Timberhill is cursed!"

Blinking, Carolyn felt a degree of her composure return as mysteriously as it had ebbed. Concluding that her aunt and cousin were slaves to the same foolish notions as Lizza, she was able to relax.

"Regardless of how your thoughts about Timberhill may differ from mine, it's lost to us both. I intend to go away from here the very moment my questions are answered to my satisfaction. Will you help?"

"I'll tell you nothing!" Verity snapped, glaring at Carolyn in a most unsettling manner.

Carolyn's hands ceased shaking. In spite of her aunt's open hostility, she proceeded without fear. "When I was only twelve, my mother and father were driven away from Timberhill. I recall a mob, and I remember that they bore torches. They threw stones through our windows. They burned the surgery to the ground. Tell me why, and I'll leave you both in peace."

Annatie gripped the back of her mother's rocker. "You must go now, before my mother suffers an attack."

"I wish you no ill effects from my questions, but that flight to Philadelphia caused the deaths of my parents. I beg your indulgence, but as you might imagine, this is important to me. Should you begin to feel ill, Aunt Verity, I might be able to assist," Carolyn said, watching the woman's bright eyes and her erratic manner. "My father was a physick, as was my late husband. I have attended many patients. I wish you no harm. I want only rest from these events haunting me."

"They haunt here, as well," Verity whispered, struggling to her feet.

"Then you do know what happened to cause simple villagers to drive one of their own into the woods?"

"Orion Adams was not one of our own! He was an outsider, an interloper, mere a…indenture, likely from an English convict ship!"

"Shush, Mother! We were never able to prove that."

"Nor would you be able to!" Carolyn cried, astonished.

Annatie abandoned her mother's side, crossing the parlor in an angry rustle of skirts. "You have the gall to come here demanding answers of strangers. Go back where you came from. The events you ask about are in the past!"

"If you refuse to help me, I'll find those who will help," Carolyn said, seething. "Do you wish for others to be reminded that you fought bitterly with my mother over which of you should live at Timberhill?"

"That had nothing to do with—"

"Then why did we not seek refuge here with you?" Carolyn demanded, reckless in her anger.

Verity's voice became ragged. "Get out!"

Alarmed, realizing she was antagonizing her most important source of information, Carolyn tempered her fiery attack, but only a little. "I'll find my father's first medical apprentice, John Rasner. I'll ask what he knows of that night. I'll find Katarinia Ebey's mother. She'll tell me what I want to know."

Annatie's eyes swelled. Crossing her arms over her chest, she spun away. "John Rasner left Eudoxia and was lost in the war. His father bears only hate for the Adams family. He'll tell you nothing. And his sister, Helen, is a fool."

Carolyn stepped back, a sudden sinking sensation in her stomach. John, dead? Was there no end to her disappointment?

Was this the real reason she had felt compelled to return to Timberhill, not to learn truth so much as to see John Rasner's face again, and whisper his name? Were her feelings for Evan merely a displacement for an infatuation begun when she was twelve, for John?

Frightening in her intensity, Verity made her way toward

Carolyn. "You should never have come back here! Lucile Ebey hates Timberhill and those who once lived there. Go to her, and you'll rue the day! Listen to me now, Carolyn. I warn you, as I once warned my sister years ago: Orion Adams was an evil, dangerous man. In his wake, he left unhealed grief. As his daughter, you're not welcome in this town. Nothing has been forgotten, nor can it ever be."

Shaking with confusion and fright, Carolyn suddenly longed to run. Forced to stand fast with her crutch and the remains of her dignity, she faced the two raging women.

"Then tell me what happened and I'll remove to Philadelphia within the hour!"

"You're the same mindless simpleton as your mother," Verity rasped, dismissing her with a flick of her hand.

Carolyn would allow no further slur against either of her parents. "I'll ask Ona Ruby!"

"Ona will tell you nothing. What happened was the devil's work! Those who still serve him are watching you. Beware the wildman. He awaits the unwary. Go from here! Go now!"

Wildman, indeed! Carolyn's fists clenched. Did they think her so stupid as to believe superstitious threats? How could she abandon her quest now, after hearing such a condemnation of her beloved father?

Hobbling into the chilled hallway, Carolyn watched the bright-eyed maid scuttle toward the door. Turning, Carolyn fixed blazing eyes upon her aunt and cousin. "I might have gone from Timberhill after today, but now *nothing* will make me leave. Until I have satisfied my every curiosity, you'll find me underfoot. You both have made me ashamed to be of the Tilbury line, and proud to be an Adams. I believe Eudoxia is sorely in need of a new clergyman. The one you have must be surely at his wits' end, having you two among his congregation!"

Thinking she had had the last word, she found her aunt and cousin unmoved. Their dark stares gave her gooseflesh.

Wrenching her eyes from their deadly expressions, Carolyn fled the house as fast as she could swing the crutch.

• • •

With trembling, shriveled hands, Lucile Ebey clutched the mended china teacup and sucked noisily at the warm liquid. In moments, she felt somewhat restored. She raised farsighted eyes to the blurred objects surrounding her.

All was well, she assured herself, momentarily forgetting what had driven her into such a frenzy this day. She struggled to her feet, her back racked with arthritic pain, and crossed the chamber to the bright glow of the window.

The drapes felt dusty to the touch, but she paid them no mind. No one would care if her house was dirty, because no one ever came to see her. She was mad, she knew, and had been left to her musings and memories. In any case, no one could be persuaded to clean the Ebey house. Joseph was her only servant, and he would not do the work of maids. It was beyond his capacity.

Almost miraculously, she could see clearly beyond the filmy windowpanes to the treetops, and the vast forest that spread before her fine old brick house. She could see nothing clearly up close, only those things in the distance, like the forest or her past.

In recent years her world had narrowed to this one upper-story chamber where she slept and took her meager meals. She had no entertainments save for her fancies and the moments of her past so clear now as to be like playacting in her imagination.

Long ago she had exceeded her usefulness. She had been driven beyond the pale, and yet she continued to exist within this gnarled body. Her thoughts scurried among much-traveled corridors of memories, back to the days when her children were living—

Abruptly, like a bright flame among the shadows, she remembered her unexpected morning visitor. Why had one of the Followers come? The delicate balance of her aging thoughts had been disturbed. The Followers went only to that wicked, horrible place…that place of death! But today that one had come…to talk to her, to tell her someone was at Timberhill.

Turning away from the window, she called out "Joseph!" in a

frightened screech.

She heard no answer. Struggling to make her stiffened legs move, she crossed the chamber. She clutched the door frame, calling frantically for Joseph.

At last she heard him starting up the creaking stairs.

"What did I tell you to do this morning?" Lucile demanded, unable to remember, and hating herself for forgetting.

"I—uh, I…" He stammered helplessly.

He was a wretched simpleton, she thought, enraged to be so like him in the witlessness of her old age. "Wretch! Oaf!" she cried, flailing at him with her fist. Where was the walking stick? She'd beat some sense into him! "What did I tell you to do?"

"I c-can't…" he muttered, hanging his head. His dark clothes were odorous and ragged, his face a blur of eye sockets and his mouth like a shadow turned down in helpless resignation.

What other person for miles would employ such as he? his expression asked. Where else might he find work to occupy his drab days if not for this woman?

Imperceptibly, he moved out of the range of her fist, like a child grown weary of abuse.

"I want her gone!" Lucile cried, remembering suddenly her visitor and the news of someone at that place…that evil place where…She advanced on Joseph's blurred shape, seizing his sleeve and jerking him about. "You remember what I told you?" she demanded. "I want her gone!"

Nodding, frightened, he bowed and backed away. "Yes, ma'am! Yes! N-now I remember."

He tumbled down the staircase as fast as he could, driven by her madness to a madness of his own. He left by the front door, forgetting to close it, and ran down the weedy coachway where it cut beneath the arching oaks.

The coachway led out to the lane where carriages and wagons no longer passed. He didn't go so far as the slouching brick posts, but cut into the dense trees, moving through the forest along a faintly discernible deerpath until he was panting and disoriented.

The blaze of his mistress's command dimmed in his mind. He paused among the briars, trying to recall her words. Then he remembered and paused a while longer to wring his hands as he tried to puzzle out what to do.

He had to obey his mistress, Joseph told himself. He had no life without her, but what she asked…*Could he do that?*

Plodding dejectedly through the dense undergrowth, he came eventually to the forest surrounding a forlorn stone house. A well-bred horse grazed alongside the house, and a wagon stood in the coachway.

A thin trail of smoke drifted from the stone chimney in the rear of the house. Moving along the edge of the clearing, pausing to blend his movements and tall frame with the trees, Joseph could finally see a faint yellow light in the rear windows.

His heart stood shivering with surprise. Smoke from the chimney, a light in the window…How long had he waited for their return? He watched the house a long time, remembering other years and better days when he had come to this place.

What his mistress wanted…He sighed, rubbing his drooping, weathered cheeks. It was a hard thing, trying to decide what to do. If only he could think clearly, make sense of it all.

Then he saw the rear door open. A woman came out, leaning against a broom handle, or perhaps a stick. Was she looking at him?

He dropped back, falling on his hindside among the weeds, frightened and cold suddenly, thinking it wasn't fair that he should always be used this way.

Was she calling to him now, coming across the grasses and chasing after him with her stick? She would beat him! His physical memories were more vivid than his fragile threads of thought. Fearfully, he scrambled to his hands and knees and scurried away until he at last felt compelled to stand and bolt, a full-grown man, forty-nine years old, and sobbing like a lost child.

• • •

Carolyn reached the edge of the clearing long after the sounds of crashing had dwindled into silence. Had it been man or animal? she wondered, her heart still racing. The shadowed shape had moved with such stealth.

Then she stopped and stared down at the soft earth. Beneath her was a huge pair of bootprints.

Gasping for breath, she whirled around and surveyed the house, wondering who the intruder might have been. He had been taller than the bearded man she'd seen with Ona. And his face had been an unearthly white, she'd seen that as she watched him stalking through the wood.

Unnerved but unwilling to reconsider her decision to remain at least a few more days at Timberhill, Carolyn went back to the verandah. She wondered if the mysterious man had any connection with her unwelcoming aunt.

At the door she turned back one last time, scrutinizing every shadow in the trees. She heard field mice scratching beneath the warped planking on the verandah; inside the house was the crackling of the hearthfire and the fragrance of their evening meal of beans and peas.

She moved into the kitchen, thinking of closing the shutters for the night. She had not expected her questions about her family to rouse such ire, but then, clearly, she had been a fool. Her father would not have fled for his life with a sickly wife and half-grown child over a trifling conflict.

In her delight at being home once again, she had made light of her nightmares. She had ignored her confusing memories and the unexpected animosity directed toward her family by those in the town.

Easing the door closed, she knew only that quitting this place would be her sole hope of stopping events that her presence had already placed into motion.

"What was out there, Miz?" Lizza asked, eyes round.

Carolyn shrugged. "My imagination."

But Lizza was no fool. Eyes narrowed suspiciously, she turned back to the stew kettle, her thoughts wary.

Carolyn sensed the weight of the night settling by degrees around the house. It soaked into every corner of the room, devouring her courage and playing on her fears. The mob and torches might be memories, but the bootprints were real. So were her aunt's words: "Go from here! Go now!"

The two women were closing off the parlor to keep out the night chill when Lizza's head snapped up. "I feel a draft coming from the kitchen, Miz."

"That back door couldn't blow open," Carolyn assured her, thinking of those creaking, rusted hinges. "Besides, there's hardly a breeze." Then she thought of the man she had seen watching the house from the woods earlier.

Lizza listened nervously. Then she shrugged. "It's stopped now."

"Did you have a pleasant conversation with Ona's son this afternoon?" Carolyn asked, hoping to divert the girl.

Lizza smiled prettily. "Pappy would like a big strapping boy like him to marry up with me." As quickly as it had come, her smile slipped away. "I'm missing my pappy something fierce."

"I know, Lizza. We'll go home as soon as we can. I'm finding that I miss Mr. Burck as well."

With a sigh of relief, they managed to close two of the stubborn parlor shutters. Carolyn felt immeasurably safer.

Lizza peeked out one of the cracks in the shutter and sighed. "There's haunts in these woods, Miz. You know that." They started back for the kitchen, both eager to return to the warmth and assurance of the leaping hearthfire. "I feel eyes all-l-l about me. Noah says there's devil worshippers in these woods. When I told him about that bearded white man with his ma—you remember— why Noah, he acted like I was crazy in the head! 'My ma wouldn't 'sociate with the likes of him!' he says to me. Near to bit my head off, he did, till finally I had to say there weren't no bearded white man with her at all."

"How strange. We must find Ona—I'd like to talk with her. Perhaps she'll work here a few days for us."

They closed the inside door to the kitchen. The back door did, indeed, stand ajar. It was moving ever so slightly back and forth on iron hinges; Lizza hung back, afraid to approach and close it.

Sighing, Carolyn hobbled across the now tidy kitchen and pressed the heavy door closed. Fresh oil was running from the rusted hinges to keep the door from squeaking.

"Lizza, help me place the bar in the brackets, please," Carolyn said, forcing her voice to remain calm. They had not oiled the door. Who had?

When Lizza didn't answer, Carolyn turned. The girl was staring at a large, rosy Jonathan apple on the corner of the trestle table.

"Did you leave that there?" Carolyn asked, feeling the hair on the back of her neck tingle.

"No'm," the girl whispered.

Catching her breath, Carolyn hobbled over to the hearth, where she lit the pierced tin lantern. Her progress was maddeningly slow as she returned to the rear door and flung it wide.

Standing on the rear verandah, she lifted the lantern high, but the speckles of illumination did little to help her see beyond the tall meadow grasses. By moonlight she might see well into the trees, but the night was devil dark, cool and strangely silent.

She listened intently, aware of Lizza's creeping footsteps as the girl edged close. Lizza stood just behind her, as if drawing comfort from her presence, breathing in shallow gasps, ready to bolt at the slightest sound.

"I see no one about," Carolyn said softly, but she was thinking of the man she had seen at dusk. Could he have slipped inside while they struggled with the shutters?

Lizza was quivering like a frightened fawn. Carolyn thought of the unbarred front door and turned to give the girl a hug. As she lifted her eyes to look again at the mysterious apple, she saw that a two-tined iron fork with a twisted handle had been stabbed into it.

Her pulse leaped.

The door leading to the entry hall was closing with the aid of an unseen hand. Only the corner of a long dark-colored woolen cloak showed for an instant before the door clicked closed.

Someone was in the house!

Carolyn couldn't prevent her body from stiffening with shock. Lizza jerked away, looking up into Carolyn's face for reassurance. "Here." Carolyn thrust the lantern's wire handle into the girl's trembling hands. "Keep watch."

Without explanation, Carolyn hobbled back to the table, using her splinted leg as much as she could. The effort was painful, but she was able to keep herself between Lizza and the sight of the forked apple.

Whatever could it mean? she thought, scooping the apple from the table's corner as she passed. As deftly as possible, she yanked out the fork, hiding it among the folds of her skirt. To show Lizza that she had nothing to fear, Carolyn was about to bite into the apple when the absurd notion crossed her mind that it might be poisoned.

"We have plenty of apples hanging outside on the tree without keeping this mysterious one," she said with false confidence, as if it were all a joke. She tossed it into the fire.

At once the aroma of roasting apple filled her nose.

"Come away from the door now and bar it for me, please," Carolyn said. She kept her face turned away until she could erase the fear from her expression. With calm assurance she said, "With these doors blowing open, we should block them for the night, don't you think?"

Holding the fork as a weapon, she limped into the hall and crept past the parlor door. She fully expected someone to leap at her from the musty shadows, but the chambers were silent. She barred the front door, wondering if she was locking the danger out or in.

When at last Carolyn settled on her pallet before the hearth, her heart slowed. Her leg was aching from exertion and she had a knot of alarm in her stomach, but she didn't want to load the blunderbuss for fear of frightening Lizza.

Lizza tugged her pallet closer to the hearth, falling asleep so quickly that Carolyn was envious.

Alone with the silence and her thoughts, she stared at the ceiling.

What lurked in the chambers above? She ached to hear Forrest's strong, passionless voice, to feel his unshakable presence near. How comforting it would be to have him here, instead of being alone in this place that was no longer her home but a place of danger.

An apple stabbed with a fork…

Shivering, she tried to summon the strength to sleep. She was foolish to stay, she knew, and stubborn enough to keep on with her folly simply to avoid admitting that she had been wrong to come.

She still hoped Evan might come to her and insist that she go back to Philadelphia with him. What did the past matter, anyway? What could her father have done that was so unforgivable that it was remembered like a suppurating wound sixteen years later?

In spite of her dejection, she did not rise to hitch the horse to the wagon and go. She slept, at last. When the dawn came, her fears from the night seemed foolish.

By the light of day, she felt none of the unseen eyes Lizza claimed surrounded them. She felt only the desire to know the truth, to right a wrong done so long ago.

Though the sun was soon covered with a gray blanket of clouds, Carolyn felt fiercely cheerful.

It was only as she sat eating sausage and cabbage for luncheon on the verandah that she noticed the apples hanging from the single tree near the door were not of the same variety as the one she'd thrown into the fire the night before.

Six

A week had passed since Carolyn and her maid had disappeared from the house on Dewberry Lane. Evan hurried by the row of shrouded corpses at Philadelphia Hospital's cellar. The search for the women had become grim, monstrous. He made the rounds of each hospital, public and private, ending his days haggard and haunted. Convinced, finally, that Carolyn had not been brought to Philadelphia Hospital—he had already searched the wards—he strode out, his heart hardened to the pitiful wretches claimed by yellow fever.

He mounted his horse and rode down the quiet streets to his last stop at Liberty Hospital. He met Chester Gibbons just as the carter was starting out with his last load. Evan looked to Chester, hoping for any word on Carolyn's whereabouts.

Chester knew only too well what the man with the ravaged expression wanted. He shook his head, snapped the lines across his shaggy mule's back and drove his cart away.

Evan slumped in the saddle. What had become of her? He'd sent the road wagon to her, and then had gone to see if she'd reconsidered his proposal. He found the house locked and cold.

She couldn't have gone to that long-abandoned estate, not in her condition, not with a mere maid and her reckless notions about understanding the mysteries of the past. How could a woman manage that? Why would she, when she knew she was loved as patiently and completely as he loved her, here, in Philadelphia?

Carolyn could not have been so rash as that! She had to have fallen ill and been unable to get word to him. If not, then he must understand that she was grieving, wanting to be left alone. She'd been struck a blow from the grave, he knew not how deep.

He made a fist, cursing Forrest for forgetting to change his will, cursing himself for not thinking to remind him, for having sent Carolyn the wagon, and for ever thinking that he could afford to let her out of his sight for even a moment! With his miserable luck in love, he would find her married...or dead. If he ever found her.

He heeled his mount, heading for his office. He hoped that his clerk had located that damnable place called Timberhill. They had not the slightest notion where to begin looking.

Carolyn had done little horseback riding in recent years, but what she had done was on a gentle mare with a sidesaddle. To squirm atop a bulky wagon horse now, and ride astride with a splinted leg, was more adventure than she had bargained for.

But Lizza insisted the way to Ona's cabin lay back across the meadow and deep in the forest. Because Carolyn couldn't hope to find her way to the woman's cabin from the village, they were forced to take the horse through the woods. They had to go the way Lizza remembered when she was brought back from Ona's cabin their first morning at Timberhill.

Lizza led the way, holding the reins, as Carolyn struggled to maintain her balance. If her mother could see her now, riding bareback like a man, with her skirts flapping in the cool autumn breeze, she would swoon from shock!

"Are you sure this is the way?" Carolyn asked when they found a seldom-used leafy cart path beyond the trees.

Lizza turned onto it. "Yes'm."

The way was so desolate, so overgrown and wild Carolyn could not imagine why anyone would travel to Timberhill along this back way when a semblance of road existed to the south.

Lizza paused, craning to look each way down the overgrown path. "I think we came from that way," she said, starting out once again.

Gritting her teeth, Carolyn gripped onto the horse's mane and prayed she would not fall off and break her other leg.

In time, the cart path meandered into a deep glen of purpled shadows and fallen russet and gold leaves. There they found a shanty of bark-covered logs crouching among the brambles. With their arrival, a rooster crowed, and a dozen plump hens scattered. There was a goat and cow around back, and innumerable cats lurking in the shade. In spite of the neglected appearance of the cabin, Ona Ruby appeared to be a most prosperous woman.

At their approach, Noah appeared in the doorway. He grinned when he saw Lizza. "What brings you?" he called, coming and helping Carolyn to the ground. "Afternoon, ma'am."

Standing uncertainly, Carolyn nodded without looking at the young man. She was thinking that her thighs must surely be bent into bows from the difficult ride. She sagged against the nearest boulder and groaned.

"I've come to ask Ona to help us at Timberhill for a day or so. I need her to cook and to help Lizza with the heavier work. I could use someone to mend the stairs and shingles, too." She peered inquiringly at Noah. "We've seen someone watching us from the trees. Having you with us would bring us both a great deal of comfort. I don't suppose you would know who might be watching us? He appeared to be a white man, very tall."

Noah's sudden interest at being asked to work so near Lizza faded upon mention of the mysterious man in the trees. He seemed about to speak, but his mother emerged from the cabin. Her dark face sported a grin that belied her mirthless black eyes. Noah closed his mouth and moved away, his eyes veiled.

Puffing on a long-stemmed clay pipe, Ona lumbered over to where Carolyn sat, and regarded her a long moment. "You ain't gone."

"No, and I don't intend to go until I've accomplished what I came to do. Will you and your son work for me a few days? I can pay you."

Ona considered the idea with a certain amount of

surprise. "Work?"

"My ma, she doesn't—" Noah began.

Ona shushed her son. "You want me to work? For you?"

"I've been to see my aunt. I asked her about the things I want to know," Carolyn went on. "She would tell me nothing, and so I must stay. You would spare me a good deal of aggravation, Ona, if you would only tell me what you remember. What did my father do? What could possibly be so evil about a man who was dedicated to the healing of others' ills?"

Ona fixed Carolyn with a chilling look. "I already told you, I can't tell you nothing."

"But you worked for my parents! You must have been at the house the night—"

Ona shook her heavy head, her expression belligerent. "I was away."

"But it was Sunday, and a dinner was on the table."

"I was away," Ona said again, softly. She looked angry.

Carolyn feared that the woman would now refuse to help her. As Ona turned, however, her expression softened. Perhaps the woman was lonely, habitually rejecting overtures of kindness.

"Ona, what happened after my parents and I...left? Did anyone look for us? What do you do for a living now?" She indicated the cluttered yard. "You have so much."

Ona pretended not to hear. "How long you stay?"

With great effort, Carolyn rose to her feet. Grimly, she faced the horse and the prospect of the uncomfortable ride back to Timberhill. She was angry that Ona still refused to help, but felt resolved not to further alienate her sources of information.

"I may stay on until the end of the month," she replied. "I should feel better leaving my parents' house to my brother-in-law knowing that it's in reasonable condition. I'll pay Noah, too, a fair price for you both."

What money she had was precious little, she thought. Soon her funds and supplies would dwindle. How might she get on, then? Dare she ask Evan for help?

"You expect to stay until All Hallow's Eve?" Noah asked in a worried tone.

Carolyn turned in time to see a sharp glance pass between Ona and her son. Noah moved quickly to help Carolyn climb astride the horse. Then, without a word, he led her away from the shanty. Lizza waltzed at his side, sneaking sly glances at him.

"Will you help me, Ona?" Carolyn called over her shoulder, unwilling to give up hope.

"I come tomorrow."

Noah glanced back, his eyes furtive.

It appeared, Carolyn thought with a shiver of wonder, that she was taking up semipermanent residence in the shabby relic of her past.

With afternoon shadows thick around her, Ona climbed the hill. Her stout, sturdy legs carried her quickly into the dense undergrowth screening Wildman's cabin from the cart path.

He heard her coming. As she ducked into his cabin, he was waiting by the hearth. The chamber was dark in the corners, but the blazing fire outlined him in fiery silhouette.

He kept his place much like Ona's. His herbs hung in braids from the barked rafters, and his possessions were piled in disorder around the log walls. The odor of bitter wormwood tea was strong.

Unlike her cabin, his had the feel of an animal's den, with his musky male scent clinging to everything in the room. But she was not afraid of him, even though he was much larger and stronger than she.

She held out a package to him and watched him reach for it. She drew it back, giving him a silent, warning look and then let him take it. He tore into it like a bear into a honey tree, and stuffed some of the contents into his mouth. He chewed quickly until the tension in his body visibly eased.

Seeing his shoulders sag, Ona moved closer, curling her dark fingers around his muscled arm. He was thinner, she noticed, and was pleased to think that someday she might with certainty overpower him. This dominance had been long in coming, for he had proved far more difficult to control than she first expected. Now, she would let nothing and no one interfere with her power in this isolated place. "She be staying," Ona whispered, her voice low and husky.

As the wild man turned to look at her, she saw the whites of his eyes flash. She felt his excitement coursing through his veins, and she knew the power she had over him.

She smiled, enormously pleased with this man, this creature of her making, this contemptible puppet. "Do you want her?" she hissed.

His chest rose and fell at a quickened pace, and his eyes were as fathomless as her own. He was her kinsman now, her kind. He belonged to her. He needed to say nothing in reply to her question, for she already knew he wanted that woman. He always wanted the new ones.

She didn't want Carolyn Clure to stay at Timberhill; she was a risk that Ona had not anticipated, not even in her cards or her stones. But she was there now, bound to stay on, asking her questions and disturbing the balance of Ona's wood.

She knew he wanted her. "I let her stay awhile," Ona murmured hypnotically. "And you may have her." She smiled at the man. "And you will serve me and mine for all your days."

She knew he would do as she said. Such a man, she thought, laughing to herself. So easily possessed now, so easily pleased with the promise of a new body to enjoy. Perhaps, after all, she should not be so annoyed by the appearance of this woman at Timberhill. What better plaything for her pet than soft white flesh in the form of a woman?

A week had passed and another chill dawn broke over the desolate house called Timberhill. Ona crept inside the dark kitchen, shrugged

75

out of her long dark cloak and went directly to the wide hearth. She had done so for the past two mornings, and many mornings long ago.

Work, she thought with a sneer, turning vengeful eyes on the woman asleep on her pallet. Oh yes, she had work to do. She threw a log on the dwindling fire, and Lizza stirred. Her eyes flew open and she quickly rose to help Ona prepare breakfast.

Doing most of the work, she watched Ona from beneath her lashes. Outside, Noah was already chopping kindling. The sound gave the house a comfortable feeling of home. They didn't speak, for Lizza had learned quickly of Ona's dark morning moods.

When the porridge was bubbling in the kettle, and the aromatic tea simmering in the pot, Ona drew the tall, gangling girl aside.

Lizza's eyes became large, her stance respectful yet wary.

"These things will protect you from haunts tonight," Ona whispered, pulling small white bats' bones and several acorns from her apron pocket. She placed the charms into Lizza's trembling pink palm and curled the girl's fingers over them. "Keep them close. 'Tis the night the haunts be flying."

Lizza's eyes grew larger still and fairly shook in their sockets. Her lips drew back from her teeth. "Tonight?"

Ona clasped the girl's arms, giving her a gentle shake. "Don't run off, my girl. You'll be dead by midnight if you do. Witches wait for fools like you."

Lizza's eyes began rolling back.

Ona drew the girl farther from the kitchen hearth. "Listen to me, girl," she whispered, knowing that at any moment Carolyn would wake. "The devil walks tonight. He strikes without warning. Witches will dance in the treetops. They fly through the black night on charmed pigs and goats. Fools be hexed. Females be ravished. All the restless spirits of this earth be roaming free."

Lizza's chest heaved.

Ona softened her whispers. "But you, girl, you be ever safe this night if you go with my boy when he come."

Without a second thought, Lizza bobbed her head. Visibly she relaxed at the thought of being gone from this dreary house on such a night as All Hallow's Eve.

"Good, good," Ona said, smiling. If the girl was concerned for Carolyn, she had not yet given thought to it. "I be here with your mistress tonight," Ona said, finally satisfied with the girl's terrified trust.

Blinking, Lizza looked across the tidied kitchen as the whispers drew Carolyn from her sleep. Then she looked back to Ona. In so few days she had come to admire and secretly fear this solid, commanding woman like no other person she had ever met before. Ona had immense power, and second sight into things most folks new nothing about.

Ona had told her that her pappy was going to get very sick soon, but if Lizza gave her all the coin she could find, the woman promised to say a charm to save his life. Lizza had taken all the coins she could find from Carolyn's reticule. Now she wore Ona's amulet around her throat, which guaranteed her father's continued good health.

Yes, this Ona Ruby had power.

"You be good to my boy this night," Ona whispered.

Lizza nodded. "I like Noah."

Ona smiled. This creature might do her Noah much good, if only to keep him further distracted from his mother's purposes. He was her dear, her innocent, her cloak. He knew almost nothing. Who would suspect her when she had such a fool for a son? His mind was a clear, deep pool. She would drop this pebble into it this night, this girl meant to delight him. She almost laughed. All would be perfectly well. She needn't have a worry!

"Ain't nobody more willing to dole out work than one who can't do a lick of it herself," Lizza grumbled, having spent the better part of the day carting litter and fallen plaster to a corner in the rear yard. She would rather have been tidying herself for Noah's visit.

"I heard that, Lizza," Carolyn said from the kitchen. "But these chores must be done nevertheless."

Carolyn hobbled to the rear door and looked out. She wasn't certain why Lizza had been so jumpy all day. The sky was overcast, with the rich scent of rain from the night before still in the air. Drops of water still seeped from a dozen sagging places on the ceiling.

Her main concern now was to ready the upper story, and move her bedding to a more comfortable chamber above. She turned to watch Ona kneading bread at the trestle table, her wide dark brow furrowed with concentration.

Strangely, Carolyn shivered. "I'm starving for fresh bread," she said, hoping to engage Ona in conversation. But the woman kept to herself, always withdrawn, almost with a mocking air.

Sighing, Carolyn hobbled out onto the verandah and gazed out across the overgrown meadow. She couldn't keep her thoughts away from the collapsed ruin of the surgery, or from the questions now haunting her sleep.

With relentless magnetism, memories dragged her back to the past. She had spent endless happy hours in her father's surgery, reading his scholarly books, watching him write his strange script into his bound journals.

Those had been perfect days, especially when she was ten and old enough to understand much of what her father studied. "If I teach you my shortened hand, Carolyn, will you let me work in peace?" he had asked once, ruffling her curls and chucking her chin.

"Yes, Papa, and someday I can be a physick like you."

"Oh, no, my precious. You will be a good wife, and tend your children."

But Carolyn had wanted to be a doctor. She had memorized her father's manner of condensed writing, which he had developed to conserve scarce paper, planning all the while to someday apprentice him.

Then, in her twelfth summer, her father had stood her firmly before him. In the grimmest of tones, he said, "My precious, you are not to waste your time in my books any longer. 'Tis time for you to learn to be a young lady. I've taken an apprentice to assist me, and you mustn't trouble him. He's a serious lad with much misfortune behind him, but with care he'll be a good man, and a credit to me. Promise now."

She hadn't known what she was promising until John Rasner had been working with her father for a few months. She was admonished many times not to trouble John during his study hours. Her beloved papa had gone so far as to scold her. For a brief time she had hated John Rasner for taking her place in the study chair.

As Carolyn reminisced, the desolate meadow transformed into a lush lawn. The cozy frame surgery blossomed in her memory, and she could see the lamp burning in the small office window. Through the window she saw John's dark golden head bent over one of her father's medical journals. She had gone out to wander in the grass to distract him, eager to make him fail at his studies.

He had lifted his head and smiled wistfully at her through the window, obviously tired and eager for a rest.

The day had been just as damp and sunless as this. When John came out and stood on the doorstep, his white linen shirt-sleeves rolled up and his golden hair tousled, Carolyn had suddenly felt as though the day could not be brighter.

Something she could not name had come over her, changing her jealousy and resentment to heart-fluttering excitement. In an instant, she forgot that she wanted to be a physick, forgot that she wanted to be her papa's darling. She longed to be that woman her papa insisted she become. She had fallen in love!

"Let's go for a walk!" she had called, strolling along the rear path. Though she had still been in a pinafore, a mere child, in her heart she had become a woman. She was completely smitten by the studious, lonely-hearted dedication of a young man she admired far too much.

"I can't," he said. "I have so much to learn."

"But you need a rest," she urged. "A walk will refresh your mind! When you get back, you'll read twice as much."

He had been easy to lure. His dedication, though fierce, had been flawed and susceptible to insecurities. He dreamed of great skill, but found the effort involved in acquiring it almost beyond his capacity.

John had led the way into the tangled woods. Carolyn followed, unmindful of her shoes and paying little attention to the direction he led her.

"I used to live here," he said when some time later they came to a deserted cabin that was half buried in grasses. The place seemed overpowered by the dense forest. He stood, squinting into the sun, which dappled through the leafy canopy overhead. She adored his air of troubled mystery!

"Were you happy here?" she asked daringly.

"No. We nearly starved. I had to do all the hunting and planting myself." With blazing eyes, he described his hard life when he lived alone with his mother. His father had been away for years, working in Philadelphia.

When his father returned, a new house in town was built. There, John's sister, Helen, was born. "But my mother's health had been ruined by the years we lived here. She died within days, and there was nothing I could do for her. I hated my father for killing her, in body and in spirit. To spite him, I refused to go to Philadelphia to study. That's why I'm apprenticing your father, Carolyn. To learn what I wished I had known to save my mother's life."

Then, as now, Carolyn shivered with pride. She could still picture John in her mind's eye. She remembered how his muscles moved beneath the smooth linen of his shirt. She had dreamed that he would turn to her that day and kiss her, but he had been a man of twenty. She had been a child of twelve.

Now, even after sixteen years, she felt a sharp pain in her heart when she thought of him. He had been her first love, perhaps her only real love. With a wistful sigh, she wondered what he might have been able to tell her of that fateful autumn when she and her parents left Timberhill. If only he had not died in the war. He, more than anyone, would have known what turned the villagers against Orion Adams.

Twisting from the doorway, and the sight of the charred beams jutting from the meadow grasses, Carolyn fingered her bare ring finger.

How quickly Forrest had slipped from her mind, she thought. Snow had yet to fall on his grave, and yet already she dreamed of other men—truer loves lost, and those yet to come. She yearned for something long denied her, something physical, primitive.

"Miz Clure, you goin' to drink this tea Ona made for you?" Lizza asked from behind her.

Carolyn shook the memories from her mind and turned. "Yes, Lizza. And as soon as we've had a look around upstairs, you may have the rest of the day to yourself. I know I've worked you very hard."

Lizza regarded her a moment, then ducked her head with embarrassment. "I didn't mean to act so high, Miz. Thank you. If I got to go up there, then I'll go now and be done with it." She reached for the saucer-shaped bettie lamp.

"Where did Ona go?" Carolyn asked, coming back into the kitchen and sipping the soothing though bitter tea. "This isn't wormwood tea, is it?"

Lizza shrugged.

Carolyn hadn't heard Ona leave the room. The bread dough lay resting on the table, covered with a cloth. Carolyn felt an odd sense of emptiness, being alone with Lizza again. Ona had a huge presence about her, an aura that seemed to fill whatever space contained her.

Lizza looked about, momentarily tense. "Maybe she's up them stairs, getting your chamber ready."

"You'd best hurry then and help her. I hope Noah repairs the stairs very soon. I want to go up, too." She listened to the soft pecking of his hammer as he, perched atop the roof, replaced fallen shingles. "I want to be sleeping in a real bed as soon as possible. I've grown quite weary of my adventure here on the floor in front of the hearth."

"I can't think of a better place to sleep than a hearth," Lizza muttered, going into the hall. "The haunts can't get to you. They don't like fire, you know."

Weary of Lizza's prattle about haunts, Carolyn eased herself down upon the nearest bench. She listened to Lizza's hesitant footsteps going up the staircase, heard her moving along the upper hall from chamber to chamber. After a moment of silence, Lizza bolted along the hall. She tumbled down the staircase.

Though feeling strangely lethargic, Carolyn stood, reaching for her crutch. "Lizza? Are you all right?"

Following a splintering crash, Lizza shrieked. Her cries sounded suddenly muffled, as if she'd been swallowed up. Hysterical, she wailed in anguish and terror.

Putting more weight on her leg than was comfortable, Carolyn limped into the hall. She found Lizza fallen through two rotten stair treads, her feet dangling above some dark, musty stone steps leading to a cellar directly beneath. Carolyn hadn't even been aware that there was a cellar. She did not know where the door to the stairs was hidden.

"Help me!" Lizza cried, clutching at the air.

Carolyn flung down the crutch and knelt awkwardly on her left knee. Lizza grasped her shoulders, her fingers cutting into Carolyn's flesh. They struggled together, trying to get Lizza free.

The front door fell open. Noah stood in the doorway, the roofing hammer still grasped in his dark fist. "What's all the fuss?"

"Botheration! You hammerheaded sluggard! Git me out of this chamber!" Lizza railed, referring to the hole in the stairs as if it was a chamber pot.

Noah grinned. "This girl gits herself into a snit every time I'm around," he said, strutting forward and reaching for Lizza's slim wrists. "I think she's looking for my attentions!"

He yanked her from the hole, then he hugged her close as she sputtered and spit with embarrassment.

With a moan, Carolyn sank back on the floor. She leaned against the wall, willing her leg to stop throbbing.

"What was you doing, girl? Running from haunts again?" Noah asked, grinning down at Lizza.

She half clung to him and half fought his hold. He ruffled her curly hair and whispered soothing words of comfort. The way their young bodies fitted together unsettled Carolyn. She looked away, feeling a piercing longing for intimacy herself.

Lizza pointed an accusing finger at Carolyn. "She made me go up there! It ain't enough to scare my wits out and freeze myself and work my fingers to bloody nubs. I'm supposed to go traipsing about in places no self-respecting cat would go! I ain't going back up there, no sir!"

"What frightened you?" Carolyn asked.

"Ain't none of your never mind!"

Noah gave Lizza a shake. "Don't you worry, Miz Clure. Lizza will be all right. I'll see to them steps right away. Won't take no time at all."

He guided Lizza outside, chiding her softly for speaking back to her mistress.

Carolyn struggled to her feet and stumbled back to the kitchen. Momentarily forgetting Lizza's brush with disaster, she frowned at the cloth-covered bread dough. Why had Ona gone off without saying anything? To soothe her nerves, she took yet another sip of the bitter tea that the woman had left.

"Ona?" she called, going to the door and looking out at the meadow.

She felt a chill in the air and turned, expecting to find Lizza in the room. But the kitchen had a strange, ominous silence about it that unnerved her, and she hobbled back to the hall. The thump of her crutch and her uneven footsteps seemed more irritating than usual.

"Lizza?"

She found the roofing hammer lying on the porch. A chill ran along her spine as she scanned the desolate forest beyond the house. Where had Lizza and Noah gone?

Sharply, she called, "Lizza!"

Angry when no reply came, she pulled the front door closed and hobbled back to the kitchen. She settled onto her pallet, poking the hearthfire with a long stick. Why had they deserted her?

Then, as abruptly as her disquiet set in, she realized Lizza must have injured herself when she fell through the stairs. Noah had likely taken her to Ona's cabin for a remedy.

With her ire eased, she lay her head on her hands, her eyelids quickly growing heavy…

Young, golden-haired John Rasner was lifting his head from a thick medical text. His handsome face was blurred by the window glass separating him from Carolyn.

She sashayed between the beds of blooming larkspur, phlox and ambrosial lilacs, the whole of the silent, green garden enclosed in a faint mist. Her only sensation was of desire, desire for young John Rasner.

She smiled at him as he came out the surgery door. Then, unexpectedly, he was beside her, holding her hand.

She was no child now; she was herself, a grown woman. He was turning her into his arms, holding her against him, tilting her face to look into her eyes.

It was growing dark all around her, and all she could hear was the pulsing of her heart. John spoke, but she couldn't hear him. When his hands closed over her breasts, she felt as if she were melting. Almost at once she was on her back in the grass, welcoming him…or hoping to welcome him.

But darkness was creeping over them now, changing him to shadow. The sound of rain and a woman's soft mournful weeping came from far away among black, barren trees.

Carolyn's breath came in gasps. She could feel his hands on her. She had wanted him for so very long, and now at last…at last… His lips were warm and wet on hers. He knew just what to do to arouse her, and she was excruciatingly aroused, panting, straining, yearning, reaching…

The weeping grew louder. Rain fell in an icy gray curtain. The earth opened before her. She saw three narrow graves. A white face stared from the edge of the forest…

• • •

Carolyn's eyes flew open. The coals in the grate were like red eyes staring from the darkness.

Embarrassed and disconcerted by her erotic dream, and the dark turn it had taken, she struggled upright. How strange to find no lamp burning on the trestle table. How could she have fallen so deeply asleep at that time of day?

Stiffly, she found her footing, and hobbled over to look at the bread dough. While she slept, it had risen too far and now lay deflated in a lopsided lump.

"Lizza? Ona?" she called.

The kitchen was not so dark as she had first thought. It was only late afternoon, but the sky was leaden. Going out onto the verandah, she tightened her shawl about her shoulders, finally tying the end of it across her bosom to outwit the tugging, teasing wind trying to steal it.

Pulling the door closed behind her, she hobbled down to the damp grass at the side of the house. The horse was nowhere to be seen. She looked at the stone path meandering across the meadow. Without giving her actions much thought, Carolyn followed the path out to the cellar pit.

Her father's surgery had been a comfortable place. In one room he performed examinations and what surgery was possible with the limited knowledge of the times.

She remembered watching once through the window, horrified and fascinated, thinking that her father must have incredible courage to cut into the human body when he knew nothing of what was inside.

The second room was an office lined with textbooks purchased from Glasgow, Vienna and New York. John had done his studies there. Below had been a cellar where John and her father often worked long into the night.

Suddenly the wind grew chilled. Carolyn remembered watching from a rear bedchamber window as the surgery burned. Turning, she looked back at the solemn stone house. Its windows were dark, almost watchful. She remembered trembling in the circle of her mother's arms, listening as each hurled rock had shattered a front windowpane.

When the shouts and taunts stopped, Carolyn and her mother had slipped down the stairs and escaped into the darkness along the path Carolyn and John had taken to the old Rasner cabin in the woods.

Now Carolyn circled the surgery's cellar pit, remembering the run through the woods, and her nightmares. A set of worn stone steps led down into the damp gloom beside the still-standing chimney. She felt almost compelled to go down them, but knew she would find nothing but rubble in what had once been the surgery's cellar.

Unable to stop herself, Carolyn limped along the path leading away toward the woods. She would find Lizza at Ona's cabin, she knew, and would have a sharp word for the foolish girl.

Seven

With each step, Carolyn felt the tug of indecision. She should go back, for to venture alone into the forest was folly. But she went on, hobbling with the crutch, fighting the wind that pulled at her shawl. She struggled with her trailing skirts and the crutch as she walked, hoping to find Ona's cabin before dark.

Beneath her concern and irritation lurked the memory of that night she had run through the trees. She had been forced to leave her mother behind and search for her father alone. Now, as she made her way between the closely nestled, rustling trees, she realized she had come along this very cart path.

When her arm and shoulder began aching, she rested. Later, at a shadowed curve leading up a hill, she realized she'd taken a wrong turn.

Though struggling up the hill proved exhausting, she was rewarded at the top with a clear view of the surrounding wood. Just as she was about to start for the village to the east, she smelled wood smoke and heard a distant but steady sound of someone chopping kindling.

Thinking she was near Ona's cabin after all, Carolyn ventured on. The way grew dark with undergrowth and tumbled boulders in thistle beds. She came to a crude sapling fence where inside three goats watched her with disinterest. Behind them stood a huge gnarled apple tree.

Startled, she turned, almost as if knowing the tumbledown, mossy Rasner cabin stood to her right.

One side of the cabin was almost caved in. Thin smoke curled from the bent rock-and-mud chimney. The place had the air of carnivore's den about it. A heap of rubbish and bones was off to one side. Several skins and furs were stretched to the nearest log wall.

She half expected a savage to leap at her from the partially opened plank door. Trembling, she ventured closer, hearing an echoing pause in the chopping. Then it resumed.

Rounding the side of the cabin, she stopped short.

A stocky man, naked to the waist in spite of the chill wind, stood with his back to her. He set another log on a stump, swung his gleaming ax and split the wood with one powerful blow.

The muscles in his arms and shoulders rippled with precision. Before setting up another log, he shook drops of sweat from his brown forelocks and rubbed his thick reddish beard with a large hand.

His knee breeches were slung low on his hips and were worn and sat out. He was the man who had been with Ona that first morning.

Breathless at seeing him again, Carolyn watched him swing the ax a second time. Leaning heavily on the crutch, her head was suddenly reeling. To see him so unexpectedly, to be so near, was like coming upon a great bear unawares. Her eyes went over his strong thighs to his bulging calves, and then back to his taut, well-rounded backside so clearly outlined by the soft clinging fabric. Her reaction to him was purely primitive.

Without turning, he said, almost as if growling, "I'll be done in a moment."

She was startled to realize that he knew she was standing there. She thought she had made a soundless approach. "H-hello."

He was long in answering, and when at last he spoke his voice was low and rumbling. "Is the leg troubling you, Mrs. Clure? I might have something for it."

How had he known it was she?

Overcome suddenly by weariness, she found herself sagging, falling. She must have made a soft sigh, for he turned and strode swiftly toward her, scooping her against his hard, wide chest before she touched the ground. He clutched her close a moment, almost as if seizing her for capture.

For an instant her hand lay flat against his bare, muscled chest. Dampened by his sweat, she snatched her hand away. "Oh, excuse me! I'm so tired suddenly."

"You're a fool to travel about on this leg," he muttered, scooping her up into his powerful arms and carrying her inside the warm, musky cabin. All she could think about was that he was holding her.

She looked up and could see the dark curls of his beard, the sunburnt angle of his cheek, his lashes veiling his pale eyes. His lower lip was pink and moist. What would it be like...

Inside the dark cabin, he lay her on a scattered bed of fragrant dried grasses. Reaching for a frayed blue homespun shirt, he slipped it on over his sweaty muscles. Carolyn shut her eyes, grateful to be off her feet. How would she get back to Timberhill, she wondered, lacking the strength to even ask the man for help?

At the crude stone hearth, he poured hot water into a pewter mug. Taking a wooden pestle from the table, he ground something in it with a stone mortar, then stirred a pinch of the contents into the mug. With a disconcerting flash of his teeth in his bearded face, he offered Carolyn the mug. "Drink this," he commanded with that hypnotic smile.

She clutched his wrist as he tipped the heavy mug against her lips. The hot liquid flowed down her throat. Instantly, warmth flooded her limbs, making her feel tingly and relaxed. She felt afraid of nothing.

Her weariness subsided and she was suddenly invigorated. Sitting up, Carolyn cast her crutch a loathing glance. How she ached from the cursed thing!

"Let me look at your leg," the man said, taking her calf in gentle hands. "How old is the break?"

"Several weeks," she said warily, fearing heavy-handed treatment similar to Dr. Winston's. "It was badly set, and I've aggravated it."

"Indeed." He nodded, releasing the straps to examine her injured limb. "But it'll heal if you give it half a hope."

With exquisite care, he washed her leg, applied a fresh dressing of clean soft linen strips dipped in a medicinal herb mixture and then relaced the leather splint.

"Thank you," she said, feeling ever so much better. She leaned back on the grass-filled bed, her eyelids suddenly heavy. Strangely, her mind seemed unable to focus. All she could think about was this stranger and his hands on her.

She felt dreamy, and the cabin was overwarm. She plucked at the buttons of her bodice, remembering suddenly the erotic dream she had had only hours before, and her blood started rushing. She could think only of being kissed, of being loved the way she had wanted to be for so very long.

The burly man left the cabin without a word, only to return moments later with an armload of wood. He looked down at her, his expression masked by the beard. "Will you stay and eat?"

Help me back to Timberhill, she wanted to say, but he turned away and stooped before the fire, arranging the logs on the ash-heaped iron grate. The andirons were shaped like snarling dog-faces.

Mischievous orange light leaped and played about the crude log walls. When the man stood, looming over her so powerfully, as in her dream, she found herself unable to speak. She shut her eyes again, trying to quell her unmanageable sensuous thoughts. Where was her strength? Why had she come into the woods?

"I don't know your name," Carolyn whispered.

He poured water from an oaken bucket into a spider kettle. Turning away, he speared turnips and parsnips with a two-tined iron fork and dropped them into the kettle. Setting the kettle among the coals, he took a coarse loaf of bread from a basket and, with deliberate care, began slicing it. He lit the stub of a dipped tallow candle and stood the candlestick in the center of the split-log table.

Carolyn fixed her eyes on the guttering gold flame. She felt her blood slowing to molasses, felt her consciousness ebbing, her will evaporating like a pale mist. Lifting unfocused eyes to the bearded man watching her from the shadows, she felt herself floating free in darkness, released from all cares.

How strange, she thought. She felt so tired…so warm…

She knew his pale hard eyes were upon her, but the tingle of

alarm roused in her breast went unheeded. She saw his teeth flash...
and then she fell gently into a deep, dreamless sleep.

Moving like a panther, Wildman pulled a crude wooden stool
from beneath the table and positioned himself at the foot of his
grass bed.

Thoughtfully, he gazed at his unexpected guest. How was it she
had come to him? Had Ona arranged it? He had thought he was to
fetch her himself, that he would have to forcibly take her, as he had
taken the others before her. But there she lay now, sleeping with her
slim white arms crossed tightly against her inviting chest. He reached
to touch the creamy flesh of her arms, finding it soothingly cool.

Brushing her straying brown curls from her cheeks and
forehead, he studied her innocent face. His own expression grew
heavy and hungry.

So this was how a beautiful, provocative child matured. This was
to be his new conquest, this female with such a bold and willful spirit.
How pliable the drugs made her...how helpless, how appealing.

The smoky air in his cabin rushed in and out of his lungs, and
he felt a heady surge of power. How good it would be to take her,
he thought. She was so new, so unexplored. He reached out to touch
her, thought better of it suddenly, and withdrew his large, work-
hardened hand.

After a time, he rose and stirred the vegetables in the pot. He
took a tattered pieced quilt and laid it carefully across Carolyn. Then
he paused again to watch her sleep. Like a dark beast hungry for
prey, desire stirred deep within him, making him want what he must
wait to possess.

She was not a lady, by the looks of her roughened hands.
Though not dew-fresh, she had a finely drawn face. Her long waving
brown hair had come loose, and he plucked several loose pins from
it. Then, stooping over her, he lifted her in his arms just enough to
let her hair tumble freely about her shoulders.

She felt delicate in his arms. Limply she lay against him now, all
tension gone from her body, and he knew she would sleep the sleep
of the dead. For these hours, she belonged entirely to him. She was

so beautiful, he thought, watching her head loll against his hard arm. Her delicately hollowed throat was exposed, her lips were pink and moist. He leaned close enough to feel her breath against his mouth. His whiskers tickled her nose. She stirred, startling him.

Dropping her back onto the bed, he watched until he was certain she was again deeply sleeping. Only a person of intensely strong will could overcome the sleeping potion he'd given her.

When at last she was limp again, he pressed his lips to her forehead, tasting her cool, faintly salty skin. Then he kissed each delicate eyelid, and finally her slightly parted lips, so soft, so vulnerable.

He put his tongue between them, pressing it into her mouth. He grasped her jaw to open her sweet, unsuspecting mouth to his exploration. He trailed his fingers down her slim throat to the shallow hollow, still kissing her.

Her skin along her shoulders was white as marble, warm and velvety. He smoothed his hand deep within her fragrant bodice, finding so much warmth and such a heady, caressable softness. She had round, ample breasts, and nipples that twirled erect as he fondled them.

Growing needful, he unbuttoned her bodice, laying open the fabric with deliberate care, savoring each newly exposed inch of her white flesh.

She wore a chemise trimmed with inset lace. As he parted the bodice of her gown, he could see her rounded breasts swelling deliciously against the white chemise. Her pale-brown nipples pointed into the muslin, and he lowered his lips to the left one, closing his mouth over the fabric of the chemise. He felt the resilience of her flesh beneath. She smelled so sweet, so warm. He drew away, looking at the damp point of muslin.

He was incredibly aroused, wanting satisfaction far sooner than was prudent. But what difference did it make if he waited? he thought. He could have her now! Why should Ona's orders matter when he had Carolyn before him? Edging closer, he swelled with anticipation. He wanted to satisfy himself now, in the privacy of his den.

She stirred again, moaning and squirming as if she was aware of his touch. Unnerved, he let her go, covering her with the quilt. Why must she fight the effects of the drug? She would be difficult to deal with, he thought, angry suddenly. These women! These damnable Followers. He didn't know if he should want her to stay now, or to go.

Where was she? Eyes still closed, Carolyn began to stir. She knew from the smell of the woodsy fire that she could not be in her bedchamber in Philadelphia...

Her eyes flew open and she saw that she was in the murky cabin where she had fallen asleep hours before. The room glowed from a blazing hearth fire.

Wind stirred branches outside. She was alone in the dark cabin. Uneasily, she propped herself onto her elbow. She felt dizzy, as if she had drunk far too much hard cider.

In spite of the leaping hearthfire, this far side of the cabin was chilled. As her bodice gaped, Carolyn felt the chill on her bare throat. Her heart leaping in alarm, she looked down at herself, aghast.

Seizing the untied sides of her chemise and clutching them together with cold, trembling hands, she scrambled from the bed. Her splinted leg protested with a jab of pain. Breathless with shock, she hastily buttoned her bodice. She was unable to believe that, while she had slept, she had been molested!

Shaking the groggy confusion from her mind, she tried to think. Perhaps he had opened her bodice to assist her breathing. She mustn't imagine improper advances where none were intended!

But running her hands over her bosom, she felt a peculiar stirring, as if she knew that he had wantonly caressed her. How long had it been since she was loved, eight years? Suddenly she felt on fire! She went faint with a mixture of emotions so alarming she wanted only to run from the cabin...and herself. How could she want a stranger?

Perversely, her mouth watered at the fragrance of the stew. On the table stood two mugs of warm tea. Shaken, not knowing what to do or say if he returned, she sipped at one mug. She hoped the warmth would give her courage, to go or stay, she knew not which, and then she wondered, suddenly, if the herbal tea caused deep sleep—or perhaps this terrible compelling arousal.

She didn't recognize the flavor. Both drinks were equally strong. She wanted to look at the things on his worktable, but couldn't find the strength to continue standing.

Feeling sluggish, with her eyelids heavy and her body feeling as if it was weighted with stones, she dropped to the stool beside the table. Bracing, invigorating warmth began spreading through her veins again.

As she thought of struggling to her feet, the cabin door swung wide. Tart night air swirled around her, rousing her. The bearded man's broad-shouldered shadow filled the low doorway. He was silhouetted by a rising red moon glowing unnaturally large beyond the branches. Scudding clouds cut across the moon, and a sinister wind disturbed the trees.

Breathing heavily, she felt no alarm. The drug was still having a powerful effect on her. Now was her chance. It was as if the drug was bringing to life her darkest desires. Shutting her eyes momentarily, she experienced a stab of arousal stronger than any she had ever known. This man had a hypnotic power over her. Her hand, clutching closed her bodice, dropped to her lap. She was helpless to resist. This was, she thought in semiconsciousness, like a dream.

He came inside, his long dark cloak covered with bits of leaves, and his huge boots muddied to the ankle. "Did you sleep well?" His voice was as warm and enveloping as black down.

She was alone with him, alone in a place where no one would ever find her. She nodded, again finding her ability to speak beyond her strength. The passion repressed for eight years was rising in her. As he stared at her with his pale piercing eyes, her breathing became deep and even.

Her nipples felt tight, her loins aching. Her head fell back, her throat bared. Her hair tumbled heavily around her shoulders. She wanted to be taken, she thought. She wanted this stranger to take her.

He pulled off his cloak and dropped it in a dusty heap. Going to an oaken bucket on the floor, he lifted handfuls of water to his face. Then he stirred his hands in the bucket, smoothing his long fingers over his wide palms.

As he straightened, teasing silver drops coursed from his dark beard. He watched her with glowing pale eyes. He was squinting just a little, as if she was difficult to see.

She was falling backward even as he lunged toward her. He supported her fall with one forceful arm while staring down into her face with pinpoint pupils.

His arm felt wonderfully warm and hard against her back. She was close enough to smell the frosty freshness of his skin, to see the glistening moisture on his full lips and to wonder with a dreamy detachment how long he had looked at her bared breasts while she slept. It was as if all her erotic fantasies had been brought to the surface on this All Hallow's Eve.

He eased her back to the stool and stood leaning over her only an instant. Then, stepping away carefully, he looked as if he was unsure where to put his feet. "Are you all right?" he asked as if a bit dazed. Was he drugged, too?

"I don't think...I don't think I can get back to Timberhill... myself." Her tingling breasts rose and fell as she waited for him to touch her.

Darkness had changed him. His eyes looked nearly silver, like the eyes of a wild beast reflecting light from without. She felt as if she were looking through him into a bottomless, alien world beyond.

She could scarcely see his lower lip among the damp whiskers of his beard. She imagined those whiskers rubbing softly against her cheeks and breasts.

Another stab of desire shivered deep into her womanhood.

As he filled two pewter plates with stew, he remained turned away, as if unaware of her scrutiny. When he persisted in ignoring her needs, she became suddenly annoyed. Her emotions were so quick to change that she felt strange to herself. Suddenly, she felt more like herself, as if the effect of the drug was wearing off.

He was like Forrest, she thought with an edge of irritation in her mind. He was so puzzling, so quiet, so difficult to understand. For a moment the peculiar erotic lethargy, which was making her thoughts so wanton, lifted from her mind.

He saw the change in her expression as he placed the plate before her and handed her a silver spoon. She felt so disoriented, she could hardly think, much less eat.

"You didn't tell me your name," she whispered, staring at the stew. Her arm seemed made of lead.

"They call me Wildman." He seated himself and gulped the potent tea.

Wildman? Impossible! As he drank she watched for his reaction to the tea, but his gaze only intensified. How could his pupils constrict so tightly? He must be nearly blind in the dark cabin. Yet he looked at her with such unsettling intensity, she felt him peering into her mind as easily as through an open window.

He poured more tea then, spilling only a little. They both drank, smiling as the warmth spread through their bodies. Irresistible sleep stole around her like a black fog. She fought to remain awake. If he was going to…going to…

"I must go," she whispered, forcing the words out. Going was the last thing she wanted to do.

He shook his head. "Not tonight, Carolyn. I won't let you."

She wanted to stand but had no strength. "Why do you live here alone? Have you no family?" She could hardly think now.

"None that would claim me now." His expression remained grave. "Tell me of your husband. Did you love him?"

She spoke of Forrest's association with her father, skimming over her marriage, unwilling to talk of love when lust was all she felt. As she talked, her host looked distracted. He seemed to find her story of no interest. He appeared to be waiting to get on with other, more urgent pursuits.

Was he fleeing the law, she wondered? By the manner in which he tended her leg, she knew he had a smattering of medical knowledge. Perhaps he was a fugitive from Philadelphia or Boston. She had heard of more than a few notorious medical students who, after a mishandled case, disappeared forever to avoid prison. Wildman, indeed!

As their eyes locked, her suspicions evaporated. Her lungs squeezed until she was breathing in short gasps. When his hand stole across the table to grasp hers, her pulse leaped.

Stock-still, she thrilled as his warm strong hand slid ever so slowly up her arm. With the greatest of care, he circled her shoulder with his arm, slipping his hand gently around her neck. His warm palm caressed her jaw, and then her cheek. His thumb brushed ler lips, and then, fingers spread, he slid his hand around to tangle his fingers in her loosed hair.

She was on fire, starving for his mysterious stranger's kiss. She had been too timid to let Evan kiss her. Where was that timidity now? Her breasts rose and fell, tingling with awareness. Her nipples were taut, her legs aching.

He stood, leaning close. Tipping her head back, he brought her face upward to his parted lips. "If I was a gentleman," he whispered, inches from her lips, "I would not suggest that you stay with me, here, tonight. I would allow you to go back into the woods and back to that ruined house to be alone and defenseless on a night like this. I would allow the insane people who live around here to terrorize you, and I would let all of that happen in the name of honor."

Her breath came in soft gasps.

"But long ago I stopped being a gentleman, Carolyn. The only place for us tonight is here, alone, together."

His whiskers tickled her cheeks. Deliciously soft and warm, his mouth touched hers. Was this protection, or seduction? Her head was swimming, her body yielding. She could think of no words to refute his description of what might happen on this All Hallow's

Eve. She believed she was in danger. Here she was safe.

"But I-I must get back," she found herself murmuring when he released her lips. "Lizza…"

"Ona will see to her," he said, covering her mouth again. His tongue plunged deep, taking command of her. Twin fires reflected in his clear, near-white eyes.

Releasing her abruptly, he stalked to the hearth and stabbed at the flaming logs. Showers of sparks rained across the broad flat stones at his feet and chased up the chimney. The flame-lit yellow planes of his temples and cheeks looked so fine. The black hollows of his eyes made him resemble an animal.

When he turned, low-eyed and glaring, she wanted him to touch her again. Leaning toward him, she let unbidden thoughts come into her mind. Drugged thoughts of surrender, thoughts of abandon filled her being and were plainly evident in her expression.

But as she let his gaze pierce her, driving deep, an uncontrollable blackness spread through her mind. Suddenly, irrevocably, she was rendered senseless. If he touched her, she did not know it.

Laying more logs on the fire, he filled the cramped, smoky cabin with suffocating heat. Red flames flared into the room. Standing back, he stripped off his shirt and faced his beautiful captive who was sitting, senseless, at the table.

Outside, a rumble of thunder was heard in the distant hills, and a fierce rain suddenly lashed in torrents.

Settling himself beside the raging fire, his head cocked as if listening, Wildman watched Carolyn slip from the stool into a heap on the dirt floor. After a time he rose, gathered her into his arms and lay her once again on his grassy bed.

He let his gaze travel over her body. She was so utterly beautiful lying there, helpless, unknowing.

He crouched beside her, running his hand from her shoulder, along her torso to her belly and beyond. The swells and valleys of her body brought him to a peak of arousal.

He felt set free of the confines of his miserable existence. He knew nothing but this limp, helpless body beneath his eagerly exploring hand. He could envision the white skin beneath the layers of fabric and could almost taste the sweetness he would draw from her secret, treasured places.

Shuddering with the power of his conquest, oblivious to all the obligations awaiting him on this terrible black night, he began sliding the hem of her skirt up her unsplinted leg. She belonged to him. This was not part of Ona's power over him. He, alone, was in command! This woman was his, entirely. He leaned closer still, his mouth salivating, his consuming black desire driving him on relentlessly...

Suddenly Wildman froze, listening to a sound outside the cabin.

Erupting in rage, he hurled himself to the door, tore it open and flung himself into the rain-lashed darkness. He heard someone calling his name frantically from the hill and he was drawn to the sound.

The harridan appeared from the shadows, her rain-wet hair streaming down her thin cheeks and shoulders. Her cloak was drenched, her skirts weighted with mud. The chill wind made him shiver with fury as he lunged to intercept the young woman's march toward his door.

"What are you doing here?"

"Aren't you coming?" she rasped, her tone petulant.

He seized her thin shoulders, furious at the interruption. Her expression was first angry and then suddenly anxious, bordering on fear.

"Please," she pleaded, rain running in rivulets along her cheeks. "I'm the one. Don't think to change that. Please!"

He felt the power of his rage filling him with molten fire. As he saw the helpless look on her face, he wrenched the clasp of her cloak open and tore the heavy wet wool back from her shoulders. He exposed the dampened black wool of her gown's snug bodice and pushed his palms roughly against her breasts.

She didn't struggle, but stood before him, jerked this way and that until he had torn every shred of fabric from her thin white body. Naked in the rain, shivering, the touch of her flesh as cool as death, she let him grasp her to his chest, roughly, angrily. She let him shake the strength from her until she dropped, apparently senseless, into the cold mud at his feet.

But as he fell to his knees beside her, parted her legs and forced himself upon her, her eyes were slitted and she was watching him. She, *not* the interloper, was triumphant. Taking him deeply, feeling her inevitable power intermingle with his useless rage, she lay in the cold, knowing that so long as she possessed him this way, she need fear nothing, not even the specter of the past.

Eight

"You musn't trust her!"

Wildman heard his whore whisper words that he did not want to hear and twisted away. He felt himself plummeting into darkness, his mind spiraling like an eagle shot from the sky. His power was waning, his desire spent, stolen from him by this creature he had so long been bound to.

"Take this," she whispered, urging a leather pouch into his trembling wet hand.

He wanted to dash it to the mud, but he was too weak in spirit to resist. He was the slave of the Followers. He was their sniveling bounden lord who was chained to the effects of potions and powders he could not combat. Even as he stuffed some of the contents into his mouth, he hated himself.

"If you insist on using her, she'll betray you. She'll never allow herself to be possessed, not as you possess me. Listen. Listen!" she rasped, grasping his sleeve. "Don't take her. I know and understand you. I can help...but not if you use another. Think on that, my dark-hearted wildman."

He tore his arm free, lurching away. His breathing was uneven and his heartbeat erratic. "Get away! Leave me!"

"But you must come with me. *Now.* You must! There's so little time left, and if you don't, there will be danger."

He whirled, thinking how easy it would be to kill her. He longed to choke her silent. She was no better than Ona.

Carolyn would never nag and cajole him like this. She would love him. She would free him! If he wanted her, no one could say he must not have her. He was a man of absolute strength!

He advanced on the naked white body huddled in the mud. As he reached for her throat, she caught his wrists. "You must come with me!" Her nails cut crescents in his flesh.

He flung her away from him. "Go on ahead," he said, unable to defy the Followers who needed him so. They knew the depths of his drug-induced needs and the depravity of his sins as their leader and lord.

He turned, trudging into the dark, smoky cabin. Before the harridan could follow him inside, he slammed the door. He didn't want her to see who lay on his bed, half exposed, only half enjoyed. He would kill the whore! He would kill them all!

Carolyn lay as he had left her, her skirts partly up, her face slack. He had given her enough potion that she might die, he realized, feeling momentarily alarmed.

Grabbing a mug filled with water, Wildman dumped enough powder into it to make a vile drink. Nearly gagging, he downed it all. To be possessed, like a puppet...

Slowly his power returned. As it always did, the potion erased the truth of his existence and restored his virile pride, convincing him that he was all they said he was, and more.

He staggered to the door. He knew what lay ahead of him, and suddenly he felt the excruciating madness of it all.

Outside, the storm had nearly passed, and Wildman strode bare-chested through the woods. When he found the half-naked harridan still dragging her cloak behind her as she hurried up the hill, he grabbed hold of her. Shaking her soundly, he threw her down so that he might go on before her, making her follow in his masterful footsteps.

The forest was pitch dark and cold. Rain dripped through the canopy of branches overhead. Carolyn clutched her mother's hand tightly.

Three long, narrow graves stood open before them, looking like windows to hell. Carolyn felt herself starting to fall toward those open graves, felt herself being drawn to them…

And suddenly, she was running, running through the woods! Her mother's hand was cold as she pulled Carolyn through the trees. Sharp branches snatched at her arms. Behind them people were running after them, burning torches in their hands.

Her mother fell, and screamed for Carolyn to go on without her. Carolyn ran more swiftly than she ever had in her life. Finding the cart path, she ran headlong into a horse drawing a small wagon.

"Papa! Papa!" Carolyn cried.

His cold hand closed over her mouth to silence her.

Then Papa ran back into the woods. Carolyn sat alone in the wagon, waiting for him to return, his wife limp in his arms.

In the wagon, Mama lay so still, Carolyn thought surely she must be dead! The wagon rattled away into the threatening darkness.

Then they were safe, Papa said. There was a lighted window ahead. Carolyn felt relieved and wept into her mother's tangled hair. But when they stopped, a shadow appeared from among the trees. The torchbearers drew near.

Unafraid now, Carolyn waited for the shadowed man to speak, but as he did, her heart went cold with horror. He was supposed to exonerate her father, but his words were filled with rage and loathing. Those with torches gathered all around, crying in a single voice, "Tell us, did he kill her?"

The shadowed man appeared to know the answer. If he told the truth, he would be driven away too.

Carolyn saw her father's stricken face. She saw the young man's shadowed face; when he answered, the tender innocence in her heart died.

"He claimed none could save her," the shadowed man said. That was the truth.

"But did he kill her?"

"Yes, he did."

"And what do you say to all the rest of our accusations?" came the ravaged, inflamed cries.

"Yes, to all the rest as well."

• • •

Carolyn woke from the nightmare. Mindlessly, she scrambled from the shallow grassy bed and found herself on all fours, facing a dwindling hearthfire. A musky smell was all about her. Alarmed, she reared up, trying to stand.

Her splinted leg hurt terribly. She had forgotten all but that awful moment when her father was betrayed. Had the dream been mere conjecture, or was it more of that black memory coming to the surface of her mind?

Standing at the door, Carolyn looked out at the gray light of dawn. The rain had ended, turning to frost on the ground. Heaving a ragged sigh, she pressed the door closed.

Lifting a bar into the crude iron brackets so that her host would not be able to enter until she was ready to face him, Carolyn turned back to the low, cavelike den. She felt so confused. What had happened here in the night? Why did she feel like she knew Wildman, knew him from that blank time in her mysterious past?

Murder? Had they accused her papa of murder? She fell upon the stool, stunned and horrified. What physick had not faced such a situation? It was a peril of the imperfect profession. And yet, they had driven him and his wife and child away. The shadowed man in her dream might have saved them all, but he had said…

Who was that tormented man?

She strained to recall the scene in her nightmare, but found only blackness where the vivid images had been moments before. They had trusted this man. He would have known the truth.

If the shadowed man in her nightmare had been John Rasner, then he had betrayed her father. She refused to believe it. Why would John, so dedicated an apprentice, betray his master?

Wildman's silhouette passed the window. Hastily, she climbed to her feet, her heart racing. He tried the door, finding it barred.

After a thoughtful pause, he struck the door once with his fist. She flinched.

"Let me in," he ordered.

She lifted the bar and stood aside. He pushed past her, his cheeks flushed, his pale eyes wide and blazing. He regarded her without familiarity, almost as if he couldn't quite see her.

Before she could speak, he said, "You must go."

Throwing off his cold-stiffened cloak, he went to the hearth and poured steaming water into his mug. She watched him take a pinch of powder from a bowl on the mantel, stir it into the water and drink it down as if unable to feel it scalding his throat.

"Take care!" she said, watching him reach again for the kettle hanging amongst the flames. "You'll burn yourself!" she cried as he grasped the hot handle.

He snatched his hand away and looked at the angry red line raised suddenly across his palm. Could he feel nothing? Her curiosity—her strange attraction to this man—was overwhelming.

Forgetting her leg, compelled to help, Carolyn ran toward him, taking his hand and plunging it into the nearest bucket of cold water. His face betrayed no feeling of pain, but he looked at her with an unsettling intensity.

"Let me see," she said as he curled his hand into a fist and jerked away.

He shook his head once, sharply. "Go, now, before they come for me. Go, or they'll kill you, too!"

"Kill me? Why? What have you or I done?"

"Do they need a reason? They're mad, all of them—you should know that better than anyone. They once drove you away. I must leave now…for a time. I'll try to come back." He backed away from her, the expression in his eyes growing ugly. His lips curled back. "You've brought me trouble."

"But I don't understand!"

From an iron-bound trunk in the corner, he yanked a black woolen clock. "It's cold. Go back the way you came, not into the village. If they learn you were here last night, you might be…stoned."

She shuddered in disbelief. "You don't expect me to…All right, all right! I'm going," she said, seeing his wild-eyed impatience.

But before she could turn away, he seized her shoulders and held her forcibly as he glared into her eyes. Then he kissed her. His lips were cold and hard, grinding into hers until she felt only alarm and pain. He kissed her without passion. It was as if he were branding her, claiming her and then flinging her away with contempt.

He pushed her toward the door, taking little heed of her need to maneuver the crutch. Tottering on the stone doorstep, she forced herself not to turn when he slammed the door behind her and barred it.

A mare's tail of wispy clouds lay across the faded sky. Frost bristled hoary white on every branch and blade of grass. Whereas the night had been black, this morning was a dreamland of white and pearl gray.

As she made her way along the clearing to the path leading down the steep hill, her thoughts swirled. Superstitions and unreasonable fears surrounded her. Everywhere was the black, incontrovertible ignorance of simple country people. What foolishness! She wanted to be away from this wretched place.

As she walked painstakingly back to the path leading to Timberhill, she felt the forest's eyes upon her. Heaps of leaves that were no longer bright but browned and sodden hampered her progress. Why had she returned to Timberhill only to learn that her father had been accused of murder? What could she hope to do to refute that?

She paused, blowing warmth into her numbed hands. "What if…" Her voice sounded flat, frightened.

It was not impossible for a man to make a mistake. What if her father had? Could she have known or suspected, deep in her heart, all along? Was that why she was driven to return?

For more than an hour she struggled along the footpath. Often she paused to rest, her mind a maelstrom of confusion. By the time she reached Timberhill's rear meadow, she was trembling, from fear and cold. Her feet were numb, her head was swimming and her body was racked with chills.

The stone house had melded with the gray forest. It looked gloomy and uninviting in the weak sunlight. No lantern burned in the rear window, no smoke lifted from the chimney.

A tingle of alarm raced through Carolyn as she limped across the meadow. With every ragged breath, she cursed her leg. If Lizza had come to harm...

The house looked so utterly devoid of comfort, she wondered how she could stay another moment. She longed to be home again in her warm, safe bed in Philadelphia. She wanted to be reclining in her parlor, waiting to receive, kiss and marry her dear, patient Evan!

Oh, Evan, she thought. She'd been such a fool to ever leave him. She wiped her hand across her lips and scrubbed at welling tears. What shameful things she had dreamed in that man's cabin!

Whether she had dreamed that the wildman had molested her, or whether it was true, the fact remained that she had been attracted to his mysterious malignant magnetism. Had he bewitched her?

By the light of day, she had to confess to herself that she had wanted to be aroused and satisfied by him. To want that was unthinkable!

Was she going mad? Was she merely hungry for a man's touch, any man's touch? If so, she must fly back to Evan and marry him!

Close to tears, she forced herself past the gaping cellar pit. When at last she reached the rear door and threw it wide, she found no sign of Lizza inside. Her calls echoed in the empty, shabby chambers.

The ashes in the hearth were cold, dampened in the night by rain running down the chimney. Her bedding lay as she had left it. Porridge had congealed in the pot.

She dragged herself down the hall to the front door and flung it wide. Before her were the endless gray rows of leafless trees. She moved out onto the porch. How she longed to hitch the horse to the wagon and be gone, but the horse was still missing from the afternoon before.

The wind slammed the heavy door shut behind her. Startled, she whirled around.

Hanging from a rusty nail in the door was a vile knot of feathers and fur, bloodied and dripping. She let out a throat-tearing scream.

By sheer force of will, she made herself face the ugly mess.

It was intended as a warning. What a cruel, monstrous attempt to frighten her away!

But instead of feeling frightened, she swelled with anger. How dare these fools treat her so! How dare they drive her respected father from his home and send her dear, frail mother into poverty-ridden exile, and a pitiless death? Who was to say that he had made a mistake? Surely not she! Most certainly not they!

Unreasoning rage mushroomed in her breast. Blazing and powerful, it had lain dormant for so long. Now it had awakened. She would fight them all! She would show them the ignorance of their ways, and redeem her father's honor! *That* was why she had come back to Timberhill, and that was what she was duty-bound to do!

With revulsion, she yanked the torn shreds of fur and feathered skin from the door and flung them into the high weeds.

An hour later, chilled and unwell, Carolyn lay watching her dying hearthfire, when suddenly she heard hoofbeats nearing on the road. She struggled to stand and reached for the blunderbuss on the table. If the townspeople had come to drive her away, well, she would welcome them in kind.

At the front door came a timid knock. "Miz Clure?" Lizza slipped in and crept down the hall.

Carolyn was overcome with relief. She set the heavy blunderbuss aside, shaking with chills.

"Miz Clure?" The girl peeked in the kitchen door. "You won't tell my pappy, will you?" she cried, running over to Carolyn and falling to her knees. "Please don't tell him I was out all night. I won't do it again, ever. I swear on anything you say!"

Startled and confused, Carolyn patted the girl's head. "Hush, Lizza. Stand up. Where were you last night? With Noah? I expected you back." Carolyn decided not to mention that she, too, had been away all night.

"It was a terrible night to be out, Miz! Noah…he kept me at his ma's cabin…" She squirmed and twisted a bit of her skirt in her hands. Her eyes glanced about furtively.

Carolyn motioned that Lizza should close the door against

the draft.

Lizza did so and then looked up at Carolyn, her face bright. "Did you eat, Miz? Why, your skirts is all muddy. You been out walking? Why, the fire's almost out. You ain't much without a body looking after you!"

"Was Ona with you last night?"

"No'm. Didn't see her."

Heaving a sigh, Carolyn suspected the warning charm that had been nailed to the door had been Ona's doing. Has she left the forked apple, too?

"Let me see what I can scare you up to eat, Miz! I'm powerful hungry myself. Ona ain't coming this morning. She told us she had folks to meet out on the pike. A peddler, I think."

"I thought you said she wasn't there with you."

"No'm, not till dawn this morning." She shuddered. "I wish we were headed back home, excepting..." She turned, catching Carolyn's eye for an instant. "...excepting that now I can't go off from Noah."

"Oh, dear," Carolyn said, groping her way to the bench by the table. "Your pappy won't be pleased. Do you want a baby before you're properly married?"

"Oh, but Miz, Noah's a good man. He'll marry me! He says he goin' to ask his ma today!"

"He'll have to ask me as well. Your pappy put you in my charge."

Lizza looked so innocent and bewildered that Carolyn could only shake her head. Then she smiled weakly, shivering with a deep chill.

"I'm sure Noah is a very good man."

If Lizza noticed the faint bloodstains on the front door that Carolyn had tried to scrub off, she said nothing. The rest of the day she took to her work with renewed energy, seeming quite eager to please.

Ona failed to return to prepare the afternoon or evening meals.

Noah arrived late to fit new glass into the lower-story windows.

"Was there trouble in town this morning?" Carolyn asked him as he worked. She wanted to know why Wildman had feared being driven away.

"Trouble? Why, no'm, there weren't no trouble as I know about. For the devil's night, it was quiet. That's a fact."

"And you kept Lizza with you all night...at your mother's cabin?"

"Yes'm, kept her safe and sound from all them haunts achasing her." He grinned and laughed to himself. "I 'spect she told you I spoke for her."

"She did. Do you expect Lizza to take up her life here with you now? I don't intend to stay much longer, just a few weeks perhaps. I expected to take her back to her father in Philadelphia. Have you thought about speaking to him about getting married?"

"Yes'm, I'll be doing that soon enough. We're in no hurry, ma'am."

Carolyn let the subject rest. After she had slept an hour, she went out and circled the house. She was looking for footprints, hoping to determine from which direction her ghastly messenger had come.

The day was crisply cold, but clear. The barren trees were a stark tangle against the pale-blue sky. She found nothing to help her determine who had gone to such trouble to frighten her.

However, she did find the entrance to the cellar. A pair of low doors appeared to open to a flight of stone steps leading down into the foundation. She would have taken a closer look, but the doors were fastened shut with a relatively new padlock that had fresh scratches around the keyhole.

The doors had gone unnoticed until now because of bushes that grew so densely over them. They had recently been disturbed.

She suspected the person who had delivered the forked apple had entered the house by way of the cellar. And by the hardened muddy footprints around the door, she suspected someone had entered the house the night before.

Circling the house, her thoughts churned. What might have

happened if she had been alone there the night before? Wildman had been right to keep her with him. Scanning the frosted meadow, she noticed a scrap of something snagged on a twig near Lizza's rubbish heap.

With care, she tugged a yellowed paper free, and her breath caught. It was a water-stained page torn from one of her father's bound journals!

Drawn on the page in faint brown ink was a hastily sketched outline of a female body. Lines had been added to indicate several parts of the body: the throat, breasts, torso and groin. Notes regarding these areas had been written along both margins. On the right side, most of the notations had been nibbled away, perhaps by mice. Because the page had been carelessly torn out, the remarks noted on the left side of the page were probably still in the journal.

Carolyn's hair stood on end. It was her father's unmistakable handwriting, of that she was certain. But his brief notations, almost a kind of code, were so weathered as to be unreadable.

Nevertheless, Carolyn's blood raced to think that a page from one of his journals should appear here in Timberhill's yard. She had thought that all his journals were stored at her house in Philadelphia. After her father's death, she had read them all and was certain not one was missing a page.

Breathless with excitement, she hobbled as fast as she could back to the house. She burst in on Lizza and Noah whispering at the hearth.

"Lizza, can you tell me where you found this?" Carolyn asked, struggling to get herself, her skirts and her crutch inside.

Lizza's expression went rigid. Quickly, she shook her head. "No'm. No'm, I don't know nothing of that!"

Noah frowned at the faint sketch. "It looks like a conjure charm."

Carolyn fought her impatience. "No, it's from a medical report of some sort. Lizza, please, try to remember where you found this. I know you took it from the house to the rubbish heap. It's terribly important."

Carolyn watched the girl's face mirror a dozen emotions. Finally

Lizza gave a shrug. "That day I fell down them stairs I saw it laying up in the hall. I thought it was a conjure charm, too. That's how come I ran."

"By the looks of it, it was there a long while," Carolyn said, shivering as she smoothed her fingers over the faint, unreadable notations. "I can't think why a page should be torn from one of his journals. Can you tell me nothing more?"

Wide-eyed, Lizza shook her head.

"And you've found no books or other loose pages?"

Lizza hung her head.

"Mercy! What can this mean?" To find a page with a sketch of a woman's body on it, all on the heels of dreaming that her father had been accused of murder…

Her ague growing worse, Carolyn finally retired beside the hearth for the night. After a while, she fell asleep, but was troubled all night long by strange dreams of lying helpless and naked, prey to a looming vulture in a black cloak.

The following day, Ona returned to Timberhill early in the morning. She prepared the day's meals and tended to the final preparations for Carolyn's bedchamber upstairs. Ona made no explanation for her absence the day before, and to Carolyn's consternation she couldn't bring herself to question the woman about it.

The window and staircase repairs were finally completed, the lower chambers clean, if barren. They ate in the dining room for the first time.

As the days passed, Carolyn found that she woke each morning feeling as if she had dreamed of Evan in the night. She still felt disappointed that he hadn't come to lure her home, and decided the time had come to write him.

Taking up her quill and bottle of ink in the privacy of the cold dining room, she pondered her message. Dipping and redipping the quill into the pale-brown ink, she wondered what she might now write to Evan. Penning the date at the top of her stationery, she realized Forrest had been dead a month. The poor man.

At last, Carolyn began her letter. "Dearest Evan," she wrote. "Please understand my haste in leaving Philadelphia. I have taken up residence at Timberhill, and am mending well. You were right to warn me that I would not be welcome here. Much has happened to trouble me. Silas has not come, and therefore I have decided to stay on until spring. My deepest thanks for your patience. You are much in my thoughts. Carolyn."

Spring! she thought, as startled by her decision as Evan would likely be. Had she really decided to stay at Timberhill that long?

After sending the note to the village with Noah, she fretted over its safe delivery. She decided she must go into the village herself, as soon as possible, to be certain it had been sent.

Carolyn's fear that Ona wished to frighten her away began to seem ludicrous. On the contrary, the woman seemed eager for Carolyn to stay as long as she liked.

But Carolyn's dreams remained persistently provocative. She thought of Evan, or Wildman, almost hourly. She wanted word from Evan, and none came.

"What have you heard of your friend, the wildman?" she asked as they moved her bedding into the upper chamber a few days later. All the original furniture was still in place. Though several tables had been ruined by rain, and the bed drapes were brittle and brown beyond washing, the chamber was now habitable.

"You'd be wise to say nothing of that, Miz. On your life," Ona said.

"Must you be so mysterious? I must know more about this man. Who is he? Where did he come from? Why must he live in exile, and flee the villagers? What do they think he does to deserve such treatment?" She felt drawn to him, consumed by curiosity, haunted by the erotic dreams she had of a man she should fear.

The woman lapsed into silence, giving Carolyn brooding, reproachful looks.

Sighing, Carolyn resolved that she would not learn what had

become of Wildman until she saw him again for herself.

Carolyn found she could set her worries aside when sipping Ona's soothing tea. That afternoon, Ona moved about the kitchen as she had so long ago in Carolyn's childhood. Carolyn felt transported into the past. At any moment she fantasized that her mother might enter and embrace her. Her gentle, loving father might arrive home to smile at her and remove all her cares.

Carolyn could ponder her dreams—or were they nightmares?—of Wildman coming to her in some forest glen. There she imagined herself lying in the grass, powerless to avoid his caress. Her heart beat wildly. The heat of her thoughts stained her cheeks. She could almost taste his kisses…

As those forbidden fantasies filled her mind, she sipped her tea. The flavor was no longer bitter. It no longer made her more thirsty than quenched. She was glad, after all, to be at Timberhill. She had not a care in the world.

Seeing her contentment, Ona would smile. The drug was doing its work well indeed.

Nine

At times, Carolyn couldn't focus her thoughts. They felt like fireflies, flitting brightly through her mind, never staying very long.

She had nothing to occupy her mind. No word came from Evan. She had no heart for trekking through the woods in search of Wildman. Though feeling physically stronger, she simply watched the hours pass. She didn't want to think about the journal page she had found or its possible importance. Nothing whatsoever seemed urgent.

During one lazy, contented afternoon, Carolyn went up to her bedchamber for a nap. Though the room was truly dreary, she found comfort in the small hearthfire and lay remembering those long-ago days of her girlhood.

Drifting into a half-sleep, she remembered the erotic lethargy she had felt All Hallow's Eve in Wildman's cabin. Helpless to resist the undulating black silhouette of him, she lay limp and warm, savoring his dreamy, forbidden touch.

She woke tingling with alarm. Feeling bewitched, she wanted freedom from the unmentionable dreams! She wanted her energy and resolve back! She remembered Wildman pressing the warm mug of tea to her lips. Ona's tea had nearly the same effect!

She got up, craving the tea. She had suspected Ona before, and now she wondered if she was being drugged with laudanum or opium. Ona was trying to keep her at Timberhill, and Carolyn couldn't fathom why!

For the remainder of the afternoon, on into the night and all the next morning, Carolyn only pretended to drink Ona's tea. The ache in her leg returned; she grew ill and depressed. To think that, for all her so-called medical knowledge, she had no idea what she had been drinking, of its effect on her thoughts…

At luncheon the following day, she sipped her tea and was startled by the strong bitter flavor. The invigorating effect was more pronounced. Ona must have been conditioning her to greater and greater dosages!

Carolyn needed all her strength to resist draining the cup. Even with her limited knowledge of pharmacology, she knew that some herbs producing lethargy, sleep and loss of pain came from poisonous nightshade and belladonna.

Carolyn wanted to seize Ona and demand to know what was being done to her, and why, but she dared say nothing.

Deciding she needed a distraction from her worries, Carolyn slipped outside an hour later and hitched the horse to the wagon. How glad she was the horse was back. As she started down the lane, she glanced back at the house and saw Ona's startled face framed in an upper-story window.

At the gates to the Ebey estate located halfway to Eudoxia, Carolyn paused to reflect on her girlhood friend. She longed to take her condolences, however tardy, to her friend's mother.

Fresh wheel tracks turned into the weedy coachway, marking the otherwise undisturbed road dust. How desolate and bleak the forest looked beyond the gate.

Just as she was about to go on, Carolyn looked up to see a movement in the trees. Her horse snorted in alarm.

Recognizing the tall man with the gaunt white face, she shuddered. It was Mrs. Ebey's manservant, and he was holding a long walking stick.

Wanting to call out, she found her throat frozen. Unnerved, she snapped the lines, sending the horse into a frenzied gallop along the lane toward the village.

She wasn't herself, she thought. With pounding heart, Carolyn crossed the ford in the brook. Concerned about Lizza's safety, she felt torn by the desire to return at once to Timberhill, and her need to reach the village.

And yet she knew that she must continue on her way to the village, if only to spend a little time in the company of sane people! Perhaps they would keep her from fleeing back into the forest like a madwoman.

When Carolyn reached the postmaster, she determined that Noah had indeed posted her letter. With relief, she tried engaging the bespectacled postmaster in conversation, but he steadfastly ignored her until she gave up and hobbled out.

When she reined in at the white frame general store up the road, she felt watchful, speculative eyes upon her. Entering the store, Carolyn found the warm smell of wood smoke and cinnamon inviting. A plain woman, wearing a calico smock covering her daydress, looked up from measuring rice into sacks. A smile flickered on her face until she recognized Carolyn as a stranger.

Backing away, the woman glanced at the rear door as if longing to escape. "You're the one living out at the…the old Adams place?"

Wounded by the woman's frightened, reproving tone, Carolyn introduced herself, explaining that she had grown up there.

"But I've lived here all my life," the woman told her with a frown. "I don't remember you. Well, I do recall that a girl who was living out at that old estate died in a fire. A grisly tale. I was only a child. My younger brothers had both just died, so it's not a clear memory."

Carolyn edged forward. "They died? I'm sorry."

"Perhaps you went away before the putrid throat took all the village's children—well, nearly all, it seemed. Enough died to bereave a dozen families."

The woman looked a few years younger than Carolyn. How strange that Carolyn could not recall the diphtheria epidemic. Surely she would have been old enough to be impressed by the tragic effects?

"I didn't die in the fire, as you can see," Carolyn said. She hoped she sounded open enough to keep the woman pouring forth her unexpected wealth of information. "There was a fire, though. Who might tell me more of the epidemic?"

"Anyone in the town, but don't ask Lucile Ebey." She leaned forward to confide in Carolyn. "She's mad, that one. But then you must be, too, to stay in that old place. It's a ruin, and haunted, I'm told. Why, the things that go on out there on the nights of the old pagan feasts! Lights passing in the windows, screams and such…A decent Christian wants to lock the shutters and fall down to pray!"

"Nothing happened there this past All Hallow's Eve," Carolyn insisted.

The woman shrugged. "I was in bed with my Bible clutched to my heart."

"If it's any comfort, I've been readying the house for my brother-in-law, a preaching man."

"Coming here! Mercy, it'll be a blessing to have one about again! We've lost our last three, all on account of that wicked seeress, Ona Ruby. Why, that godless woman! It's a sin how she fills ignorant children with superstitious nonsense. Some believe she appeared here by magic, but we all know she fled from some terrible scandal. If we had the power to drive her out, we would.

"Ona's stories aren't helped by poor Mrs. Ebey living alone with that awful half-wit she calls a manservant. Brained him herself, some claim. If a stranger was to come to town…why, I was just saying at meeting last week that a stranger would think us a queer bunch. I can't recall who said you'd all perished in a fire. It's just a story that's been about for years. A preacher! When did you say he's arriving?"

Carolyn went on to explain, and the woman seemed to take great comfort at the promise of a new preacher. But Carolyn still had questions that needed answering. "Might you tell me where the Rasners live?"

"Oh, mercy, that poor old man, just as sour as a bad pickle. Helen's a saint with him. Do you know Helen? A dear girl, saddled with that old man's care. They live over that way." She went to the window and pointed to a distant house that was set apart from the village, not far from the Tilbury homestead. "She'd be delighted to have company. Can't find a decent man to marry her until that old goat gives up the ghost. He'll probably live to bury her. Took his leave of the family for almost ten years, leaving his wife to nearly starve to death. When he came back it's said he demanded his rights, though he was surely a stranger after so long. She bore little Helen nine months later...and died in her boy's arms. It's a scandal, to be sure. Some say that's why the boy ran off. He might've killed the old man otherwise."

"His son ran off?" Carolyn asked, her heart leaping.

"To war. The army was camped all around here then."

"But the war was years after the birth of John Rasner's sister."

The woman shook her head, as if the discrepancy bore no relation to the quality of her gossip.

At the sound of the moaning wind, the woman lifted her head. "Storm's coming, Mrs. Clure. If you expect to get back to Timberhill safely by darkfall, you'd best be on your way. You don't want to be caught alone in these haunted woods." She chuckled as if joking.

Unamused, Carolyn made her way to the door. She felt the woman watching her and she paused before going out. "Did anything unusual happen the morning after All Hallow's Eve?"

Suspiciously, the woman shook her head.

"What I mean is, was there some sort of uproar over a...a strange man in the woods?" Carolyn blushed as she said the words, feeling foolish.

The shopwoman pondered but finally shook her head again. "Not as I heard about, unless you're talking of Ona's wildman. He's the one waiting in the wood for unwary travelers at dusk." She chuckled. "It's the time of year for that sort of thing, you know. That ignorant old woman and her fireside stories...You probably haven't heard about our local ghost, Wildman.

"Some have it he's a shriveled, misshapen slave, one hundred and some years old. A conjure doctor, they call him, good for herb cures, love potions and such superstitious mumbo jumbo. Others claim he's a beggar in rags who will come to your house in the night and steal your goats, chickens...or children.

"The little ones hereabouts believe he's half bear and half man, that he roars in the wood and will eat them if they wander too far into the forest. It keeps a curious child close to the hearth.

"When I was a girl, some of my more foolish friends—those who were left after the epidemic—claimed that he was a handsome prince, bewitched and evil, of course."

Carolyn decided to hold her tongue. She would add nothing to the myths about Wildman. She turned at the sound of an arriving chaise outside.

"Oh my, Verity doesn't look well, poor old soul," the shopkeeper said, craning to look out the window at the women in the chaise.

The trees outside were swaying in a driving wind. Hard bits of angry snow raced sideways, hitting the windows and gathering in the corners of each pane.

Carolyn thought to order a few supplies while she was at the store, and dug into her reticule for the proper coin. Startled, she found her purse empty, and stood several seconds frowning in thought. Would Lizza have robbed her?

"Is there anything more I can do for you, Mrs. Clure?"

"Thank you, no. Good day," Carolyn called absently, limping toward the door.

Puzzled by her missing money, Carolyn stepped out. She tugged the wind-buffeted door closed behind her. Ducking her head, she tried to avoid the stinging bits of snow driving into her face.

Her cousin Annatie was just looping the lines and climbing down from the chaise when Carolyn left the store. Her somber skirts billowed in the wind to reveal shabby petticoats. Her nose and eyes were an unattractive red, indicating a severe case of grippe.

Carolyn's Aunt Verity was looking straight at Carolyn, a shocked expression on her powdery white face. Not having expected to encounter her aunt and cousin, Carolyn felt a momentary reluctance to acknowledge them.

Aunt Verity's eyes were hard and angry. Her words struck blows to Carolyn's confidence. "I thought I had made it clear that you were unwelcome in Eudoxia," the old woman growled.

"Hello, Aunt Verity, Cousin Annatie. How are you both today? Annatie, you look as if you've taken cold."

Carolyn's greeting was met with raised brows and hostile silence. To be shunned by her own blood kin was more than she cared to endure.

Realizing that they apparently weren't going to say more, Carolyn moved toward her wagon. The snow drove mercilessly into her eyes. Angrily, she was about to struggle aboard unassisted when she turned back. "You knew I was still at Timberhill. Ona is working for me, readying the house."

"Is she?" Aunt Verity said, edging toward the store, her worn brown cloak snapping in the wind.

"Before you go inside," Carolyn interrupted, struggling to keep a hard edge from her voice. "Could you tell me anything about an epidemic here around the same time that my parents and I left?"

Annatie cast her a sharply reproachful look, but it was her aunt's reaction that caught Carolyn's attention. Verity stiffened as if she was feeling a stabbing pain in her back.

Annatie steadied her mother. "As long as you insist on upsetting Mother, I'll tell you that I think you're horrid for not recalling that dreadful autumn or the death of my sister, your own cousin Trintie."

Blinking with surprise, Carolyn shook her head. "Forgive me. I remember very little of that time."

Her aunt recovered herself and faced Carolyn with tottering strength. "Trintie died of putrid throat, as did so many others that year, including your friend Katarinia. You…lived," she said as if condemning her.

Carolyn remembered the lonely, neglected gravestones she and Lizza had stumbled across on their first day back. "The Ebey children died of diphtheria, all three?"

Aunt Verity turned, grasping the store's doorhandle with a palsied hand. "All in one terrible night."

Carolyn sagged into the driving wind, allowing the chill of the long-ago tragedy to soak deep into her heart. So, *that* was why the townspeople had driven her family from their home. "My father was blamed…" she whispered, struggling not to weep over such devastating ignorance as these women and the villagers possessed.

Her aunt and cousin only glared at her.

Carolyn's hand went to her throat. She had a small scar there that her father had always refused to explain. Not so long ago she had learned of a rare procedure for easing breathing in the event of putrid throat, or rather the dreaded reaper, diphtheria, which carried off so many young during the winter months.

Annatie shushed her. "We have no desire to talk of those times, or of your father. Yes, he was blamed! He killed those children whom he treated with his insane practices! Now, take yourself from here before someone remembers and asks you to pay a debt no one can in this life."

The two women slipped inside the general store, shutting the door, leaving Carolyn to ponder what she had learned. Blamed for the deaths of children—her poor, poor father. Of course, she should have suspected that any one of her father's innovative procedures might have caused fear and misunderstanding.

Still, she couldn't understand why the villagers would drive a well-intentioned physician, his consumptive wife and innocent child into the woods. Surely her father's procedure had saved a few lives! It had saved hers! Was he prevented from explaining the necessity for cutting into a young throat blocked by disease?

Dreamlike words echoed in her mind. "Tell us, did he kill her?" the voices in her nightmare had demanded.

She shivered, wondering if her father might have made a mistake. Knowing anatomy of the human throat was difficult when only hanged criminals were available for study. No such cadavers would have been available in so isolated an area as Eudoxia. His knowledge gathered from textbooks and lectures in distant towns would have been dated, and certainly incomplete.

Feeling abandoned and alone, Carolyn climbed aboard her wagon. She drove on through Eudoxia, lost in thought. Before she knew it, she had come to an untidy red brick house. The sign on the gate read: Rasner.

Snow was collecting among the weeds and overlong grasses. The sky was a dismal slate gray, promising more snow would fall.

The nagging thought that her father might have caused even a single death made her uneasy. She wondered, momentarily, if she should return to Timberhill and abandon her venture now that she knew what her father had been accused of.

Undecided about what to do or where to go, Carolyn watched the door open. Out stepped a slim young woman with flyaway brown hair. She was dressed in blue and had a friendly greeting ready on her face.

In her dejected frame of mind, Carolyn couldn't resist talking to someone who remembered how to smile. "Please excuse my uninvited arrival," she said, feeling acutely weary in body and heart.

"Oh, our exciting mystery woman!" Helen said, holding out her arm to help Carolyn to the snowy ground. "Do come in, Carolyn, and warm yourself. Forgive me for not coming to call, but I can't leave my father for an hour without regretting it a month. What brings you here? Let me see if I can rouse Papa. He'll surely want a glimpse of you. When I told him that I'd heard an Adams had returned to Timberhill, he had only curses for you, but he's a dotty old fool. You mustn't take offense."

Carolyn found the woman's matter-of-fact tone startling. "You can't know what a relief it is to find a friendly face!" Carolyn said, making her way into the house and parlor. Already she felt less dismal.

"This village is stagnant, isn't it? Such a fussy place, filled with silly muddle-headed old people. There is little work left at the mill, so most of our young people have gone off. That leaves the old ones and their memories, and those of us who feel we must care for the old ones. Make yourself comfortable. I'll only be a moment."

Helen hurried out.

Though she knew some people believed that to tend another's hearth brought bad luck, Carolyn lit the logs laid in the grate. She waited on a threadbare divan, delighted to find Helen so welcoming and kind.

Helen returned quickly, carrying a plate of maple fritters and plain, bland tea. Carolyn drank it, grateful she didn't have to fear that it might cloud her thoughts or put her to sleep.

Not mentioning the strange things that had happened to her at Timberhill, Carolyn enjoyed talking with her charming hostess. She let Helen chatter on about town gossip for some time.

At length, Helen leaned forward. "I feel that you're troubled, Carolyn. What can I do to help?"

"I suppose I am. I came back to Timberhill seeking relief from the grief over my husband's death, and the horrors of the epidemic in the city. Now I find myself isolated, prey to peculiar thoughts. I-I can never be sure if I'm thinking clearly…or letting foolishness overtake me. I just learned something I think explains why my father was driven from here—an epidemic of putrid throat sixteen years ago. Do you remember it?"

"I remember only that my brother John did all he could…and when it was all over, your family had gone. More than half of the village children had been buried. John went away, and I never saw him again. I was left to tend my father. I had always looked after Papa, so that wasn't difficult to bear, but I had loved John dearly. It was a miserable time for me after word of his death came during the war."

"You survived the epidemic," Carolyn said. "Did my father tend you?"

"John would have looked after me."

"Do you have a scar on your throat, like this one?" Carolyn asked, tugging her gown's high collar aside.

"Oh, no, my brother would not have bled me to get a cure! In any event, my illness was mild. Dear me, Carolyn, might we leave this hurtful subject? The loss of my brother pains me still."

"As it does me," Carolyn said, interested to think that Helen knew nothing of the throat procedure she mistook for bleeding. "What do you think of my cousin?" she asked.

"I shouldn't speak ill of Annatie behind her back, for she is like me, caring for an aging parent who is filled with bitter memories. But Annatie is excessively religious. She wears on my patience. She is forever after me to pray with her…" Helen grinned sheepishly.

"Frankly, I would rather journey up to Henderson for a good reel with some of the country men who might be looking for a strong, patient wife."

"Patient you must be, too, to have endured my thoughtless questions," Carolyn said, struggling to rise. "I must go now. I've been warned about being on the road after dark. I don't think anything more savage than a pothole would swallow me up, but..." She shivered, remembering the tall, white-faced man in the trees.

Helen looked alarmed. "Who would warn you? These woods are harmless, except for disease, or the pinch of narrow minds."

Carolyn laughed in spite of her churning thoughts. "You've heard of the wildman, I should hope."

"Oh, what utter nonsense! Children's tales for Hallow's Eve. Surely you didn't think he could be real."

"I've met him," Carolyn said, blushing.

"I can't imagine it! You must be joking. Carolyn, my dear new friend, you've done more than break your leg! I believe your isolation has addled you!"

Carolyn laughed. "Nevertheless, I...met him, once. I'm sure. And some strange things have happened to make me think someone would like me to leave as quickly as possible. Other things cause me to think I'm being gently persuaded to stay longer than I'd like. To speak of it aloud makes me see how ridiculous it all must sound. And now that I know why the villagers harbor bitterness toward my father—"

"Forgive me, Carolyn, but the opinion of most people I know here is that he...he hastened death." Helen went pale. "Some went so far as to say he murdered those unfortunate children."

Gripping her stomach, Carolyn choked out, "I see. I know of nothing I can say or do to change such ignorant opinions. Even today, my father's practices and those he taught are still considered radical. That he saved lives, that he taught my late husband to save lives, seems to matter little to those who would most benefit from his foresight and genius. My father was a great surgeon! If the children died, it was because he was not called, or called too late."

"That may well be, given the times. Do clear your mind of it now. It's done and past." Helen assisted Carolyn to the door and draped her cloak around her shoulders. "And you cannot bring back those lost."

Carolyn sighed. "It would seem, then, that my quest is at an end. I feel rather disheartened, I must admit. I might have been spared a good deal of annoyance if I had simply been told that my father was blamed for those deaths."

"My neighbors are a superstitious lot, preferring to pray or wear a good-luck charm than allow a man with ungodly practices to save even a dying child. And as for them giving up their grudges against you, that would rob them of a much-needed source of high emotion. We're an exceedingly dull lot!"

"I appreciate your honesty, Helen, and your hospitality," Carolyn said, heading out to the snow-coated wagon.

Helen helped Carolyn into the wagon. "Will you remove to Philadelphia soon? I hear that even President Washington and his cabinet have returned. You would do better there than here, Carolyn. I might come to visit you, and you could introduce me to eligible gentlemen!"

Carolyn gave her a smile. "I would, to be sure. I know a very kind, patient man there, and I miss him greatly. I do believe I'll start home in a day or so."

"I'm sorry that you lost your parents and husband, Carolyn. Would there be anything more I could do for you?"

Carolyn snapped the lines, turning the wagon in the coachway. In the gray shadows of dusk, Helen Rasner looked small and forlorn. "Wish me Godspeed home," Carolyn called, waving her farewell.

"I wish you that, Carolyn, and a contented future!"

Annatie lashed the chaise horse, frantic to get back to Lucile's house before the snow grew too deep. Glad to have left her mother at home, determined now that she would see Carolyn driven from

Timberhill at any cost, she drove on and on, heedless of the cold.

As she drove, she thought that it was strange not to see Carolyn's wheel tracks marking the snowy lane back to Timberhill. The wretched woman! Annatie lashed the horse as if it was her contemptible rival's back.

Careening between the slouching brick gateposts, she reined before the bleak Ebey house. She had left the place only hours before with her mother, when they had headed for the store, thinking all their troubles had been solved.

But so long as Carolyn Adams still existed within the circle of Annatie's carefully structured life, she had no hope of retaining what little was hers! *All was in peril.*

Sneezing, she climbed down from the chaise and stormed to the door. Without waiting for Joseph to admit her, she flung herself inside. She sneezed again, cursing the debt she must now pay for having lain in the cold rain with her savage lover.

"Lucile!" she shouted, climbing the stairs. She found the woman cowering in her filthy, cluttered chamber. "Has Joseph come back? If he has, he must go out again. Carolyn was in the village only an hour ago. I won't have it!"

Lucile's long, tousled gray hair fluttered about her face. Her once-white ruffled cap was askew, her nightshift wretched beyond description. "I haven't seen him," she rasped, drawing up her gray tattered cover in her bed. "Has he displeased you?" She raised an arm to fend off Annatie's wrath.

"You old fool, you're drooling. I'm not going to strike you, not unless your stupid Joseph doesn't do as he's told." She paused, listening to a shuffling step somewhere in the house. Unnerved, she whirled around to the door, her cloak billowing. "Is that him? Joseph! Joseph Flies, you simpleton! Come here at once!"

Annatie waited, furious that she was forced to deal with such inept cretins. As she thought of losing her precious, virile wildman to his lust for a new conquest, she felt a welling of panic in her breast.

Damn Ona, and damn Wildman for being prey to her poisons! Damn Carolyn for tipping the finely wrought balance of her life!

What would become of her? Annatie wondered as her panic spiraled. How black a future she would face if it were devoid of the man she loved with such compulsion. What other life might she hope for now that she had so fully embraced all that was evil?

"Joseph, don't lie. I know you didn't drive her away yet. You have to go back!" She tumbled down the rotting staircase after the tall, gaunt man who fled at her threatening words.

In his reckless flight, Joseph dropped the hayfork with its wickedly sharpened tines and loped beyond the coachway into the trees.

"Damn you, you must do as you're told!" Annatie screeched. "Blithering fool! If you fail, your mistress will cane you within an inch of your life! Or I will! Come back!"

Ten

Huddled and shivering at the trestle table, Carolyn gratefully ate several slices of Ona's fresh, delicious bread. She watched as the dark-faced woman placed a cup of innocent-looking tea before her. Carolyn shook her head in refusal. "I had tea in the village."

Ona asked nothing about Carolyn's unexpected visit to the village, and she seemed unconcerned that Carolyn would drink none of the tea. She soon returned to her preparations for the evening meal.

An eerie breath of cold air teased into the hearth-warmed kitchen.

"Lizza, if you would, please take the warming pan up to my bed. I'm weary," Carolyn said, shivering in the draft. "When you're done, I want a word with you."

Lizza turned from her place by the fire. She looked puzzled, and then paused, listening to the wind outside.

Night had fallen. Belligerent wind buffeted the house from the north. Snow reflected lantern light as it swirled outside the kitchen windows. Carolyn listened to a strange creaking coming from the front of the house and wondered, momentarily, if the aging rafters and beams would hold together another night.

"Please go up now, Lizza," Carolyn said, catching Ona's eye. "Stay a moment more, Ona. I want a word with you as well."

Lizza used a pair of iron tongs to pluck several glowing coals from the grate. She deposited them in a long-handled iron warming pan, closed the pierced lid and went off, holding the pan out before her.

When they were alone, Carolyn looked at the old woman beside her. "Ona, did you lead me to believe your friend with the beard was called Wildman?"

Ona's eyes drew dark. "Why you be asking?"

"I know that he lives near here. I'd like for you to tell me his real name. I'd like to help him. It's a shame that he is forced to live as a recluse, subject to the hostilities of an ignorant village."

"That be his choice. He have no name, Miz." She glanced out the window. "Snow's afalling fast. I be going now."

"I—"

Carolyn's protest was silenced by Lizza's piercing scream.

As she sprang to her feet, she heard the warming pan clang to the floor. Lizza bolted down the staircase, wailing. Carolyn reached the door as the girl burst in, colliding with her.

Carolyn staggered back, placing too much weight on her leg. "What is it this time?" she cried, her nerves ragged.

"It's a warning, Miz! It means death! Death to you!" Lizza clutched at her curls. "Somebody wants you dead, Miz! You got to go away!"

"What possesses you, Lizza, to say such things? Show me what you've found."

"No'm! No'm!" Wild-eyed, Lizza shook her curly dark head, pointing a shaking finger at the ceiling overhead. "I'm not going back up there!"

Furious and expecting to find another gruesome charm, Carolyn hobbled down the shadowed hall and limped up the groaning stairs. At the top she saw the faint golden glow of the warming pan's coals scattered on the bare planks of her bedchamber floor. The smell of scorching wood grew stronger.

Hastily, she limped into the chamber and scooped the coals back into the receptacle. When she straightened, she saw on her bed pillow a shriveled brown organ resembling the heart of a barnyard animal. Covered with dirt, as if it had been buried and then resurrected, it now sported several thorny twigs snagged in the long-dead flesh.

Uttering a grunt of disgust, she swung her crutch and knocked it to the floor. With a shudder, she stooped and picked it up by one of the thorny twigs.

This wasn't Ona's doing. The woman had been with her in the kitchen since Carolyn had returned from the village. Carolyn had come directly abovestairs to change into a dry skirt and shoes, and had gone down again to supper. Nothing had lain on her pillow then.

This was the work of the tall, white-faced man, she thought. He could gain entry to the house from the outside cellar door. She struggled from the chamber and back down to the kitchen.

Lizza wailed, wringing her hands as Carolyn entered and flicked the death symbol to the floor at Ona's feet.

"We got to turn the curse!" Lizza cried, turning anxious eyes on Ona. "You got to help us! Tell us what to do!"

Ona silenced Lizza with a wave of her hand. She looked as surprised to see the vile charm on the floor as Carolyn. "That be a devil sign. Mighty bad."

"Hallow's Eve is done, Ona. Do you know of anyone who might have reason to frighten us with this sort of thing? The man who calls himself Wildman, perhaps?"

Ona looked darkly amused by such a suggestion.

Lizza cast her eyes to the side, twisting her skirt and working her mouth.

Carolyn seized the girl's shoulder. "You've seen someone!"

"Miz Ona, she said she'd take care of him."

"Who?" Carolyn demanded.

"A tall old haunt. Looks like a haunt, anyhow. She said his name was Flies. Or something like that."

"Who is this man Flies?" Carolyn demanded of Ona.

"Joseph Flies. He be the serving man of Miz Ebey."

"Mercy, is there no end to this nonsense?" Carolyn cried. "I should have gone to see Mrs. Ebey, but I didn't have the stomach for it. Now I must."

"But we got to get away from this house!" Lizza wailed, tugging on Carolyn's sleeve.

"And we will, the moment the snow has stopped." She limped

to the window, feeling cold drafts of wind seeping through the frame. She saw nothing suspicious outside.

"I be going," Ona said, draping herself in her dark cloak. She lifted the hood until it covered her head. All Carolyn could see were her black, fathomless eyes.

She waited for no permission. Opening the door to a blast of frigid night air, Ona went out, closing the door behind herself.

What impudence! From the window, Carolyn watched the woman's dark form drift along the dismal blue shadows of the newly fallen snow. She headed toward the surgery and finally disappeared into the darkness beyond.

"Yes, we'll go, Lizza," Carolyn said thoughtfully. "I have no more business here. If Mrs. Ebey has sent her manservant to frighten us away, it's done in ignorance. I finally understand what lies behind all that's happened here. I'm sorry to have brought you so much grief, Lizza. You're a good, brave girl. Your pappy will be proud of you. And, of course, I'll pay you very well when we get home."

Lizza looked appeased until her eyes fell on the pierced sheep's heart still lying so grotesquely on the floor. She stiffened and began weeping. "Mercy, Lord, forgive my sins!"

Carolyn bent over and plucked up the heart, giving it one hard look, as if by looking squarely at it she could neutralize its harrowing effect on her mind. She took it to the kitchen door, ready to fling it away into the snow. If the snowfall hadn't already been so deep she would have taken it to the cellar pit and burned it.

The wind was too sharp and strong, however, so she threw it away into the darkness, cursing those who dared to curse her.

Pushing the door closed, Carolyn turned, rigid with determination. "We'll latch all shutters before going to sleep, just like we have been doing. I know we'll be perfectly all right."

Lizza nodded slightly, unsure.

Upstairs, Carolyn moved from chamber to chamber, struggling to lift warped sashes and latch the shutters. With each successive window barred against the gnawing dangers of a storm-ridden forest, she felt safer.

Below, she heard Lizza doing the same. Carolyn sighed, feeling weary to her soul. She dragged herself into her bedchamber, where she revived the hearthfire, latched the shutters and then turned to ask herself if she dared crawl into a bed so recently defiled by superstitious ignorance.

Her pillow cover was unstained. Carolyn tugged it off, nevertheless, and took it down to the kitchen to be washed. She found Lizza curled like a child as close to the blazing hearth as she could get without being singed.

"Do you think a body can be hexed?" Lizza asked, her voice filled with terror.

Carolyn rubbed her burning, tired eyes. "No, I don't. You shouldn't, either."

"Ona says your mama was hexed."

"My mother had consumption. My father did all he could to learn how to save her life. He tested a thousand remedies and drugs on himself first, hoping to find a cure. He spent all he could spare on medical texts from the finest universities the world 'round in hopes of maintaining her life.

"In the end we were driven from here. He was needed for the Continental army and taken away. He was promised adequate recompense and told that we would be cared for, but Congress had greater concerns than a sickly woman and her frightened young daughter. My father was a hundred miles away when my mother died. In any case, he could have done nothing for her. That, more than anything, put him in his grave."

Sadly, Lizza wagged her head. "No'm. Your mama was hexed by her sister on her wedding day, right here in this house. Ona told me so. She was here. They was receiving the wedding gifts and your mama got this house. Ol' Verity Harpswell cursed her. God's truth."

"God has nothing whatever to do with such nonsense!" Carolyn snapped, her patience exhausted. "My mother died of lung consumption, an incurable disease, not the bitter rivalry of her sister's selfishness."

"God's got no say in suchlike as this, Miz. God's just a good old man who don't wish a body harm. It's the devil we're talking about, and he's all over these woods. If a body calls him up, he don't ever go away again. I vow he's been called upon us."

"I can't abide your prattle, Lizza. Ona didn't even work here when my mother was married! She came from whatever godforsaken place she was before to Timberhill a full ten years later. Now go to sleep."

Lizza turned her sullen gaze to the leaping, teasing flames. "If Miz Ona says she was here, she was here," she muttered.

Wearily, Carolyn climbed the staircase one step at a time, her heart feeling sore and heavy. Save for the welcoming hearthfire, her bedchamber was shrouded in shadow. Though thoroughly cleaned, there was an emptiness to the chamber caused by more than the mere shabbiness of the furnishings.

At the window, Carolyn stood looking out between the gap in the shutters. A soft snow fell against the glass, and wind drove in through tiny cracks, leaving little piles of snow on the peeling sill.

She felt the cold enfolding her, numbing her fingers, causing her leg to ache. She turned and stared at the lonely bed and breathed in the musty smell of forgotten years. She could draw no comfort from the chamber. Its beauty and life had died long ago. She could hardly wait for morning, when she could pack and leave.

Her poor papa...Poor Forrest...To be so dedicated and so misunderstood. She lit a white candle and placed the pewter candlestick on the table beside her bed. Its dim light did naught to enliven the chamber.

The walls leapt with orange shadows like those she had seen in Wildman's cabin. She *had* seen him, she thought. He had not been a dream. She had his black cloak hanging on a peg in the kitchen as proof.

With her cheeks stinging from the cold, she struggled onto the hard mattress. Stiffly, she lay between linens untouched by Lizza's warming pan; the coals lay as cold ash now in the long-handled pan by the door.

The new ropes laced in the frame beneath the mattress creaked a protest as she settled herself. Below, in the kitchen, she might imagine a thousand night sounds to fever her imagination, but upstairs she was surrounded by penetrating lulling silence.

She drifted into sleep and found herself walking in a dense wood. Feeling young and free, she began running across a sunlit meadow until she forgot why she was running, and began fleeing instead.

As the darkening forest closed in around her, she heard shouts. Ahead, in the trees, fire began leaping. She heard a wailing shriek that raised her hair.

In the distance, she saw a man watching her. His stocky body was a shadow. Should she run to him, or from him?

A short, hair-raising shriek lifted Carolyn from her dream, flinging her upright in the bed. Momentarily disoriented by the leaping orange shadows on the stained walls, Carolyn quickly cast her confusion aside and struggled to the floor.

She heard nothing. Only silence.

Her heart raced. She felt trapped and, like a child, wanted to hide beneath the bed.

Seizing control of her panic, she waited for her heart to slow. Standing at the door, she called, "Lizza? Are you all right?" Then she recalled Lizza would not answer, believing an unexpected call was Death summoning her.

Taking her crutch with her, Carolyn went down the stairs and hobbled to the closed kitchen door. That was odd, she thought. Lizza preferred having the door open in case she wanted to call out.

Carolyn pushed her weight against the door. Her pulse leapt as she felt a weight on the other side, blocking her entry.

Frantic, she threw herself against the door, finally wedging herself through the narrow opening. She found Lizza sprawled on the floor against the door.

"Oh, mercy! Lizza! Lizza!" she cried.

The girl looked as though she had been backed against the door in terror. She had shrunk down and flung up her arm to protect herself from attack.

She was sagging now by that arm. Her sleeve and upper arm were pinned to the door by one of two savagely sharpened tines of a long hayfork. Stuck fast in the wood, the fork's handle jutted obscenely before Carolyn's shocked eyes. As if it had just been thrown, it waggled just a little. The second tine had just missed Lizza's face.

Carolyn seized the four-foot-long handle and yanked it away with an infuriated yelp of anguish. "My God, is there no end?"

Her arm freed, Lizza slumped to the floor. Dazed and bleeding, she lay staring at the partially opened kitchen door.

Going out onto the verandah, Carolyn found large, shallow footprints in the freshly fallen snow. Who? *Who?* The white-faced manservant of Lucile Ebey? Wildman? Ona?

Carolyn flung the door closed and whirled around, tormented to see her maid's dazed expression. Hobbling over to the girl, Carolyn crouched as best she could and gathered Lizza into her arms. "Dear, dear thing," she crooned, rocking her.

She feared Lizza had been the unfortunate recipient of an attack meant solely for her.

Eleven

By the time Carolyn had found the medical satchel she had brought from Philadelphia, and had dressed Lizza's wounded arm, enough snow had fallen to cover most of the footprints trailing around the house from the front.

Keeping the blunderbuss handy, Carolyn resigned herself to a sleepless night in the kitchen. She fetched her bedding from her bedchamber, not daring to leave Lizza alone.

Lizza remained strangely composed once Carolyn roused her from her horrified stupor with spirits of ammonia waved beneath her nose.

"Can you tell me who did this?" Carolyn whispered, trying to keep her voice as calm as possible.

Lizza looked at her with new eyes, black and bottomless. She no longer appeared to be a sassy maidservant but suddenly a woman who had faced death.

"Did you see who came to the door and threw the hayfork at you?"

Lizza's voice was as soft as snow. "No'm."

"How did he get in? Did you hear someone, and open the door?"

Lizza's eyes glazed, and she sighed deeply. Holding her hand over the stark white bandage on her upper arm, she curled once again on the pallet. With a scowl wrinkling her brow and a pinched look at the corners of her bewildered eyes, she gazed into the leaping flames of the hearthfire. All at once her eyes closed and she slept.

Marveling at the girl's reaction, Carolyn curled once again opposite her, her body coiled with tension. Her ears strained at every patter of snow on the windowpane. In time, she slept, too, but waking she felt as weary as if she had stood vigil at the window all the night through.

By morning, Carolyn knew she would be going nowhere in the wagon. Snow had drifted in swirls and whorls of white among the trees. A single drift in front of the house was two feet high. Carolyn knew she had no strength to drive their horse through it. If they were to leave Timberhill, they would have to ride the horse double and for the time being, Lizza wasn't up to it.

After waiting for Ona, who did not appear, Carolyn warmed mush for their breakfast. She tended their horse in the makeshift lean-to that Noah had built only days before.

She saw no trace of the night attacker in the pristine, flawless layer of snow. Indeed, by noon, her own morning footprints were covered in deep fresh white.

During the afternoon, Lizza rallied. Her eyes brightened and her energy seemed renewed. Carolyn thought it best to avoid discussing the unpleasantness of the night before, and so set the girl to bringing in as much wood as she could manage. Between a one-armed girl and a one-legged woman, Carolyn thought, they made a sorry pair!

Throughout the day, Carolyn watched from the windows, hoping Noah might come to see Lizza and revive her spirits. But only the snow came, mounding on the evergreen boughs and making stark pictures in the forest.

The wind came again late in the day, stirring the drifts and rearranging them. The house was cold now, devoid of all comfort. In the parlor, where no heat from the kitchen hearth reached, hoarfrost formed around the windowpanes.

Carolyn dreaded the night. If they were murdered in the night, who would know? Who would ever care to find them?

At dusk, after they had eaten, Lizza went from window to door and back again, as if waiting for the attacker to return. Each moment was an eternity. Reaching town on horseback through two feet of snow seemed as impossible as getting to Philadelphia; they were trapped in Timberhill.

"Miz!" Lizza's hoarse whisper roused Carolyn from her thoughts. "I hear something."

Carolyn was torn between relief to hear Lizza speaking normally again and her alarm that the girl might be right. "No one would come here at this time of night, not in this snow."

Her words did nothing to ease either of them. Both stiffened, listening for noises. The fire hissed. A log burned through, dropping coals through the grate. Carolyn shook her head, telling herself how silly she was to be so fearful, when she heard a faint, keening wail in the distance.

"Haunts," Lizza whispered. "They're back for us." She began mumbling something resembling a prayer.

Carolyn struggled to her feet and blew out every candle. She had just put out the lantern in the parlor when she heard another wail. The hair stood on the back of her neck.

The house was dark as a graveyard. Chilled to the bone, Carolyn crept back to the kitchen and loaded the heavy blunderbuss. At the sound of a crack and shout, Lizza shrank as close to the hearth as she could without crawling among the flames. Carolyn mentally reviewed every latched shutter and locked door. Then she thought of the outer cellar doors…

Could that snort in the distance be a horse?

They heard a faint shout. "Hello-o-o!"

Lizza whimpered in terror, covering her head with her arms and rocking herself.

The sight incensed Carolyn. She would have none of this madness! She could not forever be ruled by fear. Flinging the entry door wide, she limped down the hall to the front door and unlocked it.

The air outside was cold and crisp as she swung the door open wide. All was sweetly silent. In the distance, down the snowy lane, Carolyn spotted the dark, oblong shape of a wagon. Standing at the seat was a man in a monstrous cloak, lashing and lashing his staggering horses.

The wagon jerked forward another few feet, its wheels unmoving. The missing boards in the wagon bed sides showed that the driver had rigged runners beneath his wheels. They must have started traveling before the snow began. Anyone else would have set out in a cutter.

"Hello-o-o!"

A faint wail accompanied his cry. Carolyn's heart leaped, and she hobbled back to the kitchen for the lantern. At the front door she watched the wagon driver force his cumbersome rig and exhausted horses to a stop in a drift only a few hundred yards from the house.

"Here!" she called, swinging the lantern in an arc. "This way!" Calling back over her shoulder, she ordered, "Lizza, set the kettle on. There's someone coming!" Carolyn couldn't be certain if the girl had heard her, or if she would respond.

The man leaped to the ground, his body a huge indistinct shape of cloak, low hat and muffled face. He took two bundles from the wagon bed and plowed through the snow like a bear.

He deposited two bundled children before Carolyn and returned at once to the wagon.

Astonished, Carolyn looked down into the huge brown eyes of a girl, perhaps six, and a boy of three. Both were wrapped in tightly buttoned, snowy coats, mufflers and mittens. The boy's tears and running nose had soaked his muffler.

Carolyn was tugging away the damp things from their red, ruddy faces as the man staggered toward the door carrying a woman. Her long, black skirts hindered his progress through the deep snow.

Through his gray muffler he said, "You must take us in. My wife is ill."

The woman moaned and leaned wearily against him.

Instantly, Carolyn recognized the groan of a woman in labor. "You need say nothing more. Please, come inside. I can feed you. You'll find a bedchamber at the head of the stairs." She pointed, shivering.

His muffler white with frost, the man stepped inside. Even his brows were white with flakes. He looked startled.

A bolt of alarm stiffened her. "Silas! What can you be doing, traveling in such weather?"

"Did you think you could take my rightful inheritance? What a time I had learning the location of this place from your attorney's clerk."

He took in the time-browned walls and aging parlor furnishings, but even in its neglected state, the house was far more grand than Silas had hoped for. His eyes widened in wonder and his brow tilted, as if he was thanking the Almighty.

Sagging, Carolyn closed the door. She plucked the damp coats from the two children. Hearing Silas's wife moan again, she asked, "How long has she been feeling like that?"

"She'll be all right. She's only weary."

With each moan, Fanny Clure curled in on herself, grasping weakly at Silas's lapel.

"How often are the pains?" Carolyn asked, herding his children toward the kitchen's warmth.

He shook his head. "It's far too soon for labor. But if it proves to be time, I'll fetch a physick as soon as—"

"Silas, I'm perfectly capable of helping Fanny through a birth!" She took several awkward, limping steps toward the kitchen. "Lizza! We must have boiled water, quickly!"

Silas looked down at her as if she had taken leave of her senses. "And when did you suddenly become a physick, or even a midwife?"

Carolyn bit back a retort. "How long has she been in labor?"

"My wife is not in labor, Carolyn. She is only seven months," Silas intoned.

"You know as well as I that a baby pays little attention to calendars, especially during hard traveling. If you will let me examine Fanny, I'll be able to tell you—"

Fanny gave a deep, grunting groan.

Silas looked stricken, a pitiable caricature of a helpless husband. "Hurry! Get her upstairs! She may be delivering in your very arms!" Carolyn waved him toward the stairs. "Go! Go!"

With teeth gritted, Silas staggered up the staircase with his heavy load.

"Here," Carolyn said gently, thrusting the lantern's wire handle into the wide-eyed little girl's hand. "Be a brave child and carry this upstairs so that your papa can see to put your mama to bed. I'll have something good for you to eat when you come down."

"Yes'm." Without a protest, the girl walked solemnly up the staircase without a thought to the unfamiliar shadows above.

Carolyn held out her hand to the sniveling boy. He had shining pale-blond hair, and he looked asleep on his feet. He regarded her hand, then placed his reddened fingers in hers. They were like ice. She led him back to Lizza, who turned from the hearth and marveled, "Lord a mercy, if it's not a cute snowbaby!"

Carolyn snatched up the medical satchel still standing on the trestle table and limped back toward the stairs. She knew for certain that she would not be setting out for Eudoxia at daybreak.

Silas shouldered his way into the bedchamber at the head of the stair. Behind him came light, and he was able to make out the bare bed across the room. Staggering, he crossed the room and lay his wife on the splotched mattress.

He dropped to his knees and whispered a desperate prayer. If, by his ignorance, he had endangered this coming child...

Alarmed to think he might have been hasty, perhaps even greedy, to come here at this time of year, and when Fanny had begged him not to make her travel, he sprang to his feet. He loosened Fanny's wraps and adjusted her to a comfortable position on the bed. He had not been wrong to bring her to this larger, finer place, he told himself. Here they would prosper.

"We'll need a fire," he said, not looking back at his small daughter, who was standing round-eyed in the doorway.

He heard the child walk wearily back to the stairs, and he blessed the girl for her obedience. His eyes strayed to his wife's swollen belly. She was only chilled, he told himself. It wasn't yet time.

Shutting his eyes, he sat heavily upon the end of the mattress, allowing himself a moment of weakness. Below, he could hear the sound of women scurrying about. He longed to let them take control of this situation facing him. Fanny might give birth in spite of his prayers.

He looked around, thrilling to the size and splendor of the house. Truly, his prayers had been answered. This inheritance was proof that Carolyn had lured his brother from his true calling. Had it not been for her, Forrest would have come home and stood beside him and their father on the pulpit.

As it was, Carolyn had corrupted Forrest. God bless him, he could not forgive it. Carolyn was probably a Christian in her own way, but because of her, his father had gone to his grave a disappointed man.

Looking at his wife's waxen face, he felt a widening abyss of fear open in his heart. Her dry lips were pressed together in an undertaker's indifferent smile. Her eyelids looked transparent. He had never seen her cheeks so sunken.

Perhaps this was another miscarriage. Their second child had been stillborn. He had delivered it on just such a night as this with no help.

Shaking his head, he tried to rid his mind of the terrible thoughts. If it be God's will that this child should also die...he must accept it. He must go on, establishing a new church in this place, ministering to the faint of heart and the sick of soul.

His sister-in-law stood at the door, reading his thoughts, he feared. She limped into the room; he had forgotten she had a broken leg. He marveled that she was walking without the aid of a crutch only six weeks after her accident.

She was smaller than he remembered, and not properly dressed for a widow. Her hair was loose, curling about her face and shoulders, making her look like a common woman. Her eyes held the same lack of respect he had always found so irritating. A woman ought to be demure and effacing, like Fanny.

He puffed his chest. "Fanny is quite recovered now. Might we go below and talk? Even though this house is mine, I will allow you to stay for a time."

Fanny groaned, curling onto her side.

"Silas, there is no doctor in Eudoxia. My cooking woman is likely a midwife, but she didn't come today. But you needn't worry. I'm quite capable."

"You jest if you think I would put my wife's life in your treacherous hands. If necessary, I myself will—"

He had put his hand on her arm, intending to steer her out of the bedchamber, but Carolyn slipped free of his grasp. She was holding a medical satchel. The sight of it sent Silas into a panic.

"Once again, Silas, I must ask that you put aside your feelings about my marriage to Forrest," Carolyn said, limping to the bed. She placed her hand on his wife's forehead, then listened to Fanny's heart. Frowning, she opened Fanny's cloak. "Light the fire, if you please, Silas."

She paused, watching Fanny as a full minute of contractions caused his wife to arch and open dazed eyes. Fanny gave a harrowing gasp that seemed to suck all warmth from the room.

He watched his wife clutch at Carolyn's arms. A wave of pure jealousy coursed through him. He wanted Fanny's reliance on him alone! Carolyn always had been, and always would be, an interloper! "Get away from—"

His words were cut short as Fanny whispered a question to Carolyn.

"I'm your sister-in-law," he heard Carolyn whisper in reply.

His wife's voice was a choked gasp. "Help…me! Two days labor…dry."

Silas felt the blood leave his face. She had not told him her waters had broken. Yet what could he have done? They had been on the road, miles from shelter.

Carolyn shook Fanny gently. "You mustn't give up!"

Silas tore to Carolyn's side and yanked her away. She winced as she stumbled heavily onto her splinted leg. "You'll not treat my wife with such callousness! She needs sleep."

Carolyn's eyes blazed up at him and she shook free of his grasp, limping into the hall. He followed, thinking she was obeying him.

But in the hall Carolyn spun around to face him. "Two days in labor! Her waters broken. A history of miscarriages and difficult births—this I remember from your letters! My God, Silas, will you give the poor woman no rest? There's no time for your ignorance now! I must help her deliver the child, or she will surely die."

She glared at Silas. She had no sympathy for him. From the bedchamber came another muffled moan, as if Fanny was holding her cloak clenched in her teeth.

Carolyn softened her tone. "Regardless of what you think of me, of the two of us, I have been present at more births. I have observed births at my father's and husband's sides, and I have read medical texts since childhood. By God, I will do my best for Fanny and your child."

His hand clamped around her wrist. She watched his lips whiten. "You'll not cut out the child. The first physick I called in when Alvah was born said he would have to—"

"I haven't the skill for that, but I can lend her the strength to endure. Silas, put aside your ignorance and place your trust in me. You have no choice!"

He bent close to her face. "I won't have any leeches on my wife!"

She pointed at the medical satchel on the floor beside the bed. "Look for yourself, Silas. My bag contains no starving leeches. I give no blisters. I will not drain her strength. I will *give* her strength with words, Silas, mere words, and the touch of my caring hand. Silas, I'm not like the old physicks, nor am I like a midwife who puts a knife beneath the bed to cut the pain. I won't be opening all the locks and untying knots to make the birth easier. Such idiocy! Forrest and I spent ten years fighting the old ways and the old superstitions! If you had cared enough about your brother to open your heart to his profession, you would know this."

With a sinking heart, Carolyn saw that she had said the worst possible thing.

Silas looked more adamant than ever. "I would rather Fanny was dead than have your hand upon her!"

"You may well get your wish!"

Carolyn remembered the chilled night her mother died. She had been powerless to help her. Overwhelmed now by that same feeling of helplessness, Carolyn began shaking. By God, she had at least enough skill in this to save her sister-in-law!

Filled with cold determination, Carolyn straightened. "Stand aside."

"No, I will not let you near her!"

"Then you are a jackass! You would do better to shoot Fanny and put her out of her misery. Stand aside!"

Through the doorway, she saw Fanny tossing and turning in agony. She was grunting, and then suddenly she started to scream. But nothing eased her pain, and Fanny fell back, writhing.

Carolyn swung, striking Silas's soft cheek. She did him little harm, but he staggered backward, thunderstruck. She limped past him into the bedchamber, slamming the door in his face.

With incredible strength, Fanny seized Carolyn's arm. "Footling!" she gasped, falling back and panting. Then her eyes rolled back, and she passed into a dead faint.

Carolyn bared Fanny's swollen body. The woman's under-things were soaked and cold. A hasty examination revealed she was surprisingly large for one only seven months with child. Silas and Fanny must have miscalculated.

But moments later, Carolyn indeed found a small footling lodged in the birth canal. The size of the tiny leg belied the size of Fanny's womb. She must be delivering twins!

Carolyn's heart leaped. Panic flooded her. She had no experience with this! She had read little on the subject. She tried to turn the baby from without, and then finally from within. The flow of blood increased. Fanny was motionless now. Her pulse slowed.

If, indeed, there was another child, she might yet save it, Carolyn thought, watching Fanny's shallow breathing. She had but one choice. To let Fanny and the second twin die was unthinkable. She must forcibly deliver the footling.

She had no time to contemplate consequences. She knew only that two more lives would soon be lost if she did not act. She had seen an illustration in a medical book once of twins locked, chin to chin. The first had been a footling and likely to suffocate. The second had been in normal delivery position and was likely to survive. She had no choice. Fanny's strength was gone.

Carolyn shut her eyes only an instant, asking for courage. Then, with all her strength, she pressed the footling back into the womb. Even unconscious, Fanny began to writhe. Fumbling, all her handholds slippery, Carolyn twisted the footling, and drew forth a waxen, unmoving child.

There was no time to try reviving the child. He was dead. For one long moment she stared at him, never having seen a stillborn child before. Suddenly she couldn't move her arms.

Fanny moaned, and her abdomen tightened. She arched, groaned, and a second child appeared in the birth canal's opening. Forgetting her witlessness, Carolyn guided the child out. Small, wet and warm, he slipped effortlessly into her hands. The chilled temperature in the chamber was enough to make him draw his first breath.

His soft mewling swelled Carolyn's heart. Scrubbing away tears, she captured his tiny flailing arm, giving him a moment's comfort.

Though small, he appeared healthy and strong. Carolyn cleared his face of moisture and then concentrated on assisting Fanny deliver the single afterbirth.

Working as quickly as possible, she tore a strip from the linen bedsheet and staunched Fanny's profuse bleeding. Doing all she knew how to cause contraction of the womb so the bleeding would lessen, she found Fanny's body responding with amazing speed.

Color returned to the woman's sunken face. Carolyn was able to dash for the lantern, oblivious to her leg, and get the fire going in the grate.

With feeble warmth beginning to fill the bedchamber, Carolyn returned to the live, squirming infant and cut his cord. He was strong, crying softly and waving his arms. She wanted to gather him up, but there was the matter of the first twin, so still, so hopeless. How would she explain this death to Silas? He would surely think she had bungled the birth and murdered it.

Could she convince him the footling had been stillborn? If she had not forcibly taken the child, it would surely have caused the deaths of his mother and brother.

Legs going weak, she sagged to the floor. Gathering the dead infant into her arms, she wept softly over him. If only Silas didn't have to know of this. He had one healthy newborn now. That was all he expected. Fanny would recover, God willing. Did they need to know of this poor thing?

Carolyn felt racked with sudden weariness. She had done what was necessary. She had saved two lives. But now her mind whirled with confusion and regret. Because of this, Silas would condemn her more surely now than ever before. She might even face prison.

Fanny stirred, making sounds as if she wanted to speak and had no strength. Carolyn struggled to her feet and forced herself to smile. She placed the squirming infant in Fanny's quivering arms.

"Thank you," Fanny breathed. "You were a...godsend."

Then with the stealth of a thief, Carolyn scooped up the shawl-covered, lifeless bundle. With an armload of Fanny's damp wraps, Carolyn limped to the door. She didn't feel like a godsend. She felt like a murderess.

Outside in the hall, Silas was sitting on the floor, leaning against the wall, his head back and eyes closed. The hearth-light from the open bedchamber door fell across him. Carolyn thought he was asleep.

"Is it over?" he whispered, his tone flat.

She gave a frightened start and turned aside so that he would not see the bundles she held. Had he gone deaf? Carolyn wondered, listening to the soft noises of the newborn infant within.

"Is she dead?" he asked softly, his pained eyes narrowing. "Did they go peacefully?"

Shuddering, Carolyn could but think she'd done the only thing possible. She feared this man now, and his pious stupidity. The dead infant she carried must forever remain her heavy-hearted secret.

"Witling, you have a healthy son! Go in to him, and Fanny. Whatever you do, don't thank me. It was all Fanny's doing. And God's."

Groaning as if fighting tears, his expression incredulous, he pushed himself to his feet. Then hearing the sounds of the suckling infant within the bedchamber, he pushed past Carolyn and rushed to his wife's side.

Carolyn sank to the top step, too weary to stand another moment. Her only thought was to get out of the house with the dead twin. Then she must bring some semblance of order back to her life. She was shaking so hard she could scarely scoot to the foot of the stairs.

She found Lizza and the children asleep at the kitchen hearth. Leaving Fanny's wet clothes on the table, Carolyn took Wildman's cloak from the peg on the wall. She was trembling, certain she would not be able to hobble through the deep snow even as far as the cart path.

Then she spied Ona's kettle and poured a cup of tea from it. She recognized at once the invigorating bitterness of the drink, and found it quickly warming her fatigued bones. Was it wormwood, morphia, nightshade? She scarcely cared.

Taking her crutch, she slipped out into the snowy night. The sky was clearing, and a crescent moon lit her way across the meadow. Each step through the snow was nearly impossible. How could she go far enough into the woods to hide what she had done?

The most logical thing to do was bury the baby in the surgery's cellar. Somehow it seemed wicked to leave the child in unblessed sleep where hatred and ignorance had brought destruction, but if she hoped to get back into the house undetected, she would have to.

Taking the stone steps one at a time, she scooted down into the snowy gloom. Stumbling over shadowed rubble, she finally crouched beside a hollow in the base of the cellar hearth. There, in the corner, the earth was unfrozen and yielded to her frantic efforts to dig.

Twelve

An eerie wind moved through the forest surrounding the surgery, disturbing leaves caught in the shadowed hollow of the cellar pit.

Not to tell Silas and Fanny of the dead infant seemed an admission that she had failed, Carolyn thought, trembling as she dug the infant's shallow grave. Afraid she would be discovered, she worked frantically, her hands numbed by the cold, her mind a mass of confusion.

How could she live with this deception? The infant's body was cold and stiff now. Carolyn's heart was breaking to think that she was being such a muddling fool as to hide it. When she lay the shawl-covered body in the grave, she prayed as never before to be forgiven, to be understood.

Finally she scraped cold earth over the shawl and patted it into place. Using a loose piece of wood that might once have been a slat in a ladderback chair, she scraped more and more earth over the grave, wishing to cover up this tragic mistake.

As she scraped, she unearthed several rusted medical instruments that must have fallen from a table or drawer when the floor above collapsed during the fire. Her blood tingled, remembering that horrible night. What more lay amidst the rubble waiting to be found?

Wanting to blot it all from her mind, she pushed snow back onto the disturbed earth, then she searched for a marker.

What was she thinking! she gasped. She couldn't mark this grave. Sinking to the ground, she sat a long while in the dark stone cellar, thinking of what she had done. She prayed God in heaven to forgive her.

As she sat on the cellar floor, Carolyn let her eyes travel across the edge of the pit. In the corner she noticed a heap of charred beams she had not paid any attention to before. Struggling to her feet, she approached the beams and bent to investigate.

Beneath the collapsed roofing slates she found what she thought might be the surface of a flame-scarred table. Looking closer, she realized that in fact it was the remains of her father's desktop. A medical text lay pinned beneath the rubble, one page flapping loose in the wind.

Crouching, she pushed the broken slates aside and dug in the soil. She found the upper portion of the desk still intact; only the lower half had burned away. The left drawer was buried in the earth. She dug until her fingers were black with dirt, but eventually she was able to pull the drawer open a few inches.

With a gasp, she discovered within it a stack of her father's journals, each half an inch thick. The once hardbound covers were now as soft as bread dough from having been damp these past sixteen years.

She pulled out one of the journals, feeling it crumble at her touch. Her heart leapt with surprise as she realized that more journals existed than she had ever dreamed was the case. That long-ago night when they escaped Timberhill, her father hadn't been able to carry away everything he surely would have wanted to salvage from his burning surgery!

The second journal was equally fragile, but she was able to pull it out without destroying it. She could lift the cover, but the pages had long since melded together and it was impossible to separate a single page from another.

The third journal proved to be in slightly better condition. She could at least tuck it beneath her cloak in hopes of reading it later in the house. The last two journals were scarcely more than moldy slime in the bottom of the drawer. She ached to think of all the years of painstaking notes lost forever.

Then, with a shudder, she remembered why she had come to the cellar in the dark of night. She twisted around to see if anyone was watching from above, and struggled to her feet.

She brushed snow around to cover her actions, then made her way back up the slippery steps. As if in answer to her prayers, new snow began to fall from the dark sky. In all likeliness, the footprints and signs of digging in the cellar pit would be covered by morning.

At the top of the stairs she straightened and looked around one last time. Somehow she could not shake the feeling of uneasiness that had caught hold of her. She felt watched.

Her skirts matted with snow, feet and legs numb, Carolyn limped back toward the house. What would she say if Silas asked why she had gone out? She could tell him she had gone to Ona for help and then realized she couldn't make the trip through the snow.

The wind drove snowflakes horizontally across the dark meadow. Ducking her head to avoid getting snow in her eyes, she caught sight of something in the opaque blue depths of the wood. It was a man, and he was watching her.

His long fair hair blew in the wind. His eyes, staring out at her, were as dark as her thoughts. Like an evil, enchanted prince, Wildman watched Carolyn from the woods.

Clutching the precious journal to her chest, Carolyn's first thought was to run for the house.

Wildman stepped from the trees, motioning for her to join him.

She shook her head. "I must get back!" she cried.

As if he hadn't heard, he crossed the snowy expanse that separated them, took her crutch and flung it away. "What are you doing?" he demanded, his tone harsh.

She felt frightened, as if she'd been caught invading his territory. "M-my brother-in-law's just arrived," she stammered, knowing she must lie to him but afraid he already knew the answer to his questions. "His wife gave birth a while ago. I-I was going for... help." Her lie sounded feeble. "Ona would surely have something for the bleeding, but I couldn't make it through the snow."

As she lifted her face, she knew the truth of her feelings for Wildman was written in her expression. He seemed to have enchanted her with his mysterious brew and his promise of forbidden love.

He stepped closer, brushing the stray curls from her face. "Why are you afraid?" He gazed deeply into her eyes, as if reading her mind. Then slowly, ever so slowly, he bent closer. His eyes locked with hers. His cool lips pressed against her mouth.

She felt a thrill of desire and was even more afraid. She didn't *really* want this, did she?

Slowly his tongue invaded her mouth. She went weak, feeling helpless to resist, her body's response overwhelmingly powerful. Forrest had never kissed her so! And certainly Evan had never been given the chance to kiss her like this.

Slowly he drew her to him, embracing her beneath her cloak until it slid from her shoulders. She was left standing unprotected in the wind, clutching the journal to her stomach.

She seemed not to feel the cold. She knew not how to respond to Wildman's slow, methodical touch. Though the wind raised goosebumps on her arms, a fire began smoldering in her.

When she started to return his kiss, the pressure of his lips lessened. As she drew back, he once again pulled her to him, exploring her mouth almost harshly. It was clear that he preferred no response from her.

"Wait for me," he whispered, moving away.

"Why?...Why must I wait?" She followed, arm outstretched. "For what?"

He turned, capturing her with his stare. "When the time is right, I'll come to you. We'll be together. Until then, you must forget you saw me here. To speak of me brings danger, to me, to yourself."

Carolyn shook her head. "You're wrong if you think the villagers hate you—"

He silenced her with a fierce wave of his hand. "You must not go into the woods!"

He turned away abruptly and escaped into the forest. She was left alone once more, shivering and wondering at her sanity.

She gathered up her cloak and searched for her crutch in the snow. The pressure of her grip was leaving finger marks in the soft journal clutched to her stomach. As she hobbled back toward the house, she had to wonder if she was dreaming.

Her strength ebbing, she struggled onto the verandah. Trying to be silent, she tiptoed inside. Lizza and the children still slept near the hearth.

Sagging with relief, she draped her snow-matted cloak over a chair back, washed her hands and limped to the entry. From above came the soft rumble of Silas's snores. She sagged against the wall, shivering uncontrollably.

Finally she made herself climb the stairs. In the bedchamber she found Fanny sleeping. The newborn lay warm and pink in the curve of her arm. Silas was slumped asleep in a chair by the dwindling hearthfire.

Hot tears sprang to Carolyn's eyes. For the first time she truly understood the weight of responsibility that had made her father and Forrest such somber, dedicated men. To cure the sick was a heady triumph, but to face unpardonable defeats...To feel responsible for even one death, even though the death had saved other lives... Could she bear it?

Leaving the bedchamber and moving wearily down the stairs, she finally took her place at the hearth near Lizza. In the light of the fire, she lifted the cover of the sodden journal she still held in her arms. Across the title page she saw the ghost of her father's neatly printed shortened hand. She couldn't make out the date.

With exquisite care, she peeled away the first page. The ink on the second page had long since soaked into the paper, leaving only faint traces of markings that were impossible to decipher. The third page came away in limp pieces, soft, damp and green with mold.

Bending the journal, she was able to open to a page well within, but there the writing was a mere blur. For all she could read, the pages might as well have been blank. Toward the back of the journal, the pages had become one—sodden, green and odorous. A tiny black bug crawled from the spine, and Carolyn shuddered.

There was nothing to be gleaned from the journal, she thought with a wash of unbearable disappointment. All she had learned was that there had been more than the seven journals stored at the house in Philadelphia. She would never know all that had been lost the night they were driven away.

Laying the journal among the flames, she felt a keen stab of grief as it smoked, dried and then burned to fire and ash. Her dear papa, his career ruined at Timberhill because of ignorance...Her poor husband, dead in a senseless accident...And what of herself? she wondered. What would become of her?

She wanted to laugh, but tears threatened instead. "I saved two lives tonight. Think of that and be glad," she admonished herself.

Wearily, she lay down and sank into a dark sleep. In her dreams, she was searching in a gloomy wood for a crying child. Behind her Silas stood, finger raised in accusation.

The days following the birth of Fanny's child were filled with such normal, everyday activity that Carolyn could scarcely recall the lonely weeks that she, Lizza and Ona had spent at Timberhill alone.

Silas tended his horses and Carolyn's. With Noah's help, he built side walls around the lean-to so that the horses wouldn't be exposed to bad weather.

Two days after Silas's arrival, Ona returned to her duties. Giving no explanation for her absence, she acted as if she were not at all surprised to find five new persons in the house. She went about her increased chores without complaint.

With the help of Ona's mysterious tea, Lizza forgot that her arm had been injured in a most vicious, mysterious attack. Neither she nor Carolyn cared to discuss it. And much to Carolyn's relief, Fanny improved quickly, her strength returning daily.

A week following his arrival at Timberhill, Silas rode into the village, returning with enough supplies to keep them until the snow lessened. He borrowed a cutter from a village elder and returned that evening to christen his newborn son Eliakim.

By his very presence, Silas seemed to purge Timberhill of its superstitious shadows. His bellowing orders filled the echoing chambers. His bold plans to make the place habitable brought life and activity to what had been a house filled with haunts and memories.

In the bedchamber at the head of the stair, Fanny's recovery progressed rapidly. Eliakim's delightful cries kept everyone busy—fetching, carrying, laundering.

But best of all were the children, Alvah and Parcy. They were bright and inquisitive when their staid papa was out of earshot, and Carolyn found them a delight, as well as a distraction from the lingering memories of Wildman's disturbing kiss and his strange, hypnotic words.

The death of the twin seemed like a vague dream to Carolyn, and at times she was almost able to forget that it happened. At times she felt she had done the right thing, the *only* thing. Because she had spared Silas and Fanny the knowledge of the death, everyone was busy and happy instead of draped in mourning black.

It was as if the clouds had lifted from Carolyn's life. She got on well with Fanny, and gave little thought to her aunt and cousin in the village.

When it was quite evident that Fanny would survive the critical second week following her confinement, when childbed fever was most likely to strike, Silas felt confident in returning his thoughts to his calling.

He passed his evenings in the dining room, surrounded by papers. Poring over his Bible, he prepared his first sermon. Christmastide was nigh, and Silas was planning a grand service to draw all sinners from miles around.

It was indeed Christmastide! Though the house still looked shabby, it had been transformed. In the parlor stood a white pine tree decorated with nuts, fruit and little birds that had been fashioned from bits of twigs and milkweed pods.

Festooned about each hearth were thick green garlands of pine that smelled spicy fresh and reminiscent of Christmases past. The furniture had been cleaned and polished, the upholstery scrubbed, the windows washed, the carpets beaten. The house was warm at last, and fragrant with the scent of delicious feasts.

Ona, in a freshly starched and ironed apron, was producing such a plenty of sweets and savories that Carolyn could scarcely believe she had ever suspected the woman of trying to drug or poison her. Though she was still somber and silent, Ona appeared patient in the extreme when fulfilling Silas's many demands.

The tea that produced such drowsy symptoms in Carolyn was daily served to Fanny, restoring her to vigor. "You should have some," Fanny often insisted. "I feel marvelous. The woman is a saint."

Carolyn always declined.

Lizza, too, enjoyed the tea. She talked no more of haunts, her mind instead occupied by her romance with Noah.

At last it was the night of the Christmas party, and guests began to fill the house. Villagers who had not given Carolyn the slightest nod previously were now crowding into the new preacher's house to welcome him and partake of his cheer.

Stationed at the front door, Carolyn admitted the guests, took their wraps and hats, gave warm greetings and directed all toward the parlor or dining room.

Fanny lay propped on a new chaise lounge, her sleeping son in her arms. She made a serene domestic picture welcoming each guest to her home.

"Carolyn, please, do come in and meet everyone," Fanny said, holding out her arm and beckoning sweetly to Carolyn. "You all must properly meet my sister-in-law. She is the most wonderful friend a woman could have in time of need. I was at death's door when she lay her gentle hands on me and helped me through my confinement. Truly, I could not have delivered this little footling without her," Fanny said, gazing down at her infant son with misty eyes.

Carolyn squirmed uncomfortably, wanting to slip away unnoticed.

"How is it, Mrs. Clure, that you are so skilled in midwifery?" one of the village women asked, her small gray eyes going over Carolyn with curiosity.

Fanny answered for Carolyn. "Her husband and father were

both physicks. But I vow, neither could have done better."

Carolyn felt her face grow warm. Oh, if they only knew what she had really done, the torches would burn again, stones would fly…

But they never would know, she assured herself, extracting herself from the guests the moment it was possible.

Carolyn heard another knock and limped to the door. Outside, the winter night was beautiful and the air crisp. The heaped, glistening snow had been much trampled by horses in jingle-belled harness. Cutters had been parked in disarray. Gold squares of lamplight fell from the windows.

"Do come in. So kind of you to come. A good Christmas to you!" Carolyn greeted cheerfully, steering a farm couple with four gawking children toward the parlor.

All eyes were round with wonder as the family entered. Carolyn knew they were thinking that the house was haunted, that they were treading on the devil's playground, risking their very souls to enter. But so long as the new preacher was living here, they felt protected.

She edged away, pained to think that Timberhill had been subject to so many years of fearful, superstitious speculation. In spite of all the laughter around her, she felt strangely alone. At times like this she missed Evan sorely and feared that she would never see him again. It had been such a dreadfully long time…

She was just turning to resume helping in the kitchen—the only place where she felt of use—when another cutter arrived from the snowy lane. Again, Carolyn opened the door in greeting, laughing to think how the villagers flocked to welcome Silas. How she envied him.

"Ah, Carolyn!" Helen Rasner cried as she climbed from the cutter and guided her bent father into the entry moments later. "So good of you to invite us! A party! And everyone's here." She came inside, craning to note every face. Then she glanced at Carolyn and smiled warmly. "You look a picture! We haven't had a time like this in ages, and it's such fun. How are you? How do the woods seem to you now that the gloom of autumn has given way to the bite of winter?"

Carolyn gave the young woman a warning smile that told her they would not speak of dangers lurking in the woods in front of the guests. "I don't believe I met your father when I came to call," she said, changing the subject deftly.

Helen gave her a private smile. "No, that's true. Father, this is Orion Adams's daughter."

The man had once been tall, but now he was nearly bent over with age. He looked racked with rheumatism and had hard eyes. He gave Carolyn a contemptuous look, and was shaken gently by his cajoling daughter. With effort, he grunted, "Good tidings, Mrs. Clure."

"Thank you for coming," Carolyn said. She couldn't bring herself to say she was glad to meet such an unpleasant man.

"I heard that your aunt and cousin refused their invitations," Helen whispered as she and Carolyn assisted Mr. Rasner to a chair in the parlor. Looking around in surprise, Helen asked, "Where did you get all this furniture?"

"It's been here all the while. It belonged to my parents and grandparents. But don't look closely, for everything's warped and spotted. My brother-in-law doesn't mind. He and his family lived in a two-room rectory in New York. To them, this seems quite luxurious."

"We're more than a bit desperate for a breath of God's grace, I should say," Helen said, chuckling. "But I would be willing to wager Lucile Ebey won't break her long exile to show her face here. I once heard that she had cursed God, poor old soul."

Carolyn wanted to quit the subject. "In my first weeks here, I managed to meet only the gloomiest residents. I thought Eudoxia was inhabited by madwomen and 'haunts,' as my maid calls them."

Helen patted her shoulder. "All that's behind now—" They heard the jingle of sleighbells. "Ah, another guest! I wonder who this might be." Curious, she went to the frosted parlor window and peered out into the dark. "My, my, a closed city cutter! How exciting! Are you expecting a rather fine guest, Carolyn? Might you introduce us?" She laughed gaily. "Isn't he a marvelous figure of a man! Come and look. And he has such an attentive driver. I do hope he's not an invalid. I dare say we haven't a single man for fifty miles who wears a cloak half so well! Carolyn, where have you been hiding him?"

Her heart leaping, Carolyn limped to the door and threw it open wide.

Evan was just gaining his feet at the side of the cutter, his long navy cloak brushing the drifts. He lifted his hat, craning to observe the looming stone house burdened with foot-long icicles along the eaves.

Carolyn hurried onto the porch, her heart racing. Clasping her hands like an eager schoolgirl, she debated whether to dash to him and fall into his arms, or keep a reserved stance. With hesitant steps forward, she watched his gaze find her. Their eyes met in wonder.

Carolyn couldn't help but notice the change in him. His cheeks were pale and had thinned alarmingly. Even his fingers looked bony. His manservant, a freckled lad in an oversized livery, lent his arm.

"Evan, you've been ill!" she cried, racing to his side as fast as she could. She clasped his cold hand and felt his weak squeeze. Then she hugged him, tiptoeing to kiss his cheek. Oh, how thin was his flesh over those beautifully molded bones!

"Carolyn," he murmured, laying his thin cheek against hers, trembling slightly. "I had the devil of a time finding you! I would scold you for leaving as you did, but I'm certain I haven't the strength," he admitted with a feeble smile. "Thank God I found you."

Her eyes were quick on his face, looking for telltale signs of fever. "Hurry inside, Evan. I know just the thing to give you strength. My cooking woman's tea has the most marvelous healing properties. You'll feel wonderful and then sleep like a child. You didn't travel straight from Philadelphia without a stop?"

He nodded.

"But then you must rest immediately! I can see that you're weak. What happened? You shouldn't have come—but I'm so glad you did!"

He laughed, his summer-blue eyes shining. "How could I not come after finding that you were alive after all?"

"You thought me dead?" Her heart twisted to think of the suffering she had caused him. Never had she imagined he would think…And yet, with the epidemic…"What a horrid fool I was! Forgive me!"

"Forgiven," he whispered. "If you kiss me."

She did, lightly, on his cheek, and heard the whispers of the guests even as they entered the hallway. "You must tell me what happened."

"I had been searching for you when I was called away on business. I fell ill in Boston and was confined to bed for almost three weeks. When my clerk received your letter, he was able to find Timberhill, but I was so long in returning, and so weak, I couldn't come at once."

"Oh, my dearest!"

How wonderful it was to see him! Despite the signs of ill health, Evan looked more handsome to her than ever. Perhaps it was the driven quality in his eyes, the determined set of his mouth, the craggy planes of his face that lent him such power.

Closing the door against the dark and cold, Carolyn stayed close to Evan's side. She took up his hand, blushed at her audacity and then let it drop. Then she took it up again, feeling as foolish as a girl.

His cheeks and neck reddened. She wanted to kiss him again, but the house was filled to the rim with villagers, all with keen eyes.

Smiling her gratitude, Carolyn ushered Evan's footman back to the kitchen. "Eat what you will!" she told him, steering Evan to the crowded parlor.

"Everyone, listen! This is Evan Burck, just arrived from Philadelphia!"

There was excited clamor all around.

"What news have you from Philadelphia, good sir?" one of the elders asked.

"The talk is of nothing but the execution of the French queen, for treason," Evan said, launching into a discussion of the recent news of the revolution.

Carolyn stood in Evan's shadow, reveling in his warmth. She

felt delighted beyond words that he had finally come.

"You look weary," she said at length. "You must eat and rest."

Begging the indulgence of his news-hungry audience, Evan gratefully allowed her to draw him away and into the nearly empty dining room, where she heaped a plate and sat watching him eat.

Between mouthfuls, he told her of his illness and his return to Philadelphia. "After three weeks my servants had left. I had to hire a new housekeeper, cook, butler, even the lad who drove me here."

"If only I had known."

"And now that you do, what can I say to lure you back to Philadelphia?"

Aching for a kiss, she dropped her gaze. Dare he give her one when the house was so crowded? If he would but kiss her, perhaps it would exorcise the wildman from her thoughts.

"Carolyn, you're so beautiful. Surely you know how mad I am for you! I've come to insist that you marry me." He reached for her hand. "I'll not take no for an answer. I can't wait another day. I nearly lost my mind looking for you. I believed you dead, lost! To find that you left, with no word…You can't reject me again, Carolyn. I won't allow it!"

"I never rejected—"

He silenced her with a startling, electrifying kiss. And then, as if the house were suddenly empty, he stood and swept her into his arms. His touch was warm and commanding.

She could not doubt his passion. Nor could she ignore her own response!

"I love you, Carolyn!" His mouth closed over hers again. His conviction gave his kiss a force neither of them had known could exist.

She was lost! She clung to him, wanting to say yes, finding her mouth otherwise occupied.

When he released her, she was laughing breathlessly. As she staggered back, her fingertips pressed against her tingling lips, she caught sight of Ona in the doorway holding a tray of sweetmeats. The woman's bottomless black eyes were locked with hers.

Carolyn tore her eyes away. She would not have the woman spoil this moment! "Leave us, Ona. Close the door, if you please."

The woman retreated and obediently shut the door. Carolyn and Evan were alone in the dining room.

"Where did everyone go?" Carolyn asked, breathlessly aware of the gossip she would cause. She gave a soft laugh and looked at Evan with mischief.

"I saw no one of importance in here." His eyes danced. He sank back to the chair, patting his lap. "Come to me, Carolyn. I haven't the strength to stand just now. You've made me weak from wanting you."

Blushing, she edged closer until he tugged her down. She had her hands in her lap, but he gathered her close, turning her toward him. Her wrist brushed against his trousers. He was fully erect, smiling deeply into her eyes.

"I love you, Carolyn. You must marry me!"

Her breath coming in tingling gasps, she nodded without another thought. "I will. I will!"

Thirteen

"Am I interrupting?" Silas asked, sliding the dining-room door open.

Carolyn sprang from Evan's lap, her cheeks flaring hotly. "Oh! Silas, you startled me!"

"I daresay." Silas's tone was droll.

"You're just the man I need to speak to," Evan said, rising somewhat unsteadily. "You may think me hasty, sir, but I wish to have your blessing on my marriage to Carolyn."

Carolyn chafed to think that Evan should ask Silas for her hand. She was not under Silas's stewardship!

Silas looked a bit undone, as if he were regretting the loss of a rather handy servant who required no pay. But he hadn't forgotten that Carolyn had bested him. Always wary of her now, he smiled as if having her gone were exactly what he wanted.

He extended his hand, shook with Evan and nodded. "God's blessings for you both."

Evan apparently found the parson's agreement only a formality, for he was already turning toward Carolyn. His smile was heavy with unspoken meaning. "How soon can you be ready to leave, Carolyn? It's a long, hard ride back to Philadelphia."

She laughed to see his impatience, and blushed again. "You'll need to rest, but I can be ready as soon after as is necessary."

Silas stepped forward. "But you can't think to travel together... unmarried!" He puffed himself up like a turkey. "I won't allow that. I'll marry you myself, this sabbath."

About to protest, Carolyn could suddenly think of no reason why she should not allow Silas to marry her to Evan, and so quickly. She smiled at Evan. "Does that suit you?"

Evan's eyes glowed with delight. "Nothing would please me more!"

With a rousing bellow of merriment, Silas drew them into the parlor. "My dear new friends, I have an announcement! My treasured sister-in-law has just consented to become the bride of our fine guest, Mr. Burck. A toast!"

Flushed and happy, Carolyn stood beside Evan, her arm linked with his. They drank the toast with laughter and good wishes all around.

In the entry, Ona listened to what was being said. Then she hurried to place the tray she was carrying in the dining room. Moments later she had thrown on her cloak and was swirling out the kitchen door into the snowy night.

Leaving the cheery house behind, she plowed along the path that her daily footsteps had made through the snowy meadow back to the trees.

So intent was she on delivering this bit of unexpected news to her wildman, she didn't see him standing like a shadow among the trees just beyond the reach of the moonlight. His nightly trek to stand and watch the house had worn a path too.

"Why you be here? Get back!" she said, pushing at him forcefully. "I have much to tell you. Come."

With the last of the guests gone, the house at Timberhill was silent. Lizza was asleep in the kitchen. Fanny had long since retired to the chamber at the head of the stairs to suckle her babe and sleep. With a warm toddy, Evan had been put in Carolyn's bedchamber at her insistence.

Little usable furniture graced the third bedchamber, where Carolyn stripped off her gown and donned a warm nightshift. Every fiber of her being was aware that Evan slept only a room away! He had refused all medicinal teas, saying he could not yet bring himself to trust anything but a stout whiskey.

Outside, the night was hushed and cold. The fire hissed and crackled in the grate. She could still smell the delicious fragrances from their dinner, and the lingering warmth of bayberry candles.

With a contented sigh, she drifted into sleep. She dreamed of a great snowy wood where on one side was the warm sun of day, and where on the opposite side was the dark, mysterious cold of night. For all her desire to walk toward the warm sunlight, she found herself stumbling deeper and deeper into the dark wood.

And then she was lost, fighting her way through snagging branches. She felt drawn down until her feet were stuck fast in cold mud. Struggling, crying out with no sound, she was awakened suddenly by Lizza shaking her sleeve.

"Miz! Miz! You've got to come!"

"Oh! What is it?" Carolyn mumbled, shaking off already fading memories of the unpleasant dream.

"They's somebody outside the house. Miz! Come quick!"

"We must wake Silas, then."

"No'm. Just you. Come now!"

Lizza tugged Carolyn to her feet and fidgeted as she pulled on her wrapper and mules to follow her out into the dim hall. She could hear Silas snoring in the front bedchamber. Pausing at Evan's door, Carolyn found herself yanked along toward the stairs.

"Just you, Miz!" Lizza hissed, tiptoeing down the stairs.

When they reached the kitchen, Carolyn felt only annoyance as she limped to the door and stepped out onto the snowy verandah. With Evan and Silas in the house, she felt no fear. She wanted to be done with these gloomy pursuits!

With bulging eyes, Lizza eased the kitchen door closed behind Carolyn leaving her in cold blue darkness. It was then that Carolyn saw the broad-shouldered silhouette of Wildman standing to the side of the cellar pit.

Shivering, her heart leaping, she turned to go back inside. He was a man of the night. She wanted nothing more to do with him.

"Carolyn!" came his hushed call. "I've come."

Breathing hard, she hesitated. She recalled his hard, insistent kiss that strange night in his cabin when he had molested her, and her most unthinkable response. Was she mad to think even for a moment that she might be willing to speak with him again?

She heard the crunch of his footsteps nearing in the snow. She wanted to go inside, but a strange curiosity made her wait by the door. If she was to marry Evan in a few short days, she must be certain she had no lingering feelings for Wildman.

He stopped only a few feet from her. "I said I would come."

"I can't go with you," she said, gazing at the planes of his cheeks and the curls of his beard illuminated by the pale light falling from the kitchen windows.

"I need you," he hissed, taking a step closer.

She shook her head. "I'm sorry. If you wish to talk to me, you'll have to come inside—"

"Carolyn!" He was beside her then, enveloping her with arms she couldn't resist. It was like a dream...

She looked up into his pale eyes, and wondered what it was about him that held her so. He bent over her, mesmerizing her. Then his cool lips were on hers. He was arching against her, making his intentions clear.

Alarmed by the leap of response in her blood, she pushed him away. "No! I've had enough. Go from me! I'm leaving Timberhill, and I'm never coming back." She pushed hard enough that he staggered back and finally tumbled off the verandah into the snow. She reached for the doorhandle, frightened and disgusted with herself. She had promised herself to Evan!

"You be a fool," came Ona's deep voice from the shadows nearby. "This man, he be the one for you."

Whirling, Carolyn balled her fists. "What are you doing here? You dare to interfere in my life now? Why should I listen to anything you say when all my questions to you went unanswered? I've found what I came to learn. I've been ready to go from here a long time. And now I will go, happily! Leave me alone, the both of you!"

"This man be your first love," Ona hissed. "He be your one true love. You cannot marry that other."

Carolyn's blood went cold. "What are you saying?" She took a step toward Wildman. "What is she saying? I don't know you!"

"Ah, but you do," he said softly. "I've known who you were from the moment of your return, but you didn't remember me. Look into my eyes, Carolyn. Your heart knows me. That's why you're drawn to me. What we felt so long ago, it can't be forgotten. A marriage to another man didn't make you forget. Ten lonely years in these woods, waiting for you to set me free, didn't make me forget."

Carolyn went cold. Was this the bewitchment, that she had once known him?

Ona made a threatening move toward them.

"Carolyn, one more marriage won't make a difference either! You've always loved me!" he said in a rush, as if trying to outwit the dark woman prowling closer.

Carolyn stared into Wildman's eyes. Those strangely hard, mocking eyes were so chill. She saw nothing familiar. She couldn't have known a man like this! "No! No!"

He held up his hand at Ona's effort to speak. "Don't go back on your agreement! I will have her."

Ona's black eyes became veiled as she gave the appearance of obeying Wildman's command. "Miz, this be your own John," Ona whispered gently, as if persuading a child to understand.

Carolyn stared at him in disbelief. "It can't be...John? John Rasner? Your own sister said you were dead in the war. Did she lie?"

He shook his head. "Come with me and I'll explain."

"No! You'll explain now! You would have your own sister and father believe that you were dead for all these years? And all the while you've lived in these woods, so near to them? You're some kind of monster!" And he had bewitched her, filling her mind with those scandalous thoughts!

"It's all on account of your father that I have to live the way I do!" he cried. He stepped forward, menacingly. "And for that you owe me...everything!" His teeth gleamed, and he reached for her arm.

She backed away from him, shaking her head. Betrayed! John

had betrayed them all! "Why? Why did you betray us?"

Ona stepped forward, shushing her. She caught Carolyn's right arm. Wildman—John Rasner—seized her left arm. Together they drew Carolyn off the verandah.

Carolyn was so dumbfounded that she momentarily felt too weak to protest. This was the man she had loved as a girl! This was the looming, shadowed man in her dream, she thought, beginning to struggle. This was the apprentice her father had trusted to defend his actions, whatever they had been, and this was the man in her nightmare who claimed her father had done murder!

"Let me go!" Carolyn cried, fighting against them, finding that they held her fast.

From the house came a flood of gold light as the kitchen door was quietly opened. "Carolyn, what is it?" Evan called, his face dark with concern.

Ona's strong grip relaxed on Carolyn's arm. At once, the woman melted into the darkness and scurried away. She looked like a shadow moving swiftly across the blue-tinged snowy meadow as she disappeared beyond the dark, yawning cellar pit.

With the slightest hesitation, John Rasner, too, released Carolyn's arm. He fled, his cloak billowing like wings. Enchanted, evil prince...

With a whimper, Carolyn threw herself into Evan's strong, warm embrace. "It's madness! Pure madness! I'm not sure I believe it, even now."

"Come inside and tell me what they wanted with you," he said, drawing her into the kitchen. He closed the door, barring it. "I'd go after them—"

"No, you're too precious to me. I am such a witling! How could I not recognize him? And he was even living at the old Rasner cabin! I should have guessed! I must learn to trust my instincts, and to think, Evan! To think!"

Shaking, Carolyn sagged to the bench alongside the trestle table. Finally, she put her face in her hands. What a fool she was!

"The sooner I get away from here the better. If you hadn't

come, I would surely have lost my mind in the end."

"Who was that man, Carolyn?"

She pressed the heel of her hand to her breast. "He said…
He said he was…but it can't be. It's too preposterous. Living in
these woods all these years…Evan, if I didn't know better, I would
say this house is cursed. I want to be away!" She waved off his
additional questions. "None of that is important now. All I care
about is leaving. They would have me believe that that man was my
father's first apprentice, a man I once found infatuating. Supposedly,
he's been dead more than ten years. I—I was nearly taken in, Evan!
Thank God you came here when you did! They might have…" She
shuddered. "I don't know exactly what they might have done to me.
I think tonight they might have carried me away! Am I mad? Did any
of this truly happen?"

He took her wrists and pulled her to her feet. His eyes were
narrowed with worry. "This is no place for you. It destroyed your
father. If you don't come away at once, it will destroy you! You're
overtired, Carolyn. You have had two miserable months alone. You
have lost your secure way of life, and what is more, you have lost
your past."

She nodded, realizing he was only too right. She had lost her
most comforting childhood memories to a bewildering, tragic reality.

"Can you leave this place with a clear heart?" he asked. "I don't
want you haunted any longer by thoughts of Timberhill."

"I leave it gladly. Silas is welcome to it!"

"And you love me?"

"I wasn't sure before, but I am now!" she said, sincerely.

He gathered her tightly against him, wrapping his arms fully
around her until she was breathless and warm. "I would die before
allowing anything to harm you, Carolyn. Promise me something."

"Whatever I can," she whispered, fighting tears.

"Never run off from me again. Never."

"I promise."

"Whatever you want, you need only tell me. Don't think of
me as you would other men. I want for you more than you have

ever dreamed. I'll do nothing to stand in your way. I've waited too long…"

She tipped up her head, touched beyond words by the sweetness of his love. "I'll make you glad you did, Evan."

"You already have, my love."

Evan had little time to make inquiries in Eudoxia, but he was determined to learn more about the mysterious man in the woods. The place was so primitive, the farms so scattered and isolated, it was little wonder a man could live a mythlike existence in the nearby forest for so long.

Though his inquiries raised brows aplenty, Evan didn't mind. He wanted to know if, indeed, Carolyn had been harassed by a bearded man who had once been her father's apprentice. He found no satisfactory answers. He was told only that John Rasner had disappeared, presumably to the war a few weeks following the departure of Orion Adams and his family. And then word had come that he was dead.

"The Adamses driven out?" an elder asked, askance. "Preposterous! A mob with torches? I should say not. We're peace-loving people. Farmers! We would wish no one harm."

Helen Rasner and her father were even more incredulous. "My son is dead, sir," the old gentleman said gruffly, though neither he nor his daughter would confess whether they had seen John Rasner's body. They claimed he had been buried somewhere in New Jersey.

Satisfied only that he had stirred the imaginations of a number of widows and oldsters, Evan was glad to be taking himself away from such a dismal place. He married Carolyn that Sabbath morning, considering himself the luckiest of men.

Carolyn wore a very plain gown donated by her sister-in-law, Fanny. Evan wore his tailcoat and snug buff knee breeches. The ceremony was brief, not at all the grandiose affair he would have wanted.

But Carolyn looked happy, and that was his primary concern. Her aunt and cousin were absent, so he was informed by various whispering ladies of the village. And the madwoman couldn't be pried from her estate. He was glad.

The so-called Wildman was nowhere to be seen. The cooking woman, Ona, did not return to Timberhill for the wedding dinner. Evan couldn't bear it when Carolyn and Lizza prepared a simple meal themselves, but Carolyn glowed with delight. As he watched from the table, she often touched him. He hungered for far better than food. If it pleased her to prepare her own wedding dinner, so be it. Soon enough he would have a host of servants for her.

Now shivering, but not from cold, he gladly settled Carolyn in his cutter. They were waving their good-byes before he felt the slightest flicker of fatigue. He seemed to have gained an amazing strength from seeing Carolyn again. To have her agree to marry him—and now to have her belong to him—was better than the finest tonic!

The moment his driver cracked the whip, he could feel Carolyn relaxing against his shoulder in the snug confines of the cutter's coach.

"Happy to be going back to Philadelphia?" he asked, circling her shoulder with his arm and drawing her tightly against him.

"Very," she sighed, snuggling closer.

He tipped up her face for a kiss that immediately stirred him. "When I started out, I only hoped to find you. I can hardly believe that I've claimed you for my own. Do you love me, Carolyn?"

"I have for a long time. I only hope people don't think me hasty for remarrying so soon."

"Soon!" he said, laughing somewhat nervously. "To me it has been a lifetime."

"I'm sorry, truly sorry, for leaving as I did," she said, her eyes round and earnest.

He adjusted her cloak high about her neck. "That's done. We have only the future before us now. Do you feel up to a Christmas party?" he asked, watching her eyes light.

"It's been a long time since I saw your country house, Evan. Will you have my things from Papa's house boxed and brought out? I'll want to sort through everything…eventually."

"Whatever you like. I remember once that you said you wished to study medicine. Have you given that more thought?"

"Since arriving at Timberhill I've given very few things thought, except for the bizarre. Yes, I still think I would like to study." She fell silent a long moment, and a shadow crossed her expression.

"I have no objections," he said, thinking she might feel hampered now by his expectations of her. "As my wife, you can be whatever pleases you most."

She looked at him with a very unsettling expression.

"What's troubling you?" he whispered, cupping her jaw and kissing her nose.

She forced a smile. "I promise to tell you another time, but this is our wedding day. I want to be happy."

He kissed her trembling lips softly. "And happy tonight you shall be," he whispered, feeling a rush of desire warm his blood.

As he drew back from her and gazed through the window to the passing snowy landscape, he felt strangely as though he had not yet completely won her. There were regions within her yet locked away and inaccessible.

If he was to have her, as his good but foolish friend Forrest had failed to do, he would have to cultivate her trust as never before. How did a man do that with the woman he loved so desperately? Was patience enough? Was this place, Timberhill, seated in her like a case of swamp fever, flaring and ebbing and flaring again, never to fully give her ease?

Millers and Spoon, an inn on the turnpike to Philadelphia, looked like a speck of light from the dusk-shrouded foothills. Evan dozed against Carolyn in the cutter as it drove, slick and swift, through the snow. His head was heavy on her shoulder, his hands limp on his lap.

Carolyn gazed through the window, unable to shake the feeling that she had left something behind at Timberhill. All had happened too quickly. Evan had come, and she had thrown herself into his arms gladly, but now that they were away, she felt at loose ends.

Carolyn had virtually run from her feelings for Wildman—John Rasner. Still, she couldn't convince herself that the two men were one in the same. The young medical apprentice she had liked so much as an innocent young girl couldn't be the same man who lived as a recluse in the woods now. His eyes were so different now, so changeable, so mysterious, so feral.

Yes, she thought, all had happened too fast. She should have talked to John. She should have learned why he had allowed his sister and father to believe him dead. Was it all because of the diphtheria epidemic and the accusations against her father? Was there still more to learn?

She buried her face in Evan's hair. Breathing in the scent of him, she thought how very glad she was that she didn't have to be in that gloomy old house another night. The lights for Miller and Spoon were distinct now, closer, like a haven.

How odd, she thought that on her wedding day she should be haunted by thoughts of the dead baby she had delivered. Perhaps it was only because she might now become pregnant herself. The specter of what she had done seemed even more significant.

Would Silas have given her quite so warm a blessing on her marriage day if he knew she had buried, unbaptized, a son of his?

"You don't look very happy." Evan's voice came to her with a startling softness. He still lay against her, his eyes wide and his expression thoughtful.

"Only musing," she said, smiling quickly. "Are you tired? You were ill a long time."

"We shall see how weak I am...very soon," he said, with a fiery light in his eyes.

At once her blood was tingling, and troubling thoughts fled. He moved tightly against her, kissing her deeply, reminding her of all the untold pleasures that could be theirs this night.

Within an hour, they arrived at the inn. Like typical newlyweds, they went to their bridal room with secret smiles and the knowing smirks of every person lingering in the place behind them. Evan's driver, Thomas, saw to the horses and bedded in the barn.

Once closed in the snug, warm chamber, Carolyn and Evan turned to each other and laughed self-consciously.

"I'll have a light supper sent up," he said, shrugging off his cloak and taking off his coat.

"I could use a toddy," Carolyn said, prowling about the chamber and inspecting the great draped bed. "We'll be warm here, at least."

"With no ghosts to plague us," Evan said, smiling.

He came up behind her and helped her off with her cloak. She was trembling, and leaned back against him, trying to find her courage.

"Are you having second thoughts?" he asked, sensing a certain aloofness about her.

"Oh, no," she said softly. "Not at all. I'm being very foolish, I suppose, but I'm thinking of my wedding night with Forrest."

Evan moved away, loosening his neck stock and taking the cuff links from his frilled wrists.

"I was a very innocent girl then. Do I need to tell you that my wedding night never...occurred?"

He paused, unable to stoop to pull off his shoes. "You're not saying you're still a virgin!"

She laughed with embarrassment. "Not so awful as that, but it was almost eight months before we...and then we weren't well-suited. A year later, Forrest ceased expressing an interest in that part of our relationship."

He straightened, his eyes wide. "Eight years, then, Carolyn?"

"Well, in a word, yes. I'm virtually untouched...except that I—I'm finding it hard to express my desire for you because of a certain night not so long ago when I was at that man's cabin—Wildman. I had gone out in search of Lizza. I thought she was at Ona's cabin. I shouldn't have been, on my leg, but at the time I was as rash and foolish as a child. I got lost..." She laughed uneasily.

"I found Wildman's cabin—John's cabin. I did not recognize him, truly, but there was something between us…He said I would be in danger if I returned to Timberhill; it was All Hallow's Eve. At the time I could believe that danger lurked in the woods. Now, of course, it seems absurd. I—I was very tired. He gave me something to drink…I remember feeling bewitched, as if that mysterious attraction I felt for him was suddenly magnified."

Evan's skin prickled. He feared what she might be trying to tell him. Suddenly his jealousy flared. Could he still love her if she had given herself to the wildman?

"The herbal tea was very powerful," Carolyn went on. "I thought at first it contained belladonna or nightshade, both poisons and used in some strong medicinal teas. I later thought it may have contained morphia. Where he would get such things is a puzzle." She paused, averting her eyes in shame. "What I'm trying to confess is that I—I was molested. I'm finding it hard to get that night out of my mind now when I want to be free with you. Can you have patience?"

Evan was so relieved to find she hadn't willingly welcomed the bearded one called Wildman that he momentarily overlooked the fact that she had endured what appeared to have been a terrifying assault on her person.

Then, as he watched her stand, head down, in a shadow near the bed, he had to wonder if she was asking that he keep himself from her while she got over the shock of it. Was she in her right mind at this moment?

He crossed the chamber slowly, watching her shrink before him. He marveled that so intelligent and lovely a woman should be so frightened in the face of lovemaking. "Carolyn," he murmured. "Are you afraid of me suddenly? You weren't the night I arrived in Timberhill."

"I know, but we were in the midst of a crowd then. I had no hope of being alone with you to fulfill my desires. Now…" She laughed at herself, but tears were filling her eyes.

"Now we're alone. I wouldn't force you, darling, but you must know how very much I want you."

She searched his eyes a moment and then dropped her gaze, shivering. "I don't know how to behave, Evan."

He save a soft, incredulous laugh. She was worse than a virgin! He would have to seduce her as if she were a frightened stranger. "What can I do to make you trust me?" he whispered, laying his hands softly on her shoulders.

Wordlessly, she shook her head. The poor darling didn't know what she wanted or needed. Suddenly he felt like a fool, for he was little better prepared for this than she! He had kept himself for her a good while, venturing into brief liaisons for the mere relief of tension. The last had been more than a year ago.

He slid his hand to her neck and held her gently. He kissed her, drawing her close and making no effort to touch her in a way that would alarm her. He was growing erect, but could do nothing to quell it. He would be patient. He would be more patient than he had ever dreamed he would have to be. Already he was bracing himself for the possibility that he would not satisfy his needs this night. His future happiness with Carolyn depended on it.

He kissed her until he felt her melting against him. As she returned his kisses, he ran his fingers through her hair, sorting away pins that dropped softly to the floor planks.

Behind him, the hearthfire hissed and snapped. Golden shadows leaped around them. Her face was bathed in gold, her hair catching the dancing lights. She was so beautiful, so vulnerable. He lost himself in her, wanting only to do soft, gentle things to her. He wanted only to savor her as the delightful treasure that had so long been denied him.

It was some time later that Evan realized she was not protesting any of his most natural movements against her. His hands brushed softly against her breasts. She nuzzled her face against his chest and finally pulled away the fabric of his shirt.

When he looked at her face, he saw that she had shed her fears and her memories. She was immersed in him, abandoned to him in a way he had not expected, nor dared hope for. When he felt her breath against his bared chest, his ardor leaped to a new awareness.

He felt a burning urgency to claim her.

With exquisite care he led her to the bed. Standing over her, he bared her breasts to his eyes and lips. He could not have imagined them more beautiful, they were so warm and responsive. She laced her fingers in his hair as he kissed her full breasts.

And then there was no more thought. He was pulling away his knee breeches and she shed her skirt and petticoats. If he thought to hold back, he forgot now. If she was remembering other, less satisfying times, he couldn't detect it in her eyes.

Her eyes were golden warm and liquid with desire. He was on her, absorbing her, drawing in so close to her that they were one in heart long before he allowed himself to seek the final refuge. With one triumphant plunge he laid claim to her as his woman, his wife.

He lost himself to her, thinking only that this was what he had waited for, this was what he had prayed for. He committed his all to her, thrusting with the last of his frenzied strength until she was full and gasping, shuddering beneath him and stilling his raging heart.

Her body gave off a fine warmth. Her face looked radiant and was faintly moist with sweat. Her hair lay in riotous curls all over the coverlet. She was gasping, locked with him, taking her own pleasure from him and making his eyes wide to think that she could be so free.

He collapsed on her, crushing her to his body in hopes that she truly could belong to him. If he could give her this much in one night, she would never leave him again.

"Carolyn, I love you!" he whispered, rolling onto his back and dragging her atop him.

"Oh, don't!" She laughed, astride now, pressing her palms to his chest, squirming, blushing and sweetly demure.

But he held her there, and when she looked into his eyes he knew no other man had taken her to the place she had gone with him this night. She drew close against him, panting, warm and fragile to his hands.

In time he drew away from beneath her. They crawled into the bed that was already warmed by their unabashed lovemaking. She was ready for him again before the fire had begun to burn low in the grate. If they slept that night, it was only for an hour or so. By morning they lay in exhaustion, oblivious to the knocks calling them to breakfast or the road.

They lingered there three full days, and were the talk of every patron, and the bane of poor young blushing Thomas, who had to take most of the ribbing.

But for Carolyn and Evan, a thirst that had gone unquenched so many dry years had to be satisfied. Shadows and confusion had to be exorcised. When they emerged to resume their journey to Philadelphia, it was as if to a new world and a newborn day.

Fourteen

Carolyn had forgotten how grand Evan's country house was. Of Georgian design, it stood on a snow-covered rise, backed by dense woodland.

The sky was clear and pale blue as they approached in the cutter that morning. Evan had sent word ahead of their arrival; they had been traveling since just before dawn. Carolyn thrilled to see the house with its pedimented, pillared front doorway and its white shutters on the lower story.

"It's lovely," she said, hugging Evan's arm. The last time she had been there was with Forrest for a small holiday dinner party two or three Christmases before.

"What would you like for Christmas?" Evan asked, as if reading her thoughts.

She laughed gently. "I have everything I want now—a peaceful heart and a happy new life." If her dreams were still disturbing, she thought, that would pass in time.

"I've been thinking of a proper lady's chaise for you and a matched team. Would you like that?"

She patted his sleeve, embarrassed by his largess. "Tell me. I've never been in a position to ask. Where did you come by your fortune?"

Grinning, he watched the sweeping drive ahead. "I'm a rather fine attorney, in case you have forgotten. But in truth, most was left to me by my grandfather. My father died when I was a boy, my mother when I was a young man. I received some money from her people, as well. I was a romantic young blade, and used my inheritance to buy this house for my bride."

Startled, Carolyn turned to him. "You never mentioned—"

"I was only anticipating. I never found the right woman, until I met you...And you were so young."

Carolyn didn't want to go over the folly of her first marriage again. "What of this party you promised me?" She clung to his arm, the memories of Timberhill, her difficult early years in Philadelphia and the long, empty years at the house on Dewberry Lane deliberately driven from her mind.

"Ah, now, that's a subject I'll enjoy. Let me tell you what I've planned..."

Though furnished simply, Evan's house was charming and inviting. Readied for the bride, it stood warm and aglow in candlelight as they entered the central hall and greeted Evan's new servants.

Only Evan's new housekeeper, Mrs. Pepperell, had experience in a fine household. Forced to hire what help was available after the devastating sickness, Evan's butler, maids, cook and yard men were more used to cruder town occupations. Carolyn felt overwhelmed to find so many awkward servants now waiting upon her command. She greeted them with equal ineptitude.

They gawked with awe at the master, a man they surely mistook for a legislator. The women curtseyed and blushed at Carolyn. She began to feel a bit startled to think she had never truly appreciated Evan's position, and marveled to find herself now at his side.

"I would think you'd like to bathe and rest," he said, striding toward the study. "I'll have to see about my affairs in town—you can't imagine all that went undone while I was ill. But you needn't concern yourself with a single detail of the Christmas Eve party. Mrs. Pepperell has her instructions. If there's anything in particular you want changed, however..."

Carolyn laughed. "We'll talk about this later," she said, following Evan to his study, startled to find it lined with law books, nothing like a medical surgery. Everything in her life was now so different...

"I'm concerned about what to wear. Am I to hire a dressmaker? I—I've long made my own gowns, but there's only a few days until the party."

Evan turned, his face wide with delighted surprise. "I'm such a dunderhead! I forget that you're unused to even a semblance of wealth. What fun I'm going to have spoiling you! Yes, by all means, hire a dressmaker, and at least two assistants. You may order whatever you like. Don't hold back for any reason. This is Christmas, my love! You must have all your heart's desires: gowns, petticoats, the finest stockings." He swept her into his arms. "I'll send a merchant out with everything you could possibly need."

Laughing, Carolyn let him kiss her. Then her head fell back, and she left her mind swirl with thoughts of new clothes heaped on her bed as if by magic. "Oh, before you go…"

He was kissing her throat.

"Evan, you're a marvel! You've made me so happy! I want you to show me the entire house, from cellar to attic. I want this place to be my home. Always my home."

He seemed to understand what she was saying, that she wanted the memory of Timberhill buried and forgotten. She wanted it replaced with a shining, wonderful home that had awaited its mistress for almost fifteen years.

Hugging her close, he nuzzled her neck. "I wonder if I can tear myself away from you long enough to ride into town."

"You mustn't ride! You've had a long journey, and you're just not strong enough yet to bear the stress and cold. Evan, don't risk yourself, I beg you!" She shook him a little.

Looking deeply into her eyes, seeing her sudden anxiety, he closed her tightly within the circle of his arms. "I'll give you no cause for worry, my love."

Trembling, she was stunned to realize how very much she did love Evan. It was as if her capacity for it were deepening with every moment they shared as husband and wife. She had never known this kind of caring, this desperate need. Was it good, or were the dark places in her heart still alive, still haunting her ability to experience joy?

"Evan, I love you!"

"You sound as if you just realized it."

She drew away enough to look up at his dear, handsome face. "I think I'm only just beginning to realize what love feels like. My heart has been closed a long time."

A wonderful, exhilarating flush spread across his cheeks. Pulling her to the door, his hand trembling on her arm, he guided her toward the staircase and the chamber awaiting them upstairs.

They would tour the house later.

Carolyn's eyes glowed with wonder as the maids in their aprons and mobcaps carried armloads of items the merchant had displayed in the drawing room.

She had selected silk kerchiefs, ribbons, beads, combs, baubles and pins for her hair, riding boots and dancing slippers, white silk clocked stockings, embroidered and tasseled reticules, feathered and frilled bonnets, gloves of kidskin and silk, and two corsets, one for everyday and another smaller one for formal wear, plus several cashmere fringed shawls.

Feeling that she had been extravagant in the extreme, she bid the delighted merchant farewell. Moments later a dressmaker and her two daughters arrived in a cutter. They all adjourned to the dressing room off Carolyn's bedchamber.

Mary Wilson was wise not to comment on Carolyn's less than lovely remnants of her former life as the wife of a poorly paid physick. After being measured, Carolyn picked the fabrics she wished made into nightshifts, petticoats, chemises and pantaloons. Then came the more difficult task of selecting the fabrics and styles for several gowns, one to be formal for the Christmas Eve party.

She chose a flowered silk for around the house, a white satin with fitted brown velvet jacket for visiting, a silk plisse cloak with fur trim for winter, and matching fur muff. For a receiving gown she chose a dark print with a high, fashionable waist.

They debated some time over white spotted India muslin, a pink floral-printed striped cotton or a cream leno over satin for the gown. Finally, they chose the muslin, agreed on the cut and style, and the simple silver-thread embroidery to grace the hem and short puffed sleeves. Carolyn worried about the expense but decided that if she had ordered too much, Evan would surely say so.

The dressmaker removed to an attic workroom and set at once to sewing the evening gown. Her daughters returned to town for supplies and were back before dusk.

Evan had driven an open cutter into town, leaving Carolyn to her female pursuits. He returned in time to find Mrs. Pepperell directing the preparation of the dining room and lower parlors. With the lovely handpainted wallpapers depicting rural Pennsylvania hillsides, and the greenery draped all around, the long dining table and dozen chairs seemed out-of-doors.

He bounded up the stairs to the bedchamber to find Carolyn asleep amid heaps of items from the merchant. Grinning, he stood looking down at her, marveling that she belonged to him and loved him so.

Taking one of the sheer woven shawls from the heap on the bed, he covered her. She sprang upright, almost knocking heads with him. Her eyes were wide and unfocused, her expression decidedly disturbing.

"Forgive me! I didn't mean to wake you," he said, gathering her close, alarmed to find her stiff and unresponsive.

Almost at once, however, she regained her senses and melted against him. He could feel the pounding of her pulse as he pressed his lips to her neck.

"What were you dreaming about?"

She sighed. "Nothing. It was nothing."

But as he held her, she stared unseeingly across the expansive bedchamber. The memory of a dark looming shape came to her. It swooped down, driving deeply into her. She shuddered to find the terrors of Timberhill intruding on the passion of her marriage bed.

This time, in her nightmare, the cloaked shadow had raped her. She had lain unmoving, powerless to prevent the violation.

She clung to Evan, willing away the thoughts. She wanted only the beauty of his love and the delight of his generosity to fill her waking and sleeping moments. She needed time to heal, to forget, to go on now that Forrest and Timberhill were gone.

But the dream had seemed incredibly real, almost as if it had already happened, or *would* happen. She felt helpless to stop what her flight to Timberhill had set into motion.

Carolyn looked elegant beyond her wildest imaginings in the muslin gown that hung in sheer folds, accentuating her beautiful bosom, leaving her arms and throat bare. Betsy, her maid, had finished her hair and had twined a white silk rose in it, leaving a trail of curly fringes around her face.

When Evan came in, still fussing with the folds of his neck stock, he stopped short. His eyes swelled and he straightened. "My God, you're beautiful."

"Thank you, kind husband," she said, glowing beneath his praise.

She took her place at the dressing table, watching him in the looking glass as she dabbed a touch of perfume between her breasts and behind her ears. He crossed the chamber quickly, drawing a slim box from him breast pocket.

He handed it to her and nibbled her ear. "For you, my dearest wife. You drive me mad with passion. I want you. Right here, right now."

She giggled. "We would be late greeting our guests." She opened the box, finding within a stunning crystal necklace perfectly matching the silvery embroidery of her gown.

"Let me help you do the catch," he said, lifting the glittering bits of glass and draping the necklace about her creamy throat. He watched her in the looking glass as he fastened the catch. Then he slid both his wide hands over her breasts.

Catching her breath, Carolyn stared at her husband's hands on her bodice. She felt her nipples contracting with desire. Then, tantalizingly, he slipped his hands beneath her neckline, cupping her breasts even though the gown was snug and the delicate fabric was straining.

"I've never noticed that scar on your throat before," he whispered close by her neck, still watching her impassioned eyes in the looking glass.

"It's nothing, really. Might we...really steal a few moments before we go down?" she whispered, wanting him suddenly. "But I hate to muss my hair."

His warm fingers slid teasingly from her gown, leaving her bosom plumped above the neckline. He turned her on the stool so that she was facing him.

His breeches were fine white wool with a full-fall front opening. He allowed her to unbutton it. She found him more than willing to satisfy her.

When he crouched before her, eyes locked with hers, she sat very still, aware of her every breath. From head to foot, she was clothed in wonderful new things. Beneath the lovely gown were the sheerest of petticoats. His hands were warm on her thighs as he explored the construction of her pantaloons. He found the thin silk drawstring and finally tugged it loose.

With her skirts gathered high on her thighs, her pantaloons drawn low, she leaned back, bracing herself on the edge of the dressing table. He entered quickly, and then remained still, looking at her, this their first lovemaking not bathed in firelight alone.

Carolyn closed her eyes to better savor the feel of him. She was trembling, trying to remain still so that she wouldn't disturb an hour of hairdressing.

He moved ever so carefully against her, grinning as he pressed kisses to her neck, trying not to chafe her skin with his jaw.

She thought of nothing but this wonderful husband who was so eager to possess her at any time of the day or night. Though they were due in the entry to greet guests, they were instead locked together. She sat partially on the stool, feeling the gathering tremor of her crisis contracting in her loins.

Out in the hallway came the tiptoe of the maid's footsteps. The girl was tapping—Carolyn's eyes flew open and she saw the door easing open.

"Don't come in," she said softly. "Not just now!"

The door eased closed. Evan chuckled, pulsing in her and clutching her tightly.

"Oh, mercy!" Carolyn said, her voice trembling. "I love you!"

And then as quickly as it had begun, she found release. He, too, shuddered against her, laughing. It had been brief, but so simple, so easily accomplished she could only marvel at their compatibility. They would make love again after the guests had departed, she knew, but this one stolen moment seemed especially precious.

He didn't withdraw immediately, but remained slumped against her, his breath hot in her ear, his hands spread against her back. Then finally he sighed and drew away. In moments he had righted his clothes. She was standing, weak-kneed, looking up at him with love in her eyes.

"Will we ever have enough of one another?" he asked, looking pleasantly sated. He circled her waist as she brushed at the folds of her skirt, tidying them.

"I hope not," she breathed.

"Everyone will envy us this night," he said.

"A good Christmas to you, husband," she whispered, kissing his cheek. "It's a very good Christmas for me."

Fifteen

1794

For weeks Mr. and Mrs. Evan Alexander Burck were the talk of Philadelphia's social circles. Their Christmas Eve party had included some of the finest people in town, and not a one had failed to notice Evan's proud stance, nor Carolyn's flushed, lovely countenance. They made a lovely couple.

Carolyn had invited her few friends from Liberty Hospital. All of Forrest's colleagues had been invited to the party, except for Dr. Winston, and his absence was not inconspicuous.

Evan's friends came from far and wide, and included a vast range of people from all walks of life. Clients, friends and colleagues alike crowded into the large country house to catch a glimpse of Evan's starry-eyed bride, and the party had gone on past dawn.

Though Carolyn was unable to dance due to the weakened condition of her leg, she was devotedly attended by her husband. As his wife, she began adapting well to her elevated station.

As the New Year rang in the following week, Carolyn contented herself with furnishing the house, and she completed a wardrobe roughly double what she had originally ordered. Mary Wilson seemed like a permanent resident in the attic sewing room, and fittings were frequent.

Carolyn learned to direct her servants, always with some discomfiture, but by early spring the house took on the feeling of home. Evan came and went on horseback once again. Carolyn's leg was entirely healed, and ached only during a change in the weather.

Spring came with astonishing beauty that year. When the snow had nearly all melted by late March, Carolyn would often stand at one of the several front windows, gazing out across the rolling hills that belonged to her husband. The meadow land was such a tender, innocent green. The dogwood and apple trees were blooming, and all seemed right…

Except that she hadn't yet conceived, and that troubled her somewhat. She also found her sleep disturbed by nightmares still. Luckily, Evan was unaware of them.

He was the most wonderful of men, she thought as she dressed one day in April. She heard her chaise being brought round from the carriage house. Looking out her bedchamber window, she saw Thomas alighting and trotting away to tend his beloved horses. She found herself remembering the day she and Forrest had topped Washington Street hill in their shabby chaise…and, though the sun continued to shine, she felt herself cast in sudden shade.

Evan was such an understanding man. When she had suggested that she would like to go through the house on Dewberry Lane by herself instead of having an army of louts pack her father's and first husband's belongings, he had readily agreed.

Now she wondered if she was not again being headstrong and rash. She intended to return to town today and open the house, go through the chambers one by one, deciding what to keep, sell or discard. The ghost of her marriage was close at hand as she donned her traveling cloak and tied on her trimmed bonnet. Even those dismal days preceding her marriage loomed large in her mind.

Feeling glum, she set out for Philadelphia. She felt no better as she drew alongside the house some time later. Though Evan had hired a man to keep the yard tidy, no one had been inside since the day she and Lizza left for Timberhill in the roadwagon. In this house, would she do any better laying to rest the ghosts of her past? she wondered.

Inside, the townhouse was cramped and shabby. She moved swiftly from chamber to chamber, then ventured upstairs to stare a long moment at the bedchamber she had shared with Forrest for ten years. It all seemed like a faraway dream.

Impatiently, she went back down to the surgery, the only room in the house that held such interest for her. There, in a glassed case, were the precious journals her father had salvaged from Timberhill. She drew them all out and sat for a time at the dusty desk, thumbing through each, noting the dates and looking for a place that might be missing a page.

She found numerous pages with sketches of male or female anatomies, all with brown-ink notations along both margins, but nowhere did she find a page torn out. The fact niggled in the back of her mind. The page she had tucked away in her now overflowing jewel case must surely have come from one of the journals in the cellar.

Never before had she gone through the desk that Forrest had used after her father's death. Reminding herself to bring one of the maids to assist her the following day, she searched each drawer, finding mementos of long ago.

The years fell aside in misty disarray as if everything had happened to someone else. She could not believe that she had lived such a bleak existence here, except that she had expected such a life in those days. She had, in some ways, hidden from a bewildering world that had betrayed all she had ever known in one terrible night. This somber, quiet house had protected her.

How glad she was to be in Evan's house now, and bedded with such passionate regularity that she blushed even in the privacy of the surgery.

That first afternoon was spent carting her father's medical texts to the chaise. In the evening, after her return home, she told Evan some of what she'd felt while seeing the house again. And she impressed him by translating some of her father's Latin texts. They talked far into the night of her plans to pursue medicine.

For the next week she drove herself into town every day. She found, after all, that she preferred to do the tedious packing alone rather than share the intimacy of her reminiscences with a servant.

Often in the afternoon she found herself weary and would settle in her father's easy chair by the south window as she had in years gone by to read one of his journals. She had yet to take them home to Evan. She wanted to savor them all while still alone before boxing them for permanent storage in one of Evan's attics.

The ghost of the lost journals she had found in the cellar pit at Timberhill troubled her still. Those that had been damaged beyond reading would have been his earliest ones. She ached, wondering what his first years working at Timberhill had been like.

The journals he had salvaged detailed cases that he had worked on in the surrounds of Eudoxia. He had also filled two after his return to Philadelphia from the war. She was surprised to find frequent references to unpleasant encounters with Dr. Winston and his ilk.

One afternoon, she found that she felt particularly outraged by some of the practices her father had chosen to relate. They showed Dr. Winston's extreme indifference to progressive methods that were now accepted practice the world over.

Outside, a soaking spring rain had drenched everything. The house was chilled, and she decided on a fire in the surgery's grate. The woodbox was empty so she brought wood from the kitchen.

She was crouched at the hearth, trying to light the fire when she turned around to look for some tinder. She caught sight of something sticking out from the underside of her father's desk. Below the left pedestal she noted what looked like a slip of paper hanging from behind the drawer.

She felt a chill go up her spine, and she looked around. Against one wall hung the wired skeleton of some long-dead criminal. On each of the other walls were painted illustrations of bodies, muscles and organs drawn by the finest medical artists of the century. Her father's remaining books lay stacked in disarray, waiting storage or study.

Without knowing why, she felt certain that her father was near. Shaking, she crouched and reached beneath the desk to see if she could tug the paper free. Surprise blossomed in her breast as her hand brushed against two narrow wooden slats attached to the underside of the bottom drawer.

She found a slim journal tucked into the slot. The receipt that had originally caught her eye remained caught behind the drawer, forgotten, as she slid the journal from its hiding place.

The Private Journal of Orion Tunsford Adams
1765

Being an account of certain cases and occurances not meant for public scrutiny under any circumstances, to be destroyed unread upon my death by my apprentice
Forrest Clure
~~John Ephraim Rasner.~~

Sixteen

Astonished, Carolyn climbed to her feet, staring at the title page of the yellowed journal. By the date, her father had started this secret journal when she was a year old.

She sank to the chair behind the desk, pulling out the drawer to examine the underside. Her father had added the narrow wood slats to hide the journal from strangers. It was an easy matter to draw the journal from its hiding place while sitting in the chair.

With hair prickling on the nape of her neck, she turned to the first page and read:

> As a man of medicine, I am finding some of what I am forced to do beyond the understanding of most men. Only my colleagues can comprehend the prejudice and ignorance I face daily, and I have been advised by many to keep some of what I do entirely private.
>
> But as I am a man of honor, so doing leaves me in a quandary, for I want to record fully my activities and discoveries. It seems, therefore, necessary to keep a private journal for the purpose of recording that which may be found distasteful or unacceptable to those who come after me; I am thinking namely of any apprentices I may accept in the future, or my wife and child who might happen upon my effects after my death.

She turned back to the title page, noting that the explanatory paragraph below the title had been added some time later, in a darker ink. And John Rasner's name had been crossed out in favor of Forrest's.

Flipping quickly through the pages, she found widely scattered dates covering all the years until her father's death. Only a few pages toward the end remained blank. Each entry was titled and dated. Her attention was caught by several. Her pulse leaped, for she had discovered an aspect of her father she had never dreamed existed.

The first entry, dated that year of 1765 when her father would have been twenty-eight years old and married only two years to her mother at Timberhill, was titled: *An Accounting of my Increasing Battle with Morphia; Being the Addiction of a Medical Physick in Pursuit of a Cure for Lung Fever in His Beloved Wife.*

Carolyn went cold and flipped to the next entry, dated 1768. *An Accounting of Dissection; Being the Anatomical Study of a Male Corpse Unearthed Without Authorization.*

Horrified, Carolyn clapped the journal closed. Abruptly putting it on the desk facedown as if it were a work of the devil himself, she rose to stare unseeingly from the south window. Her father, addicted to morphia...and a resurrectionist?

"But what happened?" Evan asked, seated on the side of the bed, holding Carolyn's chilled hand.

"H-how did I get home?" Carolyn whispered, trying to sit up.

"When you didn't come home at the usual time, I went after you and found you in a dead faint!" Evan said, his face white.

Memory of the private journal surfaced. "I found something very important among my father's things today!" She realized Evan was terrified for her, and drew his hand to her lips, "I'm all right, truly, only shaken. Please, would you bring the journal I found today? It's lying on the desk in the surgery. It's vitally important."

"My better judgment tells me to say no, but I would do anything for you, my darling. If you promise to stay in bed, I'll fetch the journal. But I won't allow you to work at the house in town alone any longer. I want the task finished."

"You're right, of course. I've wallowed in the past long enough.

I've been neglecting you, haven't I?"

He shook his head, but his troubled blue eyes spoke otherwise. "You can do whatever pleases you, so long as you don't risk yourself."

She cupped his cheek with her hand. "You're so dear. Do hurry bringing the journal. The sooner I read through it, and the sooner I satisfy my curiosity, the sooner I can put it all to rest."

He stood, turning away from her a long moment. "You've said that before, Carolyn."

"My past is a nuisance, isn't it?"

"Not your past so much as your preoccupation with it. I thought the time spent at Timberhill satisfied you."

"Yes, it did."

Sighing, he turned and regarded her with a sadness she found greatly troubling. "I don't think so. I sense something still undone. And I'm haunted, thinking some afternoon I'll come home to find that you have gone away back there to…If only I understood what you are looking for, perhaps I wouldn't worry so."

"Evan, I've promised I'll never run off again. I love you too much!"

He looked as if he wanted to say more and decided against it. Going out, he plodded down the hall. Carolyn berated herself for troubling him; but she could no more stop herself from wondering what more astonishing secrets she would find in her father's private journal than she could stop herself from breathing.

Among the entries in her father's private journal, Carolyn found an account of a miscarriage her mother had suffered that Carolyn had never been told about. She also found two entries for additional dissections on unidentified persons who had lived near Eudoxia, plus mention of a secret unnamed assistant in addition to his apprentice.

At intervals, she found notations of her father's addiction to morphia, an ingredient of laudanum made from opium. He claimed to have it under control, and mentioned using other substances on himself, as well, in hopes of finding a cure for her mother's consumption.

In one entry written in 1770, when Carolyn would have been six, he wrote: *An Accounting of Dissection on a Female Having Recently Died of Childbirth; Being the Anatomical Study of the Lungs and Internal Organs for the Purpose of Finding a Cure for Galloping Lung Fever.*

By the date, Carolyn knew that her mother's consumption was life-threatening, but she had never dreamed of the lengths to which her father would go to save her life.

One mysterious, outraged account came in an entry for the following year. *An Accounting of Death by Induced Abortion; Being the Description of a Farm Girl's Final Agony Inflicted by Persons Unknown.*

The last account brought Carolyn upright oh her chaise lounge. *An Accounting of Morbid Addiction; Being the Adverse Effects of Morphia on an Imprudent Youthful Male.*

> It has come to my astonished attention that my apprentice, John Rasner, has subjected himself to the same morphia to which I am dependent. Without my knowing, he has used my supply until I am without, and badly in need. His condition and behaviour while under the influence differs from mine in the following manner…

Disbelieving all she was finding in the private journal, Carolyn flipped hurriedly to the next entry, and the next: *An Accounting of a Radical Treatment for Putrid Throat; Being the Desperate Attempt to Save my own Beloved Daughter.*

Following that was a lapse in the dated entries until his return from the war. His last entries were brief, unremarkable, and written in a cramped, shaking hand.

She gave a start when Evan came into the bedchamber, where she had been reading.

"You look tired," he said, taking the journal from her and setting it aside. "Won't you leave this now and come down to spend some time with me?"

"Forgive me," she said, trying to force a smile. "I suppose you can't imagine what it's like to discover a secret side of a person you thought you knew so thoroughly."

Evan looked thoughtful. "I think perhaps I can understand very well, for you are such a person to me. I feel I'm losing you again. I might even admit I'm jealous of your fascination for your father's writings."

He took up the yellow-paged journal and let it fall open in his hands. Frowning at the small script, he sighed. "I can't read this."

"I learned my father's notations as a child," Carolyn said, missing her father terribly. "I once fancied that I would be his apprentice, but as a female, that was unthinkable. I thought I knew him so well. Now, to realize that all I knew about him was overshadowed by an addiction to morphia...How could such a thing be?"

"From what I have heard about physicks, Carolyn, falling prey to their own cures is a common problem. What's this?" he asked, examining the open journal. "Pages torn out?"

"Let me see!" she said, snatching it from him. "How could I have missed this?" Her blood began to rush as she examined the jagged edges of four pages ripped from the journal. "It would have been the year we left! I can make out so little." She nearly broke the journal's back trying to read the notations on the edges. "Bring my jewel case, please!"

Evan obeyed. She pulled the weathered page she had found at Timberhill from its hiding place. Holding it alongside the private journal, she saw that the torn edges matched perfectly.

Lifting her eyes, she implored Evan. "I know my father tore this account from his private journal for a very good reason!"

"If the account had any significance, he would surely have burned the incriminating pages," Evan said, looking reluctant to disabuse her innocence.

"Why incriminating? What makes you think my father did something—Oh, because of the sketch...This must have been another accounting of a dissection. That might explain why he tore it out. We were being pursued. If he were caught and the journal read..."

"I strongly suspect, Carolyn, that your father studied someone and was found out. My own reaction to the idea suggests that simple country people would not accept such an act, not even for the loftiest reasons. Your father simply went beyond what those people could condone."

Reluctantly, she had to agree. "But he would not have destroyed the pages. They would have been proof of his intent." She closed her eyes, straining to remember that long-ago, terrifying night.

She had been ill from putrid throat but recovering, still in bed asleep when the first stones were hurdled from the lane. Her father had already departed to get a wagon, she had been told, even though they had a wagon in the carriage house. Perhaps he had gone to John's house in the village. In truth, he might have been doing anything.

"I woke and hid under the bed until my mother came for me. We watched the surgery burn until it seemed safe to run, and then finally we met my father on the cart path. I dreamed that we went to a house, that someone betrayed my father...If it was John, why would he betray us?"

"Fear, my dear. As your father's apprentice, he likely assisted with the dissection. Many of those I represent in court have acted due to reckless, mindless fear. Your father was being driven out. So would he have been."

"The more I learn about this, the more confused I become. It was truly better when I remembered almost nothing! Evan, bear with me a little longer." She hung her head, longing to know exactly what her father had done to merit such abuse. What was more, she wanted to know why he, a man of honor, would have removed pages from his private journal. Surely it was an admission of guilt.

To think that John might have assisted him, and that all along he might have known why her father was driven away...What did it matter? she demanded of herself. Why couldn't she lay it to rest? To learn the truth would not bring back her parents, nor restore her lost youth. She had now all that she could possibly want...save for peace of mind.

"Evan, you'll think me horrid, but I must return to Timberhill."

He stiffened. "You can't mean it!"

She looked at him a long while. "I love you truly. I would do nothing to trouble you, but if I am failing as your wife, it's because of this unresolved time in my past."

"You most certainly are not failing me!" he said, coming to her and gathering her into his arms. He kissed her passionately, perhaps thinking that if he aroused her, she would forget the haunting mysteries of Timberhill.

She tried to respond, but her thoughts rebelled. "I know of at least three people in Eudoxia who might be persuaded to tell what they know. Perhaps all it would take would be...money. If you would consent to take me...Please, Evan?"

"I won't hear of it. We have a new life here! What went on then is dead. *Dead*, Carolyn! Why keep digging it up? Can anything you learn there make our life better now?"

"Knowing would ease my mind."

"And if you learn your father deserved to be driven away?"

"How can you say that when you yourself knew of his dedication?" she cried, astonished by Evan's attitude.

He began pacing, as if arguing with himself. "You forget," he said at length. "I met your father during the war. I saw him perform surgery, and he was a master. No one was better, but I confess to knowing your father needed morphia, though at the time I thought it was for the pain of his wound. He was a decent man, Carolyn, I know that. But a physick is, by necessity, secretive. I would not be surprised to learn of anything your father would have done to increase his knowledge. Proof of that is in this journal. Think what the man risked..."

She was staring at him, horrified; and then her skin began to crawl because she remembered what she had done in order to save a woman and a newborn.

Quickly, Evan crouched before her. "I've said something to offend you. I'm sorry!"

She shook her head, beginning to weep. "I know I will find something that I may later wish I had never learned. I know what it is to be a doctor. I know the sacrifice. Evan, if I go back to Timberhill, it will be a risk for me. I've done something there that can never be undone. And it was absolutely necessary. I may have taken a life."

His pupils dilated. His brows came down, and then his skin went white. As briefly as possible, she explained about the birth, and then she sagged, weeping, into his arms. "I fear God's punishment is to forbid me children of my own. That's why I haven't conceived."

Evan shook her until she opened her swimming eyes. "I fear for you, Carolyn. You've grown morose since going back to Timberhill. Reading your father's journals has changed you still more. Though your life with Forrest was less than satisfying, you were once a relatively happy person."

"I suppose I was content. I wouldn't have dreamed of asking Forrest to take me to Timberhill. It seemed I was destined to do only as he wanted me to do. His death ended all I expected of myself and set me free to do whatever I liked."

"And look where it's led," Evan scolded. "You're more discontented than ever, and I'm hurt. I feel that I'm not enough for you."

She stared at him, horrified to think he might be right. "Then all the more reason to begin treatment on my illness at once, dear husband. Let's go to Timberhill together, find these missing journal pages and, perhaps not set the past to rest, but set my mind and heart to rest. I fear I can't go on unless we do."

There was a hint of spring green in the high wooded mountains. Fog hung in the cool valleys, and a halo surrounded the sun, portending bad weather.

When they paused at roughly the same spot where Carolyn and Lizza had happened upon the Ebey family plot the autumn before, Carolyn listened to an ailing wind murmuring in the treetops. She hugged Evan's arm, uneasy now. She felt as if the forest were about to swallow her up.

"You're certain you want to go on?" Evan asked, frowning

at her.

She nodded. She must be done with this business, she thought.

Taking the turn toward Timberhill, Carolyn felt relieved to notice more signs of traffic on the rutted lane. When they passed the slouching brick gateposts to the Ebey estate, she shuddered, for she intended to call on Lucile Ebey, perhaps as early as the following afternoon.

Then they were rolling to a stop before Timberhill. How the great stone house had been transformed from the gloomy neglected place she had seen in the barren autumn!

Green grass had sprouted all around, and overhead, the branches were studded with plump brown buds. The air smelled sweetly moist, though cool still and redolent of damp fertile earth.

A thin trail of smoke lifted from each of the five chimneys, and the unshuttered windows glinted. As they climbed from the carriage and approached the door, it was flung wide before them. Lizza's wide grin greeted them.

"Mercy Lord, you can surprise a body!"

"Didn't you get our message? We sent a boy ahead days ago when we set out," Carolyn said, hugging the girl and looking her over. "You're thinner, Lizza. Haven't you been eating?"

"I'm run ragged, Miz. How-do, sir," she said, bobbing to Evan. "There's sickness in the house. Come in quick. I been telling Mr. Silas that you is the only person I know of what can cure fever. He's a stupid man, Miz, pardon me for saying so. He says he wouldn't have you back in the house for nothing. He says I can take care of them babies myself, but Ona swears they got fever, and—" She looked suddenly stricken, as if she had betrayed a secret.

"Don't worry about a thing now, Lizza. What is the sickness? Can you be sure it's fever? Take me up at once. Is Ona still working here?"

"I'm not supposed to speak of her, Miz, or Mr. Silas gives me a sermon to roast my ears. Miz Ona, why she ain't been back here since you got yourself married. She wouldn't come for no reason. At first, Mr. Silas was fit to be tied. He wanted her for cooking. Said

I wasn't no use with a cook pot. But she won't come."

Lizza led the way up the staircase.

"It's both little ones, down since day before yesterday," she went on. "I can't say what's ailing them, but Mr. Silas, he's gone into Eudoxia to see about a physick. I done told him there ain't a single one, excepting Miz Ona. She'd have a cure, sure, but he won't hear of it. Calls her names that I wouldn't say over again, no sir. Why, he even called my Noah a—a bastard, and he says I can't see him no more. If you be going back to Philadelphia soon, I'm going, too. I miss my pappy, and I ain't staying here to work myself like some slave no more, no sir!"

"The baby's not sick, I hope," Carolyn said, pausing at the front bedchamber. "Ask if I may speak with Fanny. I would prefer not to treat the children without her permission, at least. Knowing Silas, he'd have me before the magistrate..."

"Carolyn, what can I do to help?" Evan asked, coming up the stairs behind her.

She paused to consider. "I'll need medicines, I'm sure, and I didn't think to bring a thing with me. I'll look in on the children, and then, if you would, you can go to the village store to fetch what I need. In the meantime, I could do with a strong cup of tea."

He grinned and caught up her hand. "I feel so very proud of you at this moment. Tea I can manage."

She was touched beyond words, and hugged him, pressing her cheek against his. "You're a dear for bringing me. Remind me to thank you properly later."

He turned away to go back down the stairs.

Carolyn was admitted to Fanny's bedchamber. The older woman lay with one limp hand dangling along the edge of a cradle, which was pulled close beside her bed.

"Carolyn, what brings you?" she asked softly, too weak to be astonished by a visitor from so far.

"You're not ill, as well?"

"Only weak, so sleepy all the time."

"I'll look after your children, if you'll have me," Carolyn said, glancing at Lizza and finding the girl's anxious expression free of any hint of guile. "Lizza, wait in the hall."

Lizza crept out, looking hurt and worried.

Though Carolyn wanted Fanny to remain lying flat, the weary woman tried to rouse herself. "Lizza's been a godsend. Of course I want you to help my babies. You saved my life. If I had dared defy my husband, I would have sent for you myself. And now, here you are. My prayers have been answered."

"You needn't worry about a thing. I can handle Silas."

Fanny's sweet pale face lifted with a faint smile. "I know you can. I never spoke of it, but I heard what you did the night my dearling, Eliakim, was born. Don't look alarmed. I have wanted to strike Silas on more than one occasion myself. A man can know only so much! You have no idea how desperately afraid a mother can become for her sick children. Go to them now, please. Then I must speak to you of something, and you must promise not to tell Silas. I beg your trust."

Carolyn felt a prickling of alarm. "You will always have it." Squeezing the woman's cool hand, she hurried out to examine Alvah and Parcy.

The two children lay in a narrow bed together, looking wan and tired. To see them so sent Carolyn into a near panic, for she had seen sick children often enough to know how little could carry them to the grave. She had lived with these two dears for only a short time, but their lives were precious to her now. For an instant she was overwhelmed by the responsibility she felt for their lives.

But to her immense relief, she found them suffering only from grippe. That would not prove fatal so long as they received proper treatment.

"Lizza!" she called, hurrying out. Finding the girl cringing in the shadows of the hall, she took her shoulders and tried to impress Lizza with some calming strength. "They're going to be just fine. Take off that fearful face and give me a smile."

"Oh, Miz, I been so afrighted!"

"Shush a moment and tell me something. Have you been giving

Mrs. Fanny and the babies more of Ona's herbal tea!"

"All I could, Miz. I done my best by them, Lord knows."

"I know you have." Carolyn struggled not to scold the ignorant girl. "But now they don't need the tea any longer. Don't give them any more, and don't drink any yourself. It's...only for special conditions."

Lizza nodded innocently.

"And now you'll help my husband fix me some plain tea, please?"

Smiling at last, Lizza hurried down the stairs.

Carolyn returned to Fanny's bedside, seating herself on the edge of the mattress. "What did you want to tell me? I've sent Lizza to the kitchen, so you can speak freely."

"You'll think me a fool."

Carolyn lifted the baby from his cradle and cuddled him. Her heart was suddenly full to see this living proof of her courage. "Whatever you may feel, Fanny, we're friends, linked by this child. I would find nothing you might want to confide foolish."

"Dear Carolyn! I've been so troubled here in this house. I think such strange, gloomy thoughts. I don't think of myself as a superstitious person, but..."

Carolyn held the baby tightly to her bosom, realizing with alarm what it might have been like for a sick woman, abed and drugged with Ona's tea, to be alone in this house for any length of time. "Has anything curious happened?"

Fanny looked away as a tear slid from her eye. "Nothing has happened that I can place my finger upon, except to say that my natural tendency to worry and brood has been greater here. I'm not used to a house so far from other houses. Silas and I have always lived in Wood River, and I had so many friends close by there. My house was always full of people, and now it's always so quiet and lonely...I'm grateful to have such a grand house, don't misunderstand. I know that the house was once yours."

"Don't let that trouble you, Fanny," Carolyn said in earnest.

"I—I'm trying to confess something to you that I can't seem to confess to my husband. In the last few days I've been so hagridden with guilt, I haven't been able to sleep."

"I'll help any way I can," Carolyn whispered.

"I confided to Lizza that I was fearful for my children's health in this drafty old house. She seemed to think I was asking for her help, and she...she brought that cooking woman you had here when we arrived. Silas has no trust in this woman since she refused to work for him. She came one day while he was out meeting his new parishioners. Of course, I couldn't bring myself to refuse to receive the woman."

"What did she say?"

Fanny frowned and brushed her hand over her eyes, as if trying to remember clearly. "It was all very vague and somewhat strange. It wasn't so much what she said but what she suggested. She may have meant me no harm...Carolyn, she spoke of help, of a source of comfort and strength...or words to that effect. She said, 'There be one who will help you. He promise health for children. He be powerful.' Carolyn, I'm a preacher's wife. I know when someone is speaking of God. This woman, Ona, was not. I'm sure of it! But I feel so foolish and guilty for my suspicions."

Sighing, Carolyn patted Fanny's hand. "Did she say anything more?"

"Yes, she said I must tell no one of her visit, that disaster would follow if I did." She began trembling. "I'm frightened! But not of this powerful person she speaks of, not of Satan, surely. I'm frightened of *her!*"

Seventeen

"I had thought we would go to see Mrs. Ebey this afternoon." Carolyn said, seated at the trestle table in the kitchen with Evan. "But now I don't think it would be wise to leave Fanny alone in the house with only Lizza and the children. I know only too well what can happen here."

"Aren't you rushing this business a bit?" Evan asked, taking her hand and warming it. "We've had a long journey."

"I suppose I might be, but I want so much to understand…and for it all to be over."

"I've been thinking," Evan said, going to stare out the window. "You told me this Ebey woman is considered mad. What can we learn from her…in view of the fact that she isn't in possession of all her wits?"

"I must ask if she thinks my father killed one of her children!"

"That's hardly an easy subject to discuss."

Carolyn wrung her hands, feeling grim. "Evan, if you want to know, I'm afraid of much more than finding out my father wasn't called to the Ebeys in time, or that his throat-piercing technique was misunderstood. You were correct to suspect that the torn page I found with the sketch on it suggests he did a dissection on someone from around here at about the time we were driven away—"

"But you said yourself only yesterday that you didn't recall the exact date you arrived in Philadelphia. Your father had only just made his medical knowledge known about town when he was impressed into the army. You might have arrived in Philadelphia before the deaths of those children. You've told me how much you have forgotten from that time."

"I don't understand what you're trying to say."

"Before we call on a madwoman and confront her with facts that surely were those that drove her mad, namely the deaths of her three children all in one night, we ought to know when they died. Investigating village records is in order."

"You're right, of course. If we find that we were forced to leave before Katarinia and the other children died, we'd be needlessly disturbing a troubled old woman."

"Exactly!" He came to her side and hugged her shoulder. "I'll help you search the records. Then we'll plan how to confront those who have withheld information so far. In the meantime, I want us both rested. This is a gloomy place. I hope you get your fill of it this time!"

Rain fell with dismal steadiness all the rest of the afternoon. Impatient for Silas to return so that she might be done with his surprise over her return, Carolyn unpacked and readied the third bedchamber for what she hoped would be a short stay.

She was glad that Evan didn't need to go into the village for medicine. The children seemed in better spirits when they woke from naps. She was with them when she heard Silas's wagon roll up outside. "Stay in bed, the both of you. I'll be up later with supper and a story."

Alvah was a brave little child. Carolyn smoothed her hand over the girl's mussed braids and kissed little Parcy's blond head. She hated to see them relegated to this gloomy, isolated house, too.

She was just starting down the stairs when Silas thundered inside, stomping mud from his boots. Behind him was a sheet of gray rain pummeling the ground. "Hello, Silas." She smiled at his start of surprise. Her guilty secret preyed on her nerves, gradually wilting her warm expression until she saw that he truly was sorry to see her.

"What brings you? If I had known you were coming back, I wouldn't have troubled this kind woman," he said, indicating a cloaked woman standing ahead of him in the shadows.

The middle-aged woman was looking about the entry with an

expression of abject terror. Carolyn didn't recognize her from the Christmas party, and wondered if she was one of the villagers who had not dared attend.

"Hello, I'm Carolyn Burck," Carolyn said, coming down the stairs, her leg aching from the change in the weather. She smiled encouragingly at the woman but received only a wide-eyed stare.

"If I'm not needed after all, Reverend Clure—"

"Nonsense, my dear Mrs. Appel. Even if I wanted to reject your kind offer to look after Fanny and the little ones, I wouldn't subject you to yet another hour in this drenching rain."

Carolyn cut in. "Silas, if I had known your children were ill—"

Silas silenced her. "I wouldn't have dreamed of summoning you from so far. Why have you come, may I ask?"

"I'm searching for some pages that I found missing from one of my father's journals. He kept meticulous notes of all his cases, you see, and I find it curious that he would remove some. Since I found one of the missing pages here at Timberhill last autumn, I felt I must return to search for the rest. You haven't, by any chance—"

The woman was gaping at Carolyn in a most distressing manner.

"Do forgive me," Silas said. "I've failed to introduce you both. Carolyn, this is Johannah Appel, a treasured member of my new congregation. Mrs. Appel, Carolyn is my sister-in-law."

The woman scarcely nodded. "Y-you're the little girl who used to live here! I—I heard you'd come back, but we all thought—That is to say, I was told you'd gone away…f-for good."

"I'm back," Carolyn said flatly, feeling ill-disposed toward the woman and not understanding why.

Visibly shaken, the woman retied her dripping bonnet ribbons beneath her chin. "I simply must get back. You are surely in the best of care with the daughter of a physick looking after your children."

"So you remember my father," Carolyn said, her heart beating more rapidly.

"No! No. I don't remember him at all, only that he was a doctor, and that was very long ago. Reverend, if you please…" She pulled open the front door and was greeted by a torrent. The wagon horse was up to his hocks in watery mud.

Closing the door, she turned back, her face ashen.

"You must stay until the rain lets up," Silas said gently, noting the woman's reaction to Carolyn. "Come into the parlor with me, and perhaps we can talk. My sister-in-law will prepare us a bit of warm tea."

He drew the woman into the parlor, settled her there by the fire and then went upstairs to check on his wife. Carolyn felt the chill of his welcome and wished she and Evan had elected to stay anywhere but Timberhill.

Carolyn went into the kitchen to make the tea. Evan was at the table, watching her as she came in. Lizza stirred a kettle standing on the hearth, her expression veiled.

"Mr. Silas has returned with a guest, Lizza. See to their coats, and then help me with a tray for them."

With Lizza moving out of earshot, Evan whispered, "I couldn't help eavesdropping on that rather peculiar conversation. I think the woman knows something."

"She was anything but happy to see me," Carolyn said, feeling like an outcast. "The sooner we finish this, the better."

Evan chuckled softly. "No one dragged you here a second time." Then he was close behind her, circling her with his warm, strong arms. "I'm not making sport of you, Carolyn. I admire your courage. Shall we search the house from top to bottom? Where might your father have hidden those pages he tore out?"

"I've tried to imagine. He kept the journals in the surgery. I told you of those I found in the desk that had fallen into the cellar pit after the fire. I wonder if we might search there. T-the night I was there I didn't have much opportunity to look around."

Evan gently turned her. "Have you thought of confessing to Silas what you did and having the child buried in consecrated ground? I think it would ease your conscience."

"I couldn't! Oh, Evan, don't even suggest such a thing. I did what I was forced to do, just as I believe my father did as he was forced to do."

"And it should remain your secret, perhaps as your father's deed—whatever it was—should remain his."

Carolyn sagged, letting Evan support her. She couldn't bear to think she might be prying into business that would bring her only more heartbreak.

"Forgive me, Carolyn. We won't speak of it again. The rain's let up a bit. Shall we go out there now, while we have a little privacy?"

Carolyn went for her cloak. "Yes, yes, anything, just so we're doing something!"

In moments they were slogging through spongy grass and mud to the stone path leading to the remains of the surgery. Carolyn circled to the stone steps leading down, but before setting foot on the steps, her heart sank. She pointed to the standing gray water below. "No wonder the journals I found here were unreadable. It probably floods here every spring." She shuddered to think the twin's secret grave now lay under water.

"Don't look so stricken, darling," Evan said, taking her shoulders and drawing her back toward the house.

"I'm afraid those pages are lost forever," she said, thinking more of her gruesome deed than the pages.

"If that's so, then we'll search the records, speak to those who might help us, and then we'll go home. Can you accept that the pages may have been destroyed in the fire, or that they were lost to a flood years ago? Perhaps they even blew away. It might be a blessing not to know."

"You saw how that woman looked at me!"

"No, I only heard her, and she's terrified. That terror is the only reason I'm not insisting that you come away with me this very moment."

"I don't understand."

"She has something to hide. Each person who has received you so badly has had reason to wish you were not here stirring up long-dead secrets. If their reactions stem from guilt over driving your father away, we know that she may have been one of the mob. I might question her, and it could prove quite unpleasant. But as I said before, we need a bit more evidence to be certain we aren't mistaken. For all you know, your father might have had an affair, and been driven out for that."

"Don't be ridiculous!"

"My point is, you may never learn all the truth, Carolyn. You may have to live with that."

"We must go into the village first thing tomorrow," Carolyn said, sick to think he might be right. To never know…

"We'll go when the rain has let up and the roads are passable." Just as he spoke, the leaden sky opened again, drenching them as they splashed back toward the verandah.

Two days passed while Carolyn and Evan waited for the rain to subside. Silas remained distant with Carolyn, and insisted that Mrs. Appel carry out the chores for which she had been enlisted.

The woman was an excellent cook, and seemed to want to lose herself in heaps of flour and kettles of steaming stews. Carolyn couldn't engage her in the slightest bit of everyday conversation and finally retired to the children's room to keep Alvah and Parcy amused.

At last, however, Evan and Carolyn set out for Eudoxia and alighted, mud-splattered and damp an hour later, before the courthouse, where village records for births, deaths and marriages were kept.

After only a bit of searching, the clerk found a ledger for the year in question. Evan flipped the pages, running his finger down columns of entries until he found the one they wanted.

"Here it is," he whispered, pointing to the names of the three Ebey children listed in a row, and marked down as victims of diphtheria.

"Look how many others there were," Carolyn said, counting the names. "Here's my cousin Trintie Harpswell. And look here, James Appel, age two."

"That woman Silas brought from the village…" Evan said, brows lifted with interest. "This may have been her child."

"How sad." Carolyn turned away, shivering. "At least now we know that my friend Katarinia died before we were driven away. If

I already suspect that my father examined her in secret…perhaps in hopes of finding a treatment or cure for putrid throat…why must I have proof?"

"To exonerate him, of course. I've known from the first that that was your true purpose. I've shrunk from telling you I think the idea is in vain. I don't see these ignorant farmers and villagers giving up their bitterness and grief simply because you prove to them that a physick they had no faith in meant their dead children no harm."

"My efforts haven't been futile!" Carolyn cried. "I couldn't bear that."

"Then let's put the idea to the test. Let's talk with Mrs. Ebey now and see if the one who lost her mind to grief can be persuaded to forgive."

"Is that what I'm seeking, Evan?"

"I fear so, my darling, and it's not for them to forgive. You and your father did as you were trained to do. The guilt lies with these people, not you."

Villagers stood in doorways, watching as Carolyn and Evan boarded their carriage and started away. "I'm feeling very peculiar, having them stare after us like that," Carolyn said, hugging Evan's arm.

"Perhaps if we eventually assure them we have no intention of bringing charges against them for driving your father away…"

"Is that what they fear?"

"I would like to think so."

They rode in silence until they reached the entrance to the Ebey estate. Carolyn shuddered as Evan turned the carriage into the weedy coachway. He brought it to a quiet stop before the looming, neglected brick house.

"I wouldn't think it possible for a place to have a more dismal feeling than Timberhill, but this place has," Carolyn said, waiting while Evan got down and came around to help her to the muddy coachway.

"We mustn't delay. I'm thinking it's going to rain again."

"I've had my fill of rain. I'm chilled through. What am I going to say to her? I'm so glad you're with me, Evan. I might have come before alone, but I lacked the courage."

"The words will come to you," he assured her.

As they approached the cold facade and weathered white door standing so forbidding, Carolyn found herself shaking uncontrollably. Wanting to cling to Evan, and feeling like a foolish child, Carolyn instead forced herself to stand fast as he knocked.

After a long wait, during which Carolyn felt eyes in every window, they heard a shuffling sound within. Evan knocked again. There followed a silence, but finally the door creaked open.

Fetid air wafted from the narrow opening. Carolyn drew back in horror to think someone could live in such a place. It must have been years since the house was cleaned and aired.

She saw a blur of a white face, and just as she gave an involuntary gasp at seeing the apparition that had stared at her from the woods, the door opened wide.

The tall, gaunt man before them had dirty white hair that added to the pasty color of his unsunned skin. His brows were drawn down as if he never smiled, as if he suffered hourly with untold mental agony. His mouth was a hurt line, marked by deep creases cutting to his chin.

Yet, strangely, she saw a light in his moist blue eyes. He looked as if he were overwhelmed with pleasure at seeing her!

"Hello. We've come to call on Mrs. Ebey, if you please," Evan said, his voice cordial but with an edge of authority that belied refusal.

The man in his ragged, filthy livery gaped at Evan as if he hadn't understood the words, as if he couldn't comprehend that someone had come to visit.

"Joseph? Joseph, you witless thing, what is it?" The voice shrieked from the upper recesses of the house.

Joseph appeared incapable of replying.

"May we come in?" Carolyn asked softly. Though the

manservant was a gruesome caricature of aged ignorance, his childlike astonishment at seeing her erased all her fear of him.

He apparently understood, for he backed away, wringing his hands and gesturing hesitantly toward a dark stairway.

"I think he expects us to go up," Evan whispered, nodding agreeably to the old servant. "Perhaps she's bedridden. I would let you go up alone, but I sense something unpleasant about this place that makes me think we're not entirely safe."

Carolyn approached Joseph and smiled up at him. She was astonished to find that such a stooped old man should still tower over her. She was even more astonished to think how intensely she had feared him all these months. "You mean us no harm, do you, old soul?" That was an endearment her father had once used for his older patients.

The effect was remarkable. Joseph's face, in spite of its torment of wrinkles and bags, lit up as if he were but a young child. He swallowed, blinking, struggling to speak. "I—I…you—you…I—I h-have something…I have s-something for your f-father." Bobbing his head eagerly, he shuffled backwards and bumped against a doorway. He scurried away down the long dark central hall and disappeared through a back doorway.

"I should have brought a pistol," Evan murmured as they started up the stairs. He tested each tread before putting full weight on it.

"He seems quite innocent. It must be a grim life living here with a crazy old woman." She felt certain he could not have thrown that hayfork at Lizza. Who else might have? Lucile herself?

"He's not in possession of all his wits, Carolyn. Remember that before you get so close next time. I should wring the man's neck if he thought to harm you in any way."

She took Evan's arm as they arrived on the upper floor. The carpet hadn't been beaten in ages. She felt as if she was back at Timberhill, seeing it as it had looked that first day in autumn. Cobwebs drooped from every corner and doorway. The rear portion of the upper hall looked as if no one had walked there in years.

Joseph's path to a single front chamber doorway was clearly

marked in the dust. Carolyn wondered if Lucile Ebey resided in just this one room.

Tapping at the door, she called out, "Hello?"

"It's no use! No use! He can't do it, the fool, the mindless fool. Stop bothering me! Go away! I won't come out again, not for anything! Do it yourself. Do it yourself!"

Evan tried to restrain her, but Carolyn opened the door and stepped in.

"Hello, Mrs. Ebey. Do you remember me? I'm a little older, but I don't think I've changed so much. I used to visit you in the summer. Katarinia and I played cat's cradle with you, and you were teaching us to embroider. I remember her pony. I'm Carolyn Adams. Do you remember me?"

"Katarinia? Is she here? My beauty, bring her in…"

The woman was a blur of gray in the huge draped bed. Her hair was a dull gray cascade down her shoulders, her face an unhealthy color of white-gray. She had tight, anxious brows, and the deeply set, wounded eyes of one having experienced intense, unending pain. Her cheeks were hollow, the bones beneath her skin sharp and brittle.

As Carolyn approached, she found the woman too odorous to bear, and recoiled as if having found something mouldering beneath a rock. "Do you know who I am, Mrs. Ebey?"

"Don't prod her too well," Evan warned softly from the doorway. "I wouldn't be surprised if she has a weapon hidden in that bed."

"Don't tease," Lucile said in a singsong tone. "I know who you are. You're Annatie, and you can't make me do anything today. I'm too sick and old. And don't trouble my man anymore. He sulks and won't feed me. If you don't go away, I'll die. And if I die, I'll haunt you. Go away." She sounded petulant.

"I'm Carolyn, and I've come to ask you about your children."

The woman squinted at her, her head shaking a bit, her lips working anxiously. "My children aren't…here."

"I don't think she can see me well," Carolyn said over her

shoulder. "She's like a child herself." She swallowed nervously, suddenly unsure that she could hope for sensible answers from a woman this far gone.

Lucile moved abruptly, throwing off her comfort, showing the truly appalling condition of her nightshift. "What do you want now? Don't I have enough to bear? Must you torment me? Go away!"

"Do you remember Orion Adams?" Carolyn blurted, worried she would be driven away before she got a shred of information.

The name captured Lucile's attention. Her watery eyes bulged. "Is he back? That butcher! Kill him! Kill him!" She leaped from the bed, teetering on her old bent legs. Then she half collapsed as if she'd forgotten she was old. "I'll have his heart! Give me his heart!"

"Listen to me—"

"It's no use, Carolyn. She's utterly mad!"

"Mad, am I? My children are murdered and I'm not entitled to madness to bear the pain? I'll have his heart! I swear by Satan, I'll have his very soul!"

"Carolyn! Come away."

She waved Evan silent, desperate to penetrate the fog of the woman's distorted perception. "Your children are ill, Lucile! Will you call the doctor? Will you let Orion Adams save them?"

The woman crouched, drooling suddenly, her hair like cobwebs, her skin dry and pasty white. "I won't let you bring that man here!" She was aiming her vehement words at Evan.

Continuing her effort to reenact the past, Carolyn pointed toward Evan. "Who is that man?"

"My husband, you twit! He wants the doctor, but I know a better way. Get that doctor out of my house. He desecrated my daughter! Kill him! Stone his wife! Burn his house! Let his daughter die!"

Shuddering, Carolyn backed toward Evan until she felt the reassuring touch of his warm hands on her shoulders. "Your husband called the doctor?"

Lucile straightened like a rearing white ghost. "But it was too late! They were all dying! I had to save them!" She gave out a shriek of grief that made Carolyn's skin crawl.

Evan whispered close to her ear. "Have you had enough? He was called too late, and the poor old thing couldn't bear her guilt. I want to get us out of here. Now, Carolyn!"

The shrieking went on and on, like a keening over a grave. Lucile stared at them as if her eyes would pop free of her head. Her contorted hands reached out, and then her voice, suddenly low, shuddered across the filthy chamber. "I will have his heart!"

Waiting no longer, Evan seized Carolyn's shoulders, swung her about and propelled her down the stairs. "I don't like the sound of this at all. I want us out of this miserable place and away from this village by nightfall."

He pushed her out the open front door. Heavy raindrops were falling in the mud.

"But what about Joseph? He had something for—"

Evan's face was dark with anger and fear. He pushed her into the carriage.

"I'm done with this nonsense! The children died. Your father was blamed. Wrongly or rightly, it doesn't matter after so very long! I want you to see what your questions are doing! That old woman is worse off, and I can see us no better for it. I've tried to be patient, I've tried to understand..." He lashed the horse, sending them careening away from the house toward the brick posts.

Behind them came a feeble shout. Carolyn twisted around to see Joseph standing in the doorway, his hand raised.

Balling her fists, Carolyn struggled against tears and lost. She was not so much frightened by what she had unearthed as angry at Evan for taking her away.

Once again, she was a man's prisoner. Yet she still loved Evan! She loved him more than ever for caring enough to want to protect her, but she was no longer his equal. He had exerted his authority over her, and now she resented him.

Her father had been right to turn her away from studying medicine. A single open book to a female spelled disaster for her, for the moment she discovered her own brain and her own will, she was doomed to struggle against it in favor of her husband, or to struggle against her husband in favor of herself!

Evan wiped the driving rain from his face and lashed the horse again. The carriage wheels wobbled through the muddy ruts, slowing their return to Timberhill. He cursed himself at every turn and found himself tightening like a watch spring as Carolyn struggled against her tears.

He knew, without knowing how, that she hadn't been frightened of that mad old woman. On the contrary, she had been as controlled as a soldier in battle, while he had quaked in his shoes, wanting to be away. In those hideous moments in that revolting bedchamber he had not wanted to see Carolyn's strength. He had not wanted to experience his own desire to flee.

He had waited ten years for Carolyn without the hope of ever having her for his own. He had admired her quiet courage from afar, had yearned to possess such an extraordinary woman. Now that he did possess her, he realized only too late that a woman was not a possession. He had wanted to be everything to her, to rescue her from the dismal marriage she had had with Forrest and to make her happy. To see that a part of her would always belong to this dripping, mouldering, gloomy past made him feel helpless. And angry.

At length he stopped the carriage in the middle of the torrent. They were already soaked through, so a moment more in the rain meant little. "I love you, Carolyn, and I'm sorry if I was harsh."

He watched her fists close and then how she hid them in her skirts.

"I'm afraid I'm losing you," he said simply, loving her too much to be proud.

She burst into tears and fell against him, pulling at his arms until he embraced her, his throat tight with emotion. She lifted her face and he kissed her. He didn't understand what she was feeling, and that lack of understanding frightened him.

"Do you love me still?" he asked softly against her wet hair.

She nodded. "I do, very much. Can we go on? I don't want us to get a chill and be forced to stay with Silas until we're well."

"Can we leave at once for Philadelphia?"

She drew away, her expression hurt. "No! Didn't you hear what she said? I *must* finish this! How, I can't begin to imagine, but I feel something…something building. I have the answer. I'm sure of it. Perhaps I just need to sort it all out in a quiet place, if only I could get away."

He remembered that look of hers, that expression of rebellion that he had seen the day he first proposed. There would be no controlling this woman he loved, he thought.

He had lashed his heart to a free spirit. Now he understood what it meant to claim that he wanted all that she wanted for herself, and more. He wanted her to feel free with him, and the price of that freedom was great, monstrously great. Because those who were free were free to go…as well as stay.

Eighteen

Evan and Carolyn were nearing a curve leading to Timberhill when they heard the slap of hooves in the mud ahead. Drawing the carriage to the side, Evan was just slowing as Johannah Appel thundered past in Silas's wagon. She was half standing, driving the horse on wildly, her plain black bonnet bobbing from its ribbons behind her soaked head.

Carolyn watched the woman thunder out of sight. "Whatever could be wrong?"

"I don't like the feel of this. Promise me that if it's nothing we can help with we'll leave."

Feeling impatient, but wanting to appease his feelings, Carolyn made a cursory nod. "Hurry on. I'm worried."

A short time later they arrived at the house and stopped in the coachway. Before Evan could help Carolyn to the porch, they heard weeping and shouts.

"Can Silas and Fanny be arguing?" Carolyn asked in amazement.

"Perhaps we should make ourselves scarce. I have no wish to intrude on private matters."

Carolyn was about to agree when she heard Lizza's wail. "That bully!" she muttered, climbing down and storming through the rain into the house. Evan followed.

Upstairs, Fanny was weeping uncontrollably, and the baby began its high-pitched wailing. Almost on cue, Alvah and Parcy began crying, too.

Silas's voice boomed from the kitchen. "What in God's name am I to do about this? I'll have her—"

Carolyn burst into the kitchen. She found Lizza on her knees near the hearth, face covered by her trembling hands, sobbing. Silas was circling the room, arm raised, fist doubled.

Hearing Carolyn, he whirled, his purpled face swollen with rage. In one arm, he was clutching something to his chest. It had been wrapped in Lizza's shawl.

"Devil worshipper!" he shouted, advancing on Carolyn as she shrank into Evan's protective embrace.

"Calm yourself, Silas, and tell us what's happened," Carolyn said, forcing her tone to remain calm while trying to figure out what he was holding. The bundle was dripping wet.

He drew back his lips over his teeth. "I always knew you were a curse upon my brother. Now you're a curse upon me! Get out of my house."

"One moment, my good man," Evan said, pushing Carolyn back so that he stood nose-to-nose with the raging clergyman. "My wife deserves your respect."

"She's a witch! Every person in the village has feared it, and now I have proof, irrefutable proof!"

Silas turned aside a corner of the shawl, revealing something white and swollen. It resembled a small human face.

Evan paled and stood back, finally turning his head and shutting his eyes.

Carolyn watched his reaction. Her heart shivered with terror until it went cold and still. For a long instant she stood still knowing without having to look that Silas was holding the remains of his dead twin son that she had buried in the cellar pit.

Silas's expression was full of loathing. "Every person in the village and all the outlying farms has warned me of this house's reputation as a devil's playground. The stories of secret rites, wailing in the night and lights in the dead of night were enough to turn my blood cold, but I thought it mere ignorance. Now I know why you were really here, alone, for so long before I arrived. And now I know why you and your family were driven from here. For devil worship!" His tone reflected absolute conviction that what he spoke was truth.

"Don't be absurd, Silas," Evan whispered.

"Absurd, am I? To find the body of an infant floating out there in that place the people tell me was burned because it was the abode of evil? Carolyn, I want you out of my house at once, or I myself will burn this house to the ground around you! What kind of heathen rite did you use this child's body for? God, I could do murder!"

Shaking with fear, Carolyn tried to think what she might do now that Silas had discovered what she had done. She lay her hand on Lizza's shoulder, but the girl shrank from her. "Oh, Lizza," Carolyn said, beginning to weep. "Don't believe him."

Lizza lifted her face, but there was no condemnation in her expression. She looked terrified and riddled with guilt, enough so that Carolyn was stunned into wondering if there might be some shred of truth to the tales Silas had heard. Was there devil worshipping in these woods? Could Lizza be involved?

"If you'd only let me explain," Carolyn began, trying to shake off her own shame and guilt.

"I don't care to hear another word you have to say. Be on your way. You're no longer welcome here, nor will you ever be. Take your love of Satan with you. I shall bury this hapless creature. I pray that I never see you again, or I shall be forced to bring charges against you. Have your attorney husband save you from the gallows then, for I'll do all I can to see you condemned!"

With eyes wide, heart suddenly thundering, Carolyn realized that Silas didn't know the infant corpse he held was his own. Thinking that she must confess to him, she turned away. He might actually kill her afterward.

"To think I let you touch Fanny the night my son was born," Silas growled.

Evan lunged, seizing the man by the throat of his shirt. "Be glad that you did, man, or the other child might have died as well."

Silas stood stock-still. As understanding dawned, he lifted his black gaze. Color rose to his cheeks and then drained away. Too stunned to speak, he took one heavy step backward, and then another. Groping for the bench, he dropped onto it. He looked down at the bundle in his arms, his eyes closing in grief.

Carolyn could stand no more. "I'll get our things," she whispered.

Feeling as if her legs were weighted in stone, she plodded to the stairs and dragged herself up. She felt so terribly lightheaded and disoriented. At any moment she expected Silas to regain his senses and come after her with a weapon—indeed, she half welcomed the idea.

But at the head of the stairs, she turned long enough to stare into Fanny's bedchamber. The woman was holding Eliakim to her breast. As their eyes met, Carolyn knew that Fanny had realized at once that the dead baby was her own.

Carolyn forced herself to enter the bedchamber. Almost unbidden, her knees buckled and she knelt beside the cradle. "The footling died. The second lived. There was nothing I could do, Fanny. You were already so weak, I thought only to spare you grief. I swear on my life I did nothing to dishonor your son's twin except bury him unbaptized. Forgive me, please."

There was no sound in the chamber save the crackling of the hearthfire. Below came the sounds of footsteps.

Softly, Fanny's hand dropped on Carolyn's damp curls. "You gave me my life, and for that I will always be grateful. Go quickly, before he thinks himself the hand of God. And Carolyn..."

Carolyn raised her face, her own cheeks tear-stained.

"I do forgive you, with all my heart."

Her strength ebbing, Carolyn hurried toward her bedchamber to pack. She had done the only right thing, she reminded herself, though if she had admitted the child had died she might have spared herself, Fanny and Silas a great deal of shock and grief.

She was just opening Evan's carpetback when she heard the first distant shouts. A tingle of terror crawled along her spine. In the waning afternoon light she experienced a feeling of having lived this very moment once before.

Seconds later, several panes of glass in a lower window shattered. Eliakim started his feeble wail, and the alarmed children cried out from the rear bedchamber.

"Silas, what is it?" Fanny called, her voice raised in panic.

Forgetting the carpetbag, Carolyn dashed into the hall and ran to the front window overlooking the coachway. Three men had driven a wagon close to the house. One had climbed down and was reaching for another rock. He hurled it, shattering more panes below.

She heard Silas thunder to the front door and go out, his arms wide.

"Gentlemen! Gentlemen! Fellow Christians! What is the meaning of this?"

"We know she's in there. Send her out! She and her kind have to be stopped. There's only one way. We mean you no harm, Parson, unless you take her side. Send her out!"

Torn by indecision, Silas stood facing the men. The rain soaked his thinning gray hair and darkened the shoulders of his frock coat.

Three more wagons slogged up the muddy lane, filled with shouting men and women. They were carrying torches.

Turning away from the window, Carolyn pressed her icy fists to her mouth. It was happening again! She was filled with numbing terror, incapable of determining what she must do to save herself.

They would hang her, burn her, murder her in a dozen different ways. And this time...this time, she was guilty!

Evan took the stairs two at a time. Finding her by the window, he seized her arm. His face was a twisted mask of anguish. "We've got to get out of here!"

Another volley of rocks shattered the glass in the lower windows. The children shrieked. Now Fanny was throwing back her comforter. She gathered squawling Eliakim to her breast and made her way to the door, still wearing only a thin flannel nightshift.

"Go, Carolyn! Forgive them, they're frightened fools. I'll do what I can. You saved me and now I'll try to save you. Go! Go!"

Evan took Carolyn's hand, tugging her roughly toward the stairs. "Will you trust me, Carolyn? Will you let me lead you away to safety? You must! It means our lives!" He spoke as if he thought she had lost her senses and might be expected to do something rash.

Woodenly, she followed him down the stairs, past the open

front doorway where the driving gray rain pummeled the stone doorstep and spattered inside.

She paused long enough to look into the tidy parlor that they had restored. On the carpet lay glinting shards of window glass and the hurled stones.

Head whirling, she allowed Evan to drag her back to the spinning kitchen.

Evan jerked a sobbing Lizza to her feet. "Go upstairs and put wraps on the children. You may all have to flee."

Lizza had that mindless expression that made Carolyn think the girl would be incapable of doing as she was told.

Another window shattered. Starting, she looked wildly about for a hiding place. Now the odor of burning wood began wafting through the lower chambers. She heard a soft crackling. Swirls of white smoke blossomed from the parlor.

Fanny gave a shriek. "Fire! Silas, come help me!"

Evan propelled Lizza toward the doorway. "Get those children out!"

"I have to help them," Carolyn said, feeling a portion of her reason returning. She started after Lizza.

Evan grabbed her, pulling her back. Frantically they struggled, until Evan forced her to look him straight in the eye. "You're coming with me!" he ordered, trying to shake some sense into her.

"But..." She stood in terror, watching Evan dash for the pegs by the back door. Unable to find her cloak—she had left it in Fanny's bedchamber—Evan threw his own cloak about Carolyn's shoulders and forced her out the kitchen door into the gathering darkness.

"Evan, I can't leave them!" she cried desperately.

"Silas is perfectly capable of taking care of his own family! Go! I'll find a safe place for you, and then I'll come back to reason with these people." He grabbed the nearest lantern.

They stumbled across the soggy meadow, the rain heavy and cold as it soaked through the cloak around her shoulders. The lantern made wildly gyrating arcs of light across the grasses.

Behind them the mob in front of the house increased to six

wagons filled with frightened, shouting villagers. To the side stood a tall, shadowed man too terrified to venture after the swooping lantern light. He hailed the two figures retreating into the ebony woods to the south, but they didn't turn.

Helplessly, he watched those in the wagons throwing rocks and torches. The pastor who had come out to speak to the intruders had raced back inside the house.

Moments later he emerged with a frail woman carrying a baby, a shrieking maid, and two wailing children. The man clutched something wrapped in white in his arms. He drew his family around to the lean-to shed, where he released the frightened horses.

Everyone retreated as smoke began gushing from the shattered front windows.

Joseph watched tongues of orange flame begin leaping from the windows. Smoke blackened the gray stone wall, and flames eagerly reached up to shrivel the budded branches overhead.

Though past darkfall, the coachway was bright as day in the leaping yellow light. Those who had arrived in wagons were silenced silhouettes now, standing as he was, watching the great house burn and fall.

Softly, on the night wind, came the high wail of an infant. Joseph sighed, weeping to himself and not knowing why. He was already tired from having run through the muddy forest to find the woman who had come to visit.

With rain running from his stringy white hair and his dark ragged coat soaked, he tightened the frayed lapels about his scrawny neck. He hoped the brittle papers he had kept for so long and now wore tucked inside his shirt would not get wet. The good doctor had entrusted them to him, and he had sworn on his life that he would never show them to a soul.

All he could do now was continue following her until he could give them back. She would give them to the good doctor. Joseph was certain of that, and then he could die in peace. He knew the time was coming fast.

"Evan, I simply must stop for a moment. My leg's aching. I believe I've twisted it."

They staggered to a stop beyond some dripping black branches. Looking back through the tangle of trees behind them, they saw a ruddy glow where Timberhill had once stood.

A dull roar filled the sinister night. Carolyn heard the destructive roar of flames engulfing what had been her beloved home, and wept.

She shut her eyes, wanting to blot everything out. "My father's house...How can I bear it?"

"It doesn't matter so long as we can get safely away."

"I'll never know. I'll never understand..."

"Carolyn, if I could shake this obsession from you, I would do it! It's enough to know that the people who live around here will go to any lengths to drive out what they don't understand. They're not worth your life, nor mine!"

"How can they be so stupid?" She wept, letting him drag her on, her feet heavy with mud. "I might have been able to explain."

"My God, let it rest, Carolyn!"

They emerged on the dark, muddy cart path and walked for some distance, grateful that at least the rain was letting up.

"You know, it probably doesn't matter that I don't find out what my father did to provoke the attack that drove us away. What he did has no bearing in the matter. It's what they think he did. They think he desecrated a body. That's enough."

"Yes, Carolyn, yes. Now, wipe your mind clean of it. I'm done with the whole matter."

She hardly heard him. "I wonder how they came to think he did such a thing?"

"Lucile Ebey must surely have invented the story to cover the fact that she didn't do everything she could to save the lives of her children."

"Poor woman."

Evan halted, his head cocked as if he was listening. "Did you hear something?"

"I was so deep in thought…"

"That's what galls me, Carolyn! You're so consumed with the past that you're missing all that's happening in the present. For the moment we're in grave danger! Give me your attention, and your ear."

A deadly silence settled in the wood. Then came the soft dripping of raindrops slipping from dark, gnarled branches, falling to the forest floor like tiny, cautious footsteps.

"Where are you thinking of taking me?" Carolyn whispered, shivering. She edged closer to Evan as a twig nearby snapped.

"To the village. If all of those people burning Timberhill tonight are ignorant and insane, then those left may have sense enough to help us. Surely someone will be left in the village."

The dark purple shadows of night closed around them. The lantern shed light around them, but it reached only a few yards. They moved along the uneven ruts of the cart path, sensing a lurking presence watching them.

By turns, Carolyn's heart leapt and slowed and leapt again as they made their way through the darkness. Trees loomed, and branches snatched at them. Everything seemed alive, hostile, taunting.

"I feel we're going the wrong way," Carolyn whispered.

"Then in time we'll come to some other village where we might find help. The point is to escape Timberhill and the madness there."

"Do you smell wood smoke?" Carolyn said. "Wait, sh-hh! It could be Wildman's cabin—I mean, John Rasner's cabin. We mustn't go there! He'll…"

Evan bent over and, holding the lantern high, felt about in the grasses for a stone. Hefting it, settling it in his hand, he then made a few vicious swipes through the air. "We're going to survive this, Carolyn. When we're finally home safe in our bed, you'll never want to think of Timberhill again."

"No, never," she said, knowing even as she spoke that the ghosts would live on in her forever now that her last efforts to learn the truth had been thwarted.

Before them in the branchy shadows, something dark and furtive moved. Carolyn was filled with alarm, and she drew back, trying to stop Evan. Before she could utter a warning, something— man or beast, she couldn't determine—gave a growling shout and leaped at them, crouched in their path.

For a terrifying instant his grimace was illuminated in stark yellow. He was wearing a shaggy cloak and looked half human.

Carolyn shrieked.

Instinctively, Evan cried in alarm, then swung with his rock weapon. The highlighted shadow lunged. Evan yelped, doubling over. The lantern toppled from his grasp, spilling oil onto the ground.

The oil caught and flared, outlining Evan's inert body heaped on the cart path. Carolyn was too aghast to utter a sound. With nightmarishly slow moves, she lifted her eyes to their attacker. He snatched up the lantern and thrust it toward her startled face with a fierce growl.

She screamed.

The dark human shape before her struck Evan viciously, as he lay unmoving. Heedlessly, Carolyn reached toward the dark shape, her teeth clenched, her mind empty of all but the desire to defend the one she loved.

A metal object caught the lantern light and glinted. "No, wait!" Carolyn begged.

She felt something cold slice across her palm. She recoiled with a squeal of pain and terror as warm blood began spreading between her fingers.

"Don't kill him!" she screamed, falling across Evan's still body. There was life in him, she thought, pressing her face close to his. "D-don't strike again. He's...he's already dead," she lied.

It was like a nightmare, she thought, lying motionless, her bleeding fist pressed tightly into her belly. She hoped the attacker would retreat into the wood, but she heard his footsteps approaching in the sucking mud, heard his panting breath over her, felt his murderous eyes upon her.

Something clutched her hair. Her head was lifted and her face turned. She moaned from the pain of her hair being pulled from her scalp. As the creature leaned close, his blackened face came near enough that she could smell his musky scent. Then from the corner of her eye, she glimpsed another movement in the trees.

There was a figure lurking not far off, but it did not approach. Carolyn heard the furtive retreat of footsteps in the forest, and then all was quiet except for the creature breathing so near her cheek and mouth.

"Stand carefully," the beast hissed.

She struggled to her feet, feeling weak from trembling.

Something cold pressed against her cheek. It was hard and sharp. It moved slowly along her jaw and then pressed against her throat. She felt a prick of pain and realized the coldness was a knife blade.

"Come with me," the creature whispered.

And she obeyed.

Nineteen

Would Evan die, lying alone in the cold mud? Carolyn staggered ahead of the shadowed creature who was prodding her along the cart path with his blade.

In spite of her own imminent danger, she knew she must protect Evan. She wanted to be sure they were as far from Evan as possible. Then, if he could escape...

"Please, can I stop to bind up my hand?" she asked at last, when they had traveled some distance. "It's bleeding badly."

The shadowed creature came up behind her, seized her wrist and held up her sliced palm. The guttering light from the lantern outlined her spread hand and revealed the blood running freely.

As if annoyed, he released her wrist. With shaking hands, she tore a strip of fabric from one of the unmuddied ruffles of her petticoat. The pressure of the binding against her open wound gave her some relief from the pain.

Her skin crawled as she tried to puzzle out what was going to happen to her now. "Wildman?" she whispered, feeling his breath on her neck. "John?"

"I knew you would return," he said, closing muscled arms around her shoulders.

Her heart shivered with terror. As he turned her to face him, she found herself scarcely able to breathe. Then his cold, hard, unfeeling lips were closing over her mouth. He held her with cruel fingers.

"Where are we going?" she asked when he stopped kissing her.

"To make you mine," he hissed against her lips.

His body was hard and insistent against hers. Her first thought was to bolt, but she knew she'd never be able to outrun him.

Spinning her around, he pushed her onward into the cloying darkness. She stumbled over the ruts and roots, holding her arms out before her to fend off scratching branches.

After a time she saw a faint light in the distance. Soon they came to Ona Ruby's small cabin. The single window cast feeble yellow light across the weedy dooryard, illuminating the tangle of branches and looming tree trunks crowding in around the place.

Roughly, John pushed her toward the door. She stumbled, falling to her knees. Sharp pain sparked in her weak leg. Panting, she decided to remain on her hands and knees. Ahead, the cabin door creaked open. Carolyn saw Ona's muddied skirts, and then beyond into the cluttered, smoky cabin.

"Ona, if you ever had any feeling for my father or mother," Carolyn said softly, the urgency in her voice betraying her fear, "please tell Wildman to let me go."

She saw a huge hand reach down to her. With a feeling of hope, Carolyn grasped the strong hand and got to her numbed feet. Smiling, she looked into Ona's face.

"Your papa..." The woman's lip curled back with contempt. "He say I be as human as the next sinner." Her eyes were black slits.

"My father showed respect for all people!" Carolyn said, not understanding the significance of Ona's words.

"I be better than a beast in the field by far," Ona sneered, nodding, showing her teeth. "Damned fools! I be better than all. My grandfather be a priest! He teach me his way in dreams. He be living in this man now, his spirit and his power." She gestured grandly toward John.

Carolyn looked up into John's bearded face, still incredulous that it was he, the one she had found so enthralling when she was young. He stared blankly at Ona, the maddened glint in his eye betraying consuming hate.

"Bring her in," Ona said, moving aside. "Why is she come here?" She directed the question to Wildman.

"I found her," he grunted, his eyes sharp and sly.

"Won't you please help me get away?" Carolyn said. "They

think I'm a devil worshipper. It's the same madness all over again, just like when they drove my father away. I did what I had to do. I didn't kill the baby. He was stillborn. I only buried him in secret…"

Slowly, Ona turned from the shadowed corner where she had retreated. She was laughing. "You be one of us now, then!" She made a sharp motion toward Wildman. When he failed to obey her silent signal, Ona made the same downward slashing motion again, more forcefully.

Carolyn found herself spun and thrown to the dirt floor on her back. Wildman leaped atop her, pinning back her flailing arms until his grip threatened to snap her bones.

Carolyn gave a shout, but when he only held her there like a mindless servant she felt a wave of panic. Bucking beneath him, she fought his crushing hold, only to find him horrifyingly strong.

Ona calmly stirred something into a gourd cup. After a moment, she squatted beside Carolyn. "Drink," she commanded.

Carolyn bit her lips together, twisting her face away. Unperturbed, Ona pinched Carolyn's nose, holding on no matter how violently Carolyn tried to wrestle free.

Endless seconds ticked by as Carolyn held her breath. Her head began to feel light, her heart pounded.

With determination, she held her breath until her ears began drumming and she felt faint. Finally gasping for breath, she gave a wrenching twist in hopes of escaping John's hold on her, but just when she thought she might get up, Ona poured the liquid into her mouth.

To keep from choking, she had to swallow. Then both Ona and John settled back, waiting for the effect to take hold of her. In seconds, relaxation was stealing through her blood. She felt incapable of resisting when again Ona pressed the gourd cup against her lips.

"Drink!"

She drank.

Rendered helpless, Carolyn lay thinking how hard the dirt floor was, and how sharp John's hands were on her wrists. She stared up into his small pale pupils, seeing nothing there of the dedicated young man she had once admired. "What has she done to you, John?" she whispered. "Are you her slave?"

Something flickered in John's blank expression. As if her question had penetrated some drugged fog of his own, Carolyn watched him turn his tight eyes on the stocky woman who was struggling to stand from her crouched position.

"Do you have any will of your own left?" Carolyn whispered. "Why do you serve her, John?"

Releasing her wrists with a contemptuous gesture, he stood, looming over Ona. Though the woman displayed no fear of him, she did turn and begin mixing more liquid, which she offered him.

He dashed it aside. Seizing the woman's arms and nearly lifting her from the floor in his fury, he looked eye to eye with her and growled. "Bring the followers. Give me the key."

Shaking her head, Ona backed away. She reached for a club that was standing near the door, but Wildman struck her arm, sending the club clattering away into a corner.

Raising his left arm, he hit the woman with the back of his hand, knocking her to the floor. Crouching over her as he had Carolyn, he fumbled in the woman's bodice, finally catching hold of a long iron key on a thong. Viciously, he tore it from her.

Snatching Carolyn from the floor as if she were a rag doll, he pushed her out the door. She fell headlong, too weak to find her footing.

Then he was lifting her, bearing her away in his arms. He struck out once again into the blackness of the forest. His teeth were gritted, his eyes fixed on some distant, unseen point.

"John, John, please, put me down. I'm unwell."

He went on, heedless to all she said.

Carolyn woke to the smell of smoke. Opening her eyes, she looked up at black, gaping windows in a stone wall. Gray smoke still billowed into the night sky. A faint orange glow lit the surroundings.

She was lying on the ground. All around was the bitter smell of charred wood and smoke. Nearby, John was bent over Timberhill's outer cellar steps, fumbling with the lock. The heavy planked doors opened silently on well-oiled iron hinges, falling back like an open book. He went down some stone steps into deathlike darkness.

Carolyn's first thought was to somehow struggle to her feet and escape.

Limply, she lifted her hand, but it fell back uselessly in the soft wet grass. She could no more stand than she could call out. "Evan... Evan..." she whispered. Even her fear was feeble, sifting away like mist in the night.

When John emerged from the cellar stairwell, she could see that he was grinning. "There's no one here to hear you call. They've all gone away. Come below with me, Carolyn. You'll learn why Timberhill is haunted."

He bore her down the steps and propped her against a stone pillar supporting a portion of the house's main floor. The cellar was divided into several sections, with a low beamed ceiling and stone walls. The room smelled dank and moldy, and everywhere was the faint gray veil of cobwebs.

Beyond the section where she stood was a chamber lit with the flickering light of a candle. When John had finished peering up into the blackness of the night, he drew the plank doors closed over his head and guided her into the lighted chamber.

The chamber was empty save for a four-foot circular depression in the center of the floor. It was covered with a planked lid. Next to it stood a crude wooden table.

Methodically, John went about the chamber lighting dozens of candle stubs from the one lit candlestick that had been standing on the bare table. He turned finally and gazed at her with those hauntingly pale eyes. "When I lived alone in the woods with my mother, she was all I had. I took care of her. I tried to accept my father when he returned after ten years from the city. I tried to accept the coming child, my sister Helen. But after my mother died in childbirth, all on account of a man who had abandoned us... I was wretched with grief. I apprenticed your father to learn what I wished I had known to save my mother. I thought knowing I could save others would help me become well in my heart and mind again."

"Yes," she breathed, fighting to remain conscious.

"But I did not get well. Memories haunted me. Only the morphia silenced my grief. Only Ona's Followers were able to keep my thirst for revenge satisfied. It was much later," he whispered ominously, "that I became their leader."

In the chamber glowing with strong yellow light, he removed his fur cloak, revealing a muscled naked chest. His voice rose with power.

"I have served Ona and her lord Satan these past many years. I have exacted my revenge many times, pretending each time that it was you. I did what your esteemed father taught me to do. I studied the dead. And I did what Ona forced me to—I sacrificed innocents to Satan. Now it is time for me to break free. I'm no longer her slave. I must overcome Ona's control. Tonight I seize my freedom." He smiled coldly. "And you, Carolyn, will help me."

"I won't," Carolyn whispered, confused by what he meant.

"You will because you belong to us now. It was stupid of you to return. I tried to warn you. Part of me remembered that time, long ago, when…" He shook off the memories of when she had loved him. "Why did you come back?"

"I had to find my father's secret journal." She sighed, wishing she could hold open her eyes.

John crossed to her, struck her once savagely across the face, and sent her crashing to the muddy floor.

She tasted blood in her mouth.

Stunned, reeling in her pain, she watched him straddle her, felt him tearing at her clothes. His touch was rough and cruel. She could do nothing to stop him. It was as if she was dreaming, locked in a nightmare in which she had no strength. She could only lie helplessly, receiving any and all abuse he cared to inflict upon her.

"Your father…" he hissed, with spittle spraying her face. "Your father's journal! Satan's eternal curse on him!" John's hand closed about Carolyn's throat. "I was with your father the night he was driven away. He had insisted that I stay. My sister was sick, as you were, and he said there was a way we could both learn to save the ones we loved."

Carolyn was beyond being frightened now. She listened to John's rasping, raging voice with a quiet horror.

"I was forced to stand beside your father and watch him dissect a young girl's body. When it was done, he wanted to write about it, just as he always wrote about his procedures. He said to me, 'John, bring my journal from beneath the drawer.' I had never seen such a journal, but when I looked, I found it and brought it to him. I respected him." His tone dripped with contempt.

Carolyn felt her consciousness ebbing.

"I was mad with the horror of what he had done," John went on. "I needed morphia. I took some, and then, on a whim—a whim!—I opened your father's damned secret journal. He was closing the body, wrapping it. He had learned what he needed to know. I had begun to read...I—I thought I knew everything about him, but there before my eyes was an account of a dissection just like the one we had just completed. I saw the date. I realized..." He gave a howl of anguish. "I didn't know what to do! The wretched simpleton of an assistant who dug up the bodies for your esteemed father was coming to take the body back to the graveyard. I realized your father made a regular practice of studying cadavers. I had tried to understand, b-but he had already corrupted me and desecrated the one sacred memory that I had of my boyhood."

"How else can a physick learn—"

"But to learn on my mother?" John jerked her to her feet and shook her viciously. "To do what he did to my mother? He betrayed her memory! I went mad with rage. I would have killed him then, but he escaped me. I set fire to his surgery and ran away. When he came to me, begging me to explain to the others what we had done to the body..." He smiled wickedly. "I lied. I told them he murdered the girl. That was the first moment of my revenge. After that I went away, but I came back quickly. Ona had already lured me into practices I could not resist, and I soon learned she could get the morphia I could not live without. In return for it, I agreed to lead the Followers, and impersonate her dead father at Satan's altar. Since that day I have cursed Orion Adams's name, and waited, knowing that in return for what your father did to my mother's body, I would someday do the same to you."

She could hardly see. She was shivering uncontrollably. When he released her, she dropped like a sack of meal at his feet.

Then she felt him fumbling with her ankles. He was tying her—she wasn't certain where or why.

She tried to squirm free, but she was powerless, still conscious and yet incapable of doing a thing to stop him.

Then she saw him bending over her, his eyes nearly white with hate. "And I did get my revenge on him after that," John said softly. "When they came to ask if he had killed Katarinia, when they asked me if he did it so that he could study her...to save your damned life...I said yes! Yes!"

Laughing, he pulled something from his pocket and pressed it hurtfully against her lips until she opened her mouth to avoid the pain. He tied the gag behind her head and then stood.

Her head reeling, her arms leaden and her body numbed by the potion containing morphia that he and Ona had forced on her, she lay helpless, watching him throw a rope over a rafter. He kicked aside the planked cover of the round opening. She heard distant dripping, as if into a well.

With powerful arms he began dragging on the rope until Carolyn felt something tighten around her ankles. She was being dragged, feet first, across the muddy floor. Then her legs were hoisted into the air! Higher, higher!

Dear God, couldn't she do anything to stop him? Was this to be her end, here alone in this dismal cellar?

When he had hoisted her bound feet to the rafter, she was hanging upside down over the blackness of a cistern. Her arms hung limp over her head. With the care of one who had years to perfect his rituals, John painstakingly lowered her.

She squirmed only a little. Fearing that she might fall free of the ropes and drop bound into the water, she strained to think what she might do to save herself.

Blood rushed to her head and blackness closed around her as she felt her hands slip into icy water. The ropes around her ankles cut sharply into her skin as he lowered her, hand over hand, into the black water.

Now she was in water to her elbows, unable to close her mouth for the gag, fearing he might actually lower her head into the water. Grunting, trying to convey her panic—and her compliance to whatever he might want from her if only he would stop this torture—she felt the cold touch of numbing water on her scalp.

For every fraction of an inch that she was lowered, her panic rose. Clamping her eyes closed, she felt the water settle like the touch of death's icy kiss around her nose and upper cheeks. She took a gasping deep breath…

Her head slid completely beneath the water. Her heart was already racing in terror, her blood rushing. Now the cold was on her shoulders, her breasts…All sensation was turning to ice. The cold water was in her gagged mouth, stinging up her nose. She wanted to scream, to breathe, to thrash about…

Helpless! Utterly, hopelessly helpless!

Mercy! Mercy! The water caressed her waist, and now her hips, her knees…

Mama! Papa! Oh, Evan!

Her entire body was in the black water.

Think. *Think*…

Her lungs were bursting now and she was losing consciousness. A chilling lassitude was stealing through her. Though her body shrieked for air, she refused to draw a breath.

Feeling a queer tingling beginning in her fingertips, she felt herself for one eternal moment submerged, and her will was lost to the acceptance that death had arrived.

• • •

239

Sarah Hawes paused with her darning. All was still in the great room in her farmhouse outside Eudoxia. On this rainy night, the hearth poured soothing warmth across the silent room. Her husband had just gone off to their bed in the far corner, and their children were snug in the loft.

All was safe, she told herself, once again weaving her darning needle between the threads stretched across the darning egg. Such nights were for the devil, she thought, always uneasy during a heavy rain. Always, always, it brought to mind that awful time...

She shook her head, wanting to blot out the memory, but to forget was to erase the memory of her beloved Jeremy, who had died of the putrid throat. Losing him had been punishment, and she had vowed over his grave never to forget.

Since that awful year so early in her marriage, she had devoted her entire being to the love of God and to doing good works in the community. She went to meetings, avoided gossip, bore her woes and birthings in patient silence, all to atone for one terrible night when she had lost her faith to fear and desperation.

Even after so long, she had trouble understanding how she could have fallen prey to that evil woman's urgent words. But whenever the rains came in the night, and the shadows gathered in her otherwise comfortable life, she felt the sense of fear that had once led her to slip away into the dark with several of her trusted, equally desperate friends.

How could they have let it happen? And was it true that some of them had not repented as she had, that they still met several times a year, promising their secret souls to Satan in return for favors?

She and two of her friends were the only Followers from that first night so long ago who had not profited by that woman's evil promises. Their beloved children had died, while the children of the others had lived. Yet those other women were still bound in terror to Satan and his mistress, Ona. And Sarah, blessedly, was free.

Her skin crawled as she remembered the shadows and flickering firelight of that night. She thought of the forest clearing where they had gathered, each to ask that a child's life precious to them be spared.

She remembered all too clearly the long white body lying so still in the clearing. One moment the young girl had been struggling for breath and then, after he had done the unspeakable with her, she was pledged to the evil one whom that woman claimed would save all their children. Mercy, and so many of them had died, regardless!

Putting aside her mending, she bowed her head. She was never certain that she had been completely forgiven by God for her part in it. As she began praying, a prickling of awareness crawled along the nape of her neck. A quiet tapping came at the window. Her eyes flew wide. She looked up, and she saw a woman looking in.

That woman!

Had her dismal thoughts conjured her from the darkness? Sarah thought in a panic. She wanted to whisper her husband's name, but to tell him of her fear would be to confess that horrible night and her enduring shame.

It was then she knew Ona Ruby still possessed her soul. When she opened the door a crack, seeing the black-eyed woman close up for the first time in sixteen long years, she could not refuse to go out with her.

She stood a moment, her hand reaching for her cloak. What could the woman want? Might she not break this guilty hold on this black night?

But one glance at her husband's sleeping face in the big draped bed across the way and Sarah knew that whatever the cost, she could never admit that, one night long ago, she and her friends had turned to Satan when they believed that God had abandoned them.

She went out, closing the door. She followed the stocky shadow moving away on the road. Two other shadows had been waiting nearby. As Sarah drew near, her heart drumming, her fear as real as shackles on her judgment, she didn't need to be told that the shadows were Ona's servants, Verity and Annatie.

As silently as ghosts, they made their way quickly through the village where they waited in the darkness while Annatie went into the meetinghouse. Sarah knew nothing about the town meeting that seemed to be going on inside. She heard voices raised in fear and anger, but her only concern was for herself. She was marveling at the hold Ona had over the Followers. She was marveling at the power of fear to drive otherwise decent women into the rain to hide their long-repented shame.

In moments, Annatie came out, dragging Lizza by the arm. With her were two other whispering women.

"What must you say to us that you can't say inside?" Johannah Appel hissed.

Beside her was Hope Miller who, like Sarah, had agreed to pledge her loyalty to Satan in return for the lives of two of her ill children.

"We've driven her away! There will be no more questions," Johannah cried. "You can go on as always...and leave us alone!"

Sarah shivered, tears cold on her cheeks. She longed for the courage to run away. She watched helplessly as Ona stepped forward from the shadows. It was whispered that those who did not follow Ona died horrible deaths, but somehow Sarah, Johannah and Hope had slipped from her hold all these years...because their precious children had died.

"She be here still," Ona whispered, her voice low and evil.

Hope clutched at Johannah's sleeve. "But what can be do? If we're found out, I'll die! I'll hang myself from the nearest—"

Ona silenced the hysterical woman with one savage swipe of her hand. Then she seized Annatie's arm and jerked her close. "It be you or Carolyn for Wildman. I be wrong to let him toy with her. We must see that she dies."

Annatie nodded, her young face ugly.

Johannah made a dash for the meetinghouse, but like a wolf, Ona was on her back, wrestling her to the rain-drenched ground. As she squeezed the air from the woman's throat, Hope took several steps backward, her face a white blur of horror. Then, turning, she fled straight across the commons.

"Go after her, fool!" Ona hissed, motioning to Annatie.

Nearby, the meetinghouse door fell open. "Johannah? Hope?

Where have you gone?"

With Johannah coughing and Hope pounding away into the darkness, Ona sprang up and signaled for all to follow her. Dark cloaks billowing, hearts drumming, they fled into the night.

Joseph Flies limped through the tangle of underbrush. Stopping suddenly, he shuddered with pain and fell to his knees in anguished terror. The lantern he held dipped precariously close to the mud.

He couldn't remember why he'd gone out. The rain drizzled coldly on his stubbled, hollow cheek, and ran inside his collar.

Then, blessedly, he remembered and pressed his hand to the wrapped pages tucked inside his shirt over this aching heart. Clenching his fist, he fought the unrelenting pain, afraid that after waiting so patiently, he would not be able to help his only true friend this one last time.

Though his heart was beating wildly, he finally staggered to his feet. Lifting his face into the rain, he tried with all his might to remember why he was in the wood. With nothing to give him his bearings, he feared he would drop to his death and never be found.

Quite suddenly, the confusion in his old brain cleared. He remembered following the good doctor's daughter into the woods. Taking a step, and then another, he found himself plodding onward, lantern clutched in a rigid fist. His determination was as clear in his simple mind as a single steady flame.

When he tripped and fell over the body on the cart path, he feared he had muddied the precious papers that had been entrusted to him. The pain in his chest melted away. He rolled to a sitting position and stared at the man who lay faceup in the rain.

"Thank God you found me, old soul," Evan whispered, remembering the remarkable effect the name had had on the servant only hours ago. Wincing, Evan tried to sit and found the pain in his side excruciating. "I'm wounded, friend," Evan said, panting. "Carolyn needs our help. Can you get me to my feet?"

The gaunt man stared at him in the darkness.

"Together we can help her," Evan said.

At last Joseph pushed himself to his knees and struggled to his feet. His left side drooped and, apparently, he had lost the use of his left arm.

He stood fast, however, as Evan used his legs to drag himself upright. Panting, he clung to the towering man's bony frame.

"We need help, friend. Can you help me back to Timberhill? Perhaps I can reason with those fools…"

Without mentioning that the house was in flames and that he was afraid to venture back where all those enraged people stood, Joseph lifted his head proudly. He had a new friend, one who needed him and talked to him as if he were a man. For this one, he would walk until he was dead.

Evan felt light-headed as they broke from the trees into the grassy meadow behind Timberhill. The way ahead was lit by waning orange light from all the windows. There could be nothing left of the interior, he thought.

But he kept on, leaning on Joseph, each step an effort in sheer determination. When they drew abreast of the verandah, Evan worried that the stone shell of the house would fall and crush them. He urged Joseph on around to the front.

With a sinking heart, he saw the wheel marks in the coachway. All the villagers had gone. Apparently, Silas and his family had gone with them.

Losing his strength suddenly, he dropped down, unable to determine how he must proceed. Where would he find help in looking for Carolyn? All these fools wanted her gone. If he couldn't save her, he'd go mad! But where to look? He pressed his hand to his wound. How long could he go on with his lifeblood oozing between his fingers?

"Can you make it to the village, old soul, and bring help to search for my wife? Can you tell them a madman is loose in the wood? Can you do that for me, please?"

Joseph's gaunt, pale face twitched as if from pain. He looked down at Evan, puzzlement softening his hurt old eyes. Finally he drew something from his shirt and offered it to Evan. "For the doctor," Joseph whispered.

And then he was turning away from the cart path, dragging his left foot, but moving as if nothing would stop him.

Evan sagged, letting his head rest in the mud a moment. If he could just hold out until help came, then he could lead them back into the woods. They might have a hope of finding where Wildman had taken Carolyn.

Dimly, he realized the rain had stopped. The forest was silent now, the crackling of flames within the house hypnotically soft. Then came a rumble as some interior portion of the house caved in, and a shower of sparks erupted from a shattered front window.

Evan concentrated on keeping his wits about him. He didn't want to drift into unconsciousness. He pressed the packet Joseph had given him into his wound, cursing and praying by turns. "Carolyn," he whispered. "Wherever you are, I love you."

Sighing, he slumped more heavily onto the muddy coachway, his eyes fixed in an unfocused stare up at the dark stone face of the house with its softly glowing eyes.

Six cloaked silhouettes hurried from the lane toward the side of the burning house. Evan thought he was dreaming.

Twenty

Feeling invincible strength pumping in his muscled arms, John Rasner hoisted the half-clad, dripping body out of the cistern. Gritting his teeth, he braced himself against the dead weight. Pausing, he lashed the rope in a slip knot to a bolt in the nearby wall.

Arms limp over her head, wet hair dripping softly into the black water, Carolyn hung pale and still. The sight stirred him, as it had since the first time he had seen a dead body more than sixteen years ago. He went to her then, gathering her close and gave the rope a jerk, releasing it. He caught her, teetered at the edge of the cistern and then staggered backward, lowering her to the muddy floor.

Her skin was white now, cool, and smooth as a marble headstone. He pushed back the wet curls clinging to her forehead and bent to kiss her unresponsive lips. The only woman he felt capable of controlling was a dead one.

Lifting her, he carried her to the crude table, laid her on it with care and tenderness and then arranged her lifeless arms at her sides. Deftly, he tugged the stubborn wet ribbons of her chemise and drew the wet fabric aside, baring her full, lovely white breasts. He was about to draw off her pantaloons when he heard the quiet thunder of collapsing walls overhead.

Gray smoke curled from cracks between the flooring planks above the rafters. Dust settled on his hair and shoulders. He paused, glaring up with squinted eyes. If only he could see more clearly, he thought, turning back to the woman lying on the table in the encircling golden glow of the flickering candles. The morphia rendered him almost blind.

Drawing in deep breaths, feeling his heart drumming and his

loins quickening, he gazed hungrily at her. The bright candle flames all around shrank to pinpricks of light. Darkness closed in around him like a fog. He could see nothing but the body, the breasts, the pale white arms and long slender legs. He heard a deep ringing. A strange urgent voice whispered huskily in his mind. He couldn't comprehend the words, but they made him feel agitated and jittery.

Then a draft caused all the candles to sputter. The curls of smoke seeping between the planks overhead were sucked down around his head and then drawn into the next chamber like gray spirits.

Impatiently, he whirled, watching as Ona stepped down from the cellar stairwell, her skirts and cloak heavy with rain. Behind her were five cloaked women, heads bowed. The last, Annatie, drew the doors closed and prodded the women to follow Ona into the candlelit chamber.

"We must hurry," Ona whispered, producing the leather wallet from which John drew his cold, glittering instruments.

"Why?"

"They be following. We must go. Hurry!"

He didn't want to hurry, he thought, watching as the women bared their heads. They stood in postures of submission and shame. He scarcely remembered one of them. She had been at one of their earliest meetings, years ago, back when the children were sick. Why was she here now? Had she rejoined them?

Ona was passing a gourd filled with her special potion that took away their pain and heightened their perception. He had already had enough of his own medicaments to make him feel he could overcome them all, at last, this night.

The demon spirit that Ona claimed lived within him had never existed. He had only pretended to act as she wished in order to please her. He had been forced to in order to get the morphia he couldn't obtain himself, and he had to frighten the others enough that they would never reveal his presence in the wood.

And, for this night, he would pretend a while longer.

He searched each pinched face, his own eyes squinted in an effort to see. His pupils were constricted almost to the point of blindness. He recognized the new one, the little black maid who had come to a meeting with Ona only once and had wept until the potion silenced her.

And of course there was the stupid one, Verity, who came because she didn't know how to stop herself. And there was Annatie, glancing at him and then at the still body on the table. Annatie's chest rose and fell with violent breathing, as if she were indignant or afraid. He wanted to command her away, for she had come to irritate him unbearably these past few years. She wanted to control him, too. He would have an end to it, now, if she didn't learn to obey.

Lucile Ebey couldn't see him at such close range, he knew, and he wanted to laugh at the hag. They were all such witless, spineless creatures in the face of Ona's control. The *Followers*. He'd free them from all of it! The house was burning over their heads...the time for change had come!

Ona began her chants. John took his place at the side of the table where the body was spread motionless before him. He shut his eyes, opened his arms and waited for the power of his courage to gather.

He didn't hear the gasps of the women as they stared at Carolyn lying so still and seemingly dead on the table. Her chest rose and fell in a sigh, softly.

When he opened his eyes and squinted down at her, he couldn't see her breathing.

His mind was spiraling inward, down into a black consciousness where the morphia, coca, nightshade and wormwood stirred him to power. He knew nothing of where he stood, or who was watching. He thought only of the body, the clean, white, cool body awaiting his practiced touch.

His mind was spiraling back to the first time, in a cellar so like this one, where he stood looking down on a pale-white creature he had seen only hours before in the wood. He had seen her bathed in pure moonlight, giving up her lifeblood and her virginity to him at Ona's hissing command.

He remembered the times since, when Ona brought someone

into the fold for sacrifice. His body reeled to recall the intense, rocketing release. His mind spiraled toward the moments ahead when again he would feel it, savor it, explode with it, and then lower the sacrifice one last time into the cistern. Lost. Forgotten. Forever.

Ona passed the gourd a second time, then drank deeply of it herself. As her heavy features relaxed and her eyelids drooped, she stepped forward, taking one of John's small scalpels.

He held forth his wrists, allowing her to make tiny pricks in his skin until several drops of blood fell on the torso before him. Then, lovingly, Ona massaged a powder into the openings. He felt surging exhilaration spread through him like bolts of lightning.

"I call upon you, Satan!" he shouted, causing the women to cringe and begin weeping. "This woman has brought us trouble. We offer her as sacrifice, as we have offered the others, for your favor and protection."

Lizza squealed, clutched her hair and dropped to her knees. "Mercy, Lord, save me!"

Ona crossed the chamber and cuffed her roughly about the head, but she wouldn't be still.

Sarah wept openly, her expression one of resignation and terror. Verity's eyes were riveted on John, straining to be one of those favored with protection.

Annatie turned away slightly, her eyes a stormy blur. Her mouth was tight over her teeth. Finally she crossed her arms, trying to quiet her gasping breaths. She was losing him!

Only Lucile looked on with a placid expression. She thought only of comfort promised, of favors asked for. She listened to him call upon their lord…but the chamber was so filled with smoke now she began coughing. Her concentration faltered.

She looked at the body on the table. She had seen other bodies there, and she had watched him…She never asked why or who. She had only obeyed, waiting for her comfort, favors and protection like Verity.

But this body stirred!

And where, oh where in all these years, had been her comfort?

What protection had she obtained? What favor had she but endlessly silent days alone with her crushing torment? The others had escaped. Why couldn't she?

Straining to understand, she heard a sudden rumble overhead that sent a rafter crashing through the floor into the next chamber. Smoke, flames and sparks showered behind them.

Lizza squealed again. Ona struck her down, and then as the air clouded thickly with brown smoke, the murky interior of Lucile's memory cleared.

She remembered. Like all her memories now, this one was as fresh as if she was living it all over again. She was a healthy, strong woman again as she turned confidently to watch their young lord work his magic to save their children, her children.

She saw the body lying on the table, but she didn't see brown curls. She saw soft blond ringlets. She didn't see the body of a mature woman but a slim, underdeveloped one. A young girl so precious to her...

Dying!

Deep in her being came a welling of some urgent emotion she couldn't control.

No...No-o—

Like an earthquake, she began a furious shaking. Her back straightened as if she'd been stabbed. She lifted her head, feeling the featherlike softness of her long graying hair waft against her sunken cheeks.

Past and present seemed to coexist in her mind. She knew that they had come to this place this night to save their children! There her precious daughter lay, fighting for every breath.

And Lucile knew at the same moment that he, their lord, was going to ask for favor and protection. But she also knew that Katarinia would not be spared.

She was going to die in choking agony right before her eyes just as if they had never called upon Satan at all!

If that wasn't enough she would then watch in grief-stricken silence as he...as he...

She saw him standing, arms outstretched, calling upon their lord. Then he lowered his face, spread his hands across the body. He finally focused his attention on her throat. With the grace of a skilled sculptor, he reached toward the slim young throat where a tiny white scar pulsed.

The black water was cold, soothing. She floated deep within in, relaxed, unconcerned. Strangely, she seemed able to draw shallow breaths and sighed with contentment.

What peace she had found in the darkness, she thought. No more fears, no worries, no people chasing her with torches. She felt cool, serene…

Opening her eyes to mere slits, she wondered why the water above looked gray. There was a strange echoing voice in the distance, a voice that quickened her heartbeat and troubled her serenity.

She shut her eyes again, wanting to reclaim the black sleep, but the peace and contentment were gone. Something niggled at her brain, a tiny worry that grew like a rumble of thunder until she gave a shudder.

Eyes flying wide, she saw looming over her a man of seemingly endless height. His arms were open wide above her. He called out in an echoing voice that she could scarcely hear.

In one hand he held an object that glinted. His face, lit with wavering gold light, his dark head and blurred countenance enveloped in clouds.

He bent, reaching toward her.

She tried to move, and found herself powerless.

The volcanic eruption in Lucile exploded. Her scream tore her throat, shattering the quiet.

"No-o-o!" she wailed, lunging forward through the fog of

drugged obedience, through years of unbearable remorse and regret.

She would not let him murder her daughter! Possessed of superhuman strength, she rounded the table in only a few strides, captured his wrists with gnarled hands and, with a growl, twisted until her clenched rotting teeth shot shards of pain to her brain.

John gave a cry of alarm and surprise. He hadn't expected the attack. He fell to the side as the feeble woman's body crashed against him. Even as he landed heavily, she was climbing on top of him, kicking, scrambling to wrestle the scalpel free of his hold.

When she couldn't open his fist, she sank her teeth into his tender inner arm.

Screams reverberated in the smoky chamber. More smoke gushed in as the frozen women looked on. Ona swirled around the table, her fist raised.

John twisted free of his attacker and rolled perilously near the rim of the yawning cistern.

Ona flung herself onto the flailing pair.

"I will have his heart!" Lucile shrieked, tearing at the powerful, quivering hand bending relentlessly toward her now. The gleaming scalpel was clutched in a murderous grip.

He struck, sending the fragile old woman sprawling. Blindly he thrashed, catching the side of Ona's head with his blade. He sliced mercilessly, and then wrenched away with a reverberating roar that suddenly changed to a yelp of surprise.

His head and shoulders had slipped over the cistern's edge. He wheeled for handholds, letting the scalpel drop. Grabbing, twisting, he slid farther in until he dropped headfirst…falling…into blackness.

His cry of surprise was swallowed up in the cistern.

Overhead, more of the second floor and roof crashed. The sound of straining beams groaning against the weight made the house seem as if in its death throes.

Carolyn saw tongues of flame curling between the planks now. With all her concentration, she struggled to sit. Her head pounded and her heart skipped wildly. Dazed, she clutched the edge of the table to keep from rolling off, and stared at the dark stocky woman lying in a heap near a circular opening in the floor.

Blood had pooled beneath the woman's sliced jugular. Nearby, a still form lay as if thrown there, strands of feathery gray hair dangling over the cistern's edge.

"Miz, we got to get out of here 'fore it's too late!"

With effort, Carolyn reached for the welcome sound of a voice she recognized. She tumbled off the table and collapsed to her knees. Then there were hands supporting her, guiding her toward a flame-lit doorway.

"Mother, don't! We've got to get out!" Annatie fumbled through the choking smoke. "Someone help me with Mother!"

Carolyn felt as if she were swimming in fog. Unable to feel her feet touching the floor, she let herself sag into the arms that were helping her toward the fresh air of night.

Sarah and Lizza tried to shake Carolyn back to consciousness, but she was dropping to the floor. Overhead, flames hungrily devoured the beams, eating through them.

Dropping Carolyn, Sarah sank to her knees, crawling toward the steps that led upstairs.

"Miz! Miz, please!" Lizza cried helplessly. Finally she plunged after Sarah toward the steps, scrambling up past the woman. "Someone, please!"

Screaming, she ran for the road.

Outside, in front of the house, Evan had staggered to his feet. He was still concerned that the stone shell would eventually topple on him.

More and more of the roof was crashing through now. The house was belching plumes of smoke and ash into the air. He saw Lizza running away into the darkness, her arms waving, her frantic cries muffled.

Staggering around to the side of the house, he saw another woman drag herself from an opening at the foundation. Were there steps?

Fighting his pain, he forced himself closer. He was about to speak when the woman saw him, turned and pointed back. "Help her!"

Annatie Harpswell struggled backwards up the stone steps, dragging her mother's body. Seeing Evan staggering toward her, she shoved him aside and went on dragging until she collapsed, sobbing.

Evan steadied himself. Then he saw a figure moving below in the smoky darkness. She looked like a ghost, pale and nearly naked, advancing on all fours, slowly, toward the steps.

Forgetting his wound, he made his way down to her, grasped her hand and pulled with all his might. Behind her came a roar as the main floor dropped beneath the weight of the fallen slate roof.

Smoke gushed from the stairwell as Evan helped Carolyn crawl up. Then he was pulling her to her feet, feeling too stunned to speak. Together, they stumbled away to a safe distance from the house.

"Carolyn!" he finally gasped, feeling his pain return full force. "Are you all right?"

She looked as if she could scarcely see him. Her head tipped as if she couldn't hold it still. Limply, she reached for him, trying to hold him.

He gathered her close, weeping softly into her smoky hair. He was too grieved to want anything more than to hold her and never let go.

Twenty-One

Silas leaned forward on the wagon seat. Riding along with him were those villagers willing to return to Timberhill. He was unable to explain why he felt so strongly that he must return, but something drove him on. The way ahead was murky and forboding, and he felt a chill run along his spine.

Dawn was just breaking, turning the black night sky to dark lavender. Morning birds were waking, twittering as the wagon rattled past with its load of seven elders and the pastor.

"Ahead there, in the road!" the man seated next to Silas said, pointing.

Silas reined, climbed down and found a tall bony man collapsed in the rut of the road. "Who is this?" he called back to the passengers.

One of the sober-faced elders climbed from the wagon and came to stand over the body. "Looks like Mrs. Ebey's manservant. Dropped in his tracks."

"We'll move him to the side and take him into the village later."

The man detained Silas. "Preacher, I'm not clear in my mind why we're going back there. Those folks are gone for good this time."

Silas ran his hand over his eyes. "I don't understand myself. But if my own wife can understand how my sister-in-law could take the life of a newborn baby, then I must yield to her. I know only that a while ago something struck me soundly. I knew I had to return to the house. If I'm to be your spiritual shepherd, I must face that which terrifies this community, and overcome it."

Returning to the wagon, they drove on. As they neared Timberhill, the smell of smoke was in the air. Wisps of smoke still lifted from the stone shell, with its gaping, lifeless eyes opening out to the scorched trees nearby.

Silas felt a pang of regret for losing the house. It was just punishment for his greed, he knew. But even more than regret, he felt ashamed that he'd been a party to a mob scene. He'd done nothing to protect his brother's wife, and he did have her to thank for Fanny's and Eliakim's life, after all.

They rolled to a stop in the road; Silas was reluctant to pull into the rubble-strewn drive. Almost at once a lone figure sprang from the grass to the left and staggered toward them.

"Help us!"

"It looks like Sarah!" one of the men exclaimed, vaulting from the wagon bed behind Silas. He loped toward the woman. "I thought you had run off. It's my wife!" He called over his shoulder. "She's found! What are you doing here?"

She broke into sobs. The man led her to the side, straining to hear her whispered story. At length he paused, put his hand to his temple, then turned to look at her in disbelief.

She went on speaking, pleading. Then she dropped to her knees, doubled over and rocked herself. The man stood rigidly over her, looking away.

Then finally he stooped beside her, encircling her with his arms.

Uneasily, Silas watched the sky lighten. He climbed down, seeing two shadowed figures huddled beyond a crumbled garden wall.

What were these people doing here? he wondered, glancing around him at the devastation. The wreckage of the house was complete.

He nearly stumbled over a young woman seated in the grass. She held her white-haired mother in her lap, her eyes blankly staring at nothing, her cheeks smudged with soot.

"I beg your pardon! Can I help you, sister?" Silas asked, stooping to offer the woman his hand. He didn't recognize her.

Annatie Harpswell never lifted her eyes. She only wagged her head. "She's at peace at last."

"God rest her soul," he said, turning to see who else was there beyond the wall. What had happened here? Had the hand of God led him back to give comfort, or was his purpose here larger still? Had God brought him here to rebuild the spirit of a village?

He found Carolyn and Evan huddled together against the protection of the low stone wall.

"Thank you for coming back," Carolyn whispered. She looked up, her face smudged with soot and blood, her brown curls dried in a wild tangle. "Please, Silas, forgive me. I truly don't believe I killed your son's twin. He was stillborn, and I sought only to spare you grief. It was foolish, I know, but—"

Surprised at himself, Silas found no bitterness lingering in his heart. He marveled that a woman for whom he had had such contempt and loathing mere hours before could now move him to admiration. "Carolyn, the night my sons were born, I gave you little reason to trust me. Can you forgive me my ignorance? You truly did save my beloved Fanny and Eliakim."

Her smile looked so serene that he felt ashamed.

"We both had much to learn, Silas. Help us get into Eudoxia. Evan's been stabbed and has lost a great deal of blood."

Silas noted that Evan's face was ashen as he lay with his head lolling on her arm. He crouched, unfastened his cloak and drew it around the pair. "Where can I take you?"

"Perhaps Helen Rasner..." She looked momentarily bewildered, and then shrugged. "Perhaps not. Have you seen Lizza?"

He shook his head.

"She's run off again." She looked toward the house, her expression suddenly grave. "Give Timberhill your blessing, Silas. Three people died in there last night. They're still inside, in the cellar."

He stood, scowling at the gaping stone facade. He couldn't tell her about her aunt just yet, or the manservant lying back in the lane.

Carolyn's face contorted. She bowed her head. "My search must end. I won't look any further—God forgive me. I won't rake over the past, not at the risk of losing the man I love!"

Several of the elders came up behind Silas then. There was the sound of brittle papers fluttering in the rising sweet spring morning breeze.

"We found this lying in the coachway." The foremost man held out three unfolded yellowed pages, dark with blood along one side. They had been wrapped in a leather packet.

Carolyn gasped in amazement.

"Is this something important?" Silas asked, steadying her with a hand on her shaking shoulder. "Here, you're chilled through! Let's get you into the village. There's much to talk over. You can read these later."

She reached for the pages, revealing beneath Evan's and Silas's cloaks that she was nearly naked.

Silas averted his eyes. "Give her the papers, man. And let's get them in from this chill morning."

Carolyn nearly crushed the papers in her quaking hand as she held them before her eyes in the lifting dawn light. She saw faint brown writing that was unintelligible to anyone but herself. The ink was faded but legible.

Her eyes tightened, and she coughed out a cry. "Papa! Oh, dear Papa..." Then she doubled over, pressing her face to the top of Evan's disheveled head.

An Accounting of Dissection on a Female Victim of the Putrid Throat; Being the Secret Findings Which Indicate Ritual Murder.

Without giving a reason, my apprentice has gone off, leaving me to relate this unpleasant case. My assistant shall arrive momentarily to return the body to its grave. I had it exhumed in hopes of learning how to save these dying children; I fear my own beloved Carolyn will soon succumb. The risk of resurrectionism seems small in the face of that.

As it happens, I was called to the subject's home only yesterday by a distraught, despairing father who, against his wife's and neighbors' wishes, begged me to do whatever I might to save his three strangling children.

I found all three in advanced stages of the disease, well beyond anything I might do, save piercing their throats in hopes that they might draw enough life-giving air to survive the onslaught of the reaper, diphtheria.

The youngest, a boy of five, was nearly gone, his throat almost completely clogged with the membrane characteristic of this disease. He drew but little air, and was failing as I examined him.

The middle child, a girl of nine, seemed a bit stronger, but she would soon be struggling for breath like her brother.

The eldest, a girl of twelve, was faring the best, though someone had wantonly given her too heavy a dose of the laudanum. At the time I found nothing remarkable about her person, and felt of the three that I might be able to save her.

At the last instant, however, I was driven from the house by violent means by the hysterical mother, who, upon my departure, called out that she would see her children living and completely well by morning.

As I have met with unconquerable resistance and ignorance hereabouts, I could do nothing but return home, thinking that if my own dear child should contract the putrid throat that I should have no qualms piercing her throat to prolong her breathing. It seemed to be the only logical treatment.

It happened that she, indeed, became ill. I sat at her bedside, watching her worsen. As her father, to pierce her throat or not to made me quite ill, suddenly, with indecision. To do it wrongly would surely mean her life. I realized it is folly to treat one's own.

I learned early this morning that the three unfortunate children I had examined only hours before had died. To prevent further contagion, they were to be buried this afternoon, and so they were. I gave my wife permission to attend, and then went off to contact my assistant. To me, it was imperative that I obtain the body of one of those children for study.

Imagine my horror upon returning to find my wife had taken Carolyn to the funeral, further endangering her health. By darkfall, Carolyn was in desperate condition.

I realized I had not the composure to pierce her throat; fear kept my hand unsteady and cowardly. When my assistant and apprentice arrived for the dissection, I proceeded.

Now I have just come from my daughter's bedside. She is breathing through a bit of tubing, and I am sick at heart to relate that which I found on the body of young Katarinia Ebey since I last saw her.

Her throat had been slit. Due to my shock, I examined her fully, discovering evidence of recent intercourse— possibly inflicted after death. I cannot fathom the perpetrator of such a desecration…

The entry was unfinished. Carolyn's voice trailed off. She felt numbed. "That's all," she whispered at length.

Those gathered in the bedchamber at the Rasner home remained silent, lost in thought. Standing behind her father's chair, Helen Rasner began weeping.

Annatie stared out the window, her expression blank. "Mother joined the group to save my sister and myself. If we both had died she might have broken away as Sarah, Johannah and Hope were able to do, but she had me. Ona convinced her that so long as she remained a member of the group, my life would be spared. Sixteen years we endured this hellish nightmare."

Sarah was there with her husband, her eyes still round with fright. "We were all so frightened for the lives of our children, we would have done…a-anything."

Silas motioned her silent, patting her as he stepped to the center of the chamber. "I am well aware of panic and desperation. Let me say that I think my sister-in-law has done you all a service by exposing this festering wound secreted in your community—our community. How was it that you all believed Orion Adams responsible?"

One of the many elders present, a man Carolyn didn't recognize, stepped forward. "It was a terrible time, no doubt of that. We were sick with fear, watching our children die in our arms. When Lucile came to us saying Orion Adams had examined her children but they'd worsened and died, and then that he'd been found to have dug up their bodies…We were all too ready to conclude he had killed them for study to save his own child. It was madness, but we needed a scapegoat."

Evan leaned heavily in the chair next to Carolyn's bed. He sought her hand and sighed. "I venture to guess Lucile noticed Katarinia's grave had been disturbed, realized your father had examined her after her death and had seen the evidence of murder. By then she was surely half mad, knowing her daughter had died because of her ignorance. To shunt the blame onto someone else in order to conceal her guilt must have seemed her only recourse."

Carolyn put the journal pages aside and sank back in the soft pillows. "I'm so weary," she confessed.

Silas motioned for everyone to leave Carolyn and Evan alone. He followed, murmuring comforts to those nearest.

Annatie remained by the window. When everyone had gone but Helen and her father, Annatie turned, perhaps thinking she was the last to exit. She looked momentarily startled as her eyes met Helen's.

"You knew all those years that my brother wasn't dead," Helen whispered in a reproachful tone. "You knew, Annatie, and you said nothing."

Annatie stiffened, arching her neck and looking down her nose at Helen. "I would have done anything for John. He needed protection from his part in Orion Adams's dissections. I was willing to keep his secret forever. I am not the only guilty one who took part in rituals. Even if I were, no one can prove I did anything. John was our master. Ona controlled him. If anyone should hang, it is they."

Carolyn whispered, "And they are both dead."

"Please leave my house," Helen whispered.

Annatie's hand curled into a fist. Stiffly she marched from the bedchamber, braced to face the gauntlet of elders waiting below.

Feeling drained, Carolyn shut her eyes. She heard Helen's father rise with a groan from his chair and shuffle toward the door. She couldn't bear to look at the bewilderment in his eyes.

"My brother might have become a great surgeon," Helen said, almost as if to herself.

"It was the morphia, Helen, and the nature of such an addiction," Carolyn said, gathering her strength. "Try not to blame him. I remember his dedication, too. If it hadn't been for Ona wanting everyone within her power, and, I believe, because of something quite innocent that my father once said to her, John might have gone on to do great things."

Mr. Rasner went out. Helen paused at the door. "He was so near all along. If Father hadn't left him and Mother alone all those years…If my mother hadn't borne me and died…"

Carolyn roused herself. "Oh, Helen, what good will such thinking do you?"

"I want to run away from all this shame!"

"Then go. Forget the shame, it's not yours. You've wanted to leave here for years. You told me so yourself. Make a life for yourself. A woman can, you know, if she has courage."

Evan made a careful laugh, winced and clutched his side. "And if she has stubborn, reckless pride."

Helen looked long at Carolyn. Then the corners of her mouth turned up. "If you'll excuse me, I want to stay close to Father."

"He'll be fine," Carolyn assured her. "Thank you for your hospitality."

When the door closed, Carolyn sagged against the pillows. "I want to return to Philadelphia as soon as we're feeling a little stronger."

Evan looked puzzled. "What made Silas come back for us? We might still be sitting out in that dismal meadow smelling smoke. Joseph never reached the village, poor old soul. To think he kept those journal pages all this time…" He lifted his summer-blue eyes. "How do you feel, my dearest, most precious wife?"

Carolyn searched her heart and mind, finding both peaceful and content. Sighing, she squeezed Evan's hand. "Crawl into the bed beside me, my love. I want to warm you."

"And I you," he said gently, his eyes more tender than she had ever seen them. "We can leave here forever now, can't we?"

She smiled as he slipped beneath the comfort with her. "I feel as if a new morning has dawned, that for so long I lived in twilight, that when I came here it was a bitterly endless night. Today, I feel new. I feel hope and true happiness for the first time. Thank God I didn't lose you, Evan," she whispered, enfolding him in her arms.

Gingerly, he turned toward her. "I love you, dearest. Can a wounded man make love with his wife?"

"Let's find out." She smiled.

Outside, the sun poured down on the woods, bathing the trees and fields in golden light. All was quiet and serene. The mountains in the distance were tinged with pale green, and the earth gave off its rich deep fragrance of spring and renewal.

On the rear porch step sat a slim young serving girl, her dress in tatters, her shoulder encircled by the strong arm of a brawny, dark-skinned lad with bewildered eyes.

In the village the elders were gathering for the unpleasant task of searching the ruins of Timberhill. Preacher Clure was driving his wife and children out to a small vacant farm with the thought of staying on. Nowhere else might they be more needed now than in a village purged once and forever of the demon—ignorance.

And in the guest bedchamber of a once lonely house lay two hearts beating as one, a man and a woman finding contentment in love. Of all the ghosts laid to rest in the night the haunting emptiness of their hearts had been the worst.

Carolyn held her husband, relishing his warm, life-giving touch. The shadows of her past had been replaced with light. The memories of an unhappy time long ago were fading, replaced by coming days of promise and hope.

In her heart sang the beat of strength and courage, of a world opened to her, of love enduring. With this dear man she would grow to the fullness of her womanhood, realizing at last her potential as a healer, mother, lover and wife.

Also by Samantha Harte

CACTUS ROSE

In the heat of the southwest, desire is the kindling for two lost souls—and the flame of passion threatens to consume them both.

Rosie Saladay needs to get married—fast. The young widow needs help to protect her late husband's ranch, but no decent woman can live alone with a hired hand. With the wealthy Wesley Morris making a play for her land, Rosie needs a husband or she risks losing everything. So she hangs a sign at the local saloon: "Husband wanted. Apply inside. No conjugal rights."

Delmar Grant is a sucker for a damsel in distress, and even with Rosie's restrictions on "boots under her bed" stated firmly in black and white, something about the lovely widow's plea leaves him unable to turn away her proposal of marriage.

Though neither planned on falling in love, passion ignites between the unlikely couple. But their buried secrets—and enemies with both greed and a grudge—threaten to tear them apart. They'll discover this marriage of convenience may cost them more than they could have ever bargained for.

ANGEL

When her mother dies, fourteen-year-old Angel has no one to turn to but Dalt, a gruff-spoken mountain man with an unsettling leer and a dark past. Angel follows Dalt to the boomtowns of the Colorado territory, where she is thrust into the hardscrabble world of dancehalls, mining camps, and saloons.

From gold mines to gambling palaces, *Angel* tells the story of a girl navigating her way through life, as an orphan, a pioneer, and ultimately a miner's wife and respected madam…a story bound up with the tale of the one man in all the West who dared to love her.

AUTUMN BLAZE

Firemaker is a wild, golden-haired beauty who was taken from her home as a baby and raised by a Comanche tribe. Carter Machesney is the handsome Texas Ranger charged with finding her, and reacquainting her with the life she never really knew.

Though they speak in different tongues, the instant flare of passion between Firemaker and Carter is a language both can speak, and their love is one that bridges both worlds.

HURRICANE SWEEP

Hurricane Sweep spans three generations of women—three generations of strife, heartbreak, and determination.

Florie is a delicate Southern belle who must flee north to escape her family's cruelty, only to endure the torment of both harsh winters and a sadistic husband. Loraine, Florie's beautiful and impulsive daughter, bares her body to the wrong man, yet hides her heart from the right one. And Jolie, Florie's pampered granddaughter, finds herself in the center of the whirlwind of her family's secrets.

Each woman is caught in a bitter struggle between power and pride, searching for a love great enough to obliterate generations of buried dreams and broken hearts.

KISS OF GOLD

From England to an isolated Colorado mining town, Daisie Browning yearns to find her lost father—the last thing she expects to find is love. Until, stranded, robbed, and beset by swindlers, she reluctantly accepts the help of the handsome and rakish Tyler Reede, all the while resisting his advances.

But soon Daisie finds herself drawn to Tyler, and she'll discover that almost everything she's been looking for can be found in his passionate embrace.

SNOWS OF CRAGGMOOR

When Merri Glenden's aunt died, she took many deep, dark secrets to the grave. But the one thing Aunt Coral couldn't keep hidden was the existence of Merri's living relatives, including a cousin who shares Merri's name. Determined to connect with a family she never knew but has always craved, Merri travels to Colorado to seek out her kin.

Upon her arrival at the foreboding Craggmoor—the mansion built by her mining tycoon great-grandfather—Merri finds herself surrounded by antagonistic strangers rather than the welcoming relations she'd hoped for.

Soon she discovers there is no one in the old house whom she can trust...no one but the handsome Garth Favor, who vows to help her unveil her family's secrets once and for all, no matter the cost.

SUMMERSEA

Betz Witherspoon isn't looking forward to the long, hot summer ahead. Stuck at a high-class resort with her feisty young charge, Betz only decides enduring her precocious heiress's mischief might be worth it when she meets the handsome and mysterious Adam Teague.

Stealing away to the resort's most secluded spots, the summer's heat pales against the blaze of passion between Betz and Adam. But Betz finds her scorching romance beginning to fizzle as puzzling events threaten the future of her charge. To survive the season, Betz will have to trust the enigmatic Adam...and her own heart.

SWEET WHISPERS

Seeking a new start, Sadie Evans settles in Warren Bluffs with hopes of leaving her past behind. She finds her fresh start in the small town, in her new home and new job, but also in the safe and passionate embrace of handsome deputy sheriff, Jim Warren.

But just when it seems as if Sadie's wish for a new life has been granted, secrets she meant to keep buried forever return to haunt her. Once again, she's scorned by the very town she has come to love—so Sadie must pin her hopes on Jim Warren's heart turning out to be the only home she'll ever need.

VANITY BLADE

Orphan daughter of a saloon singer, vivacious Mary Lousie Mackenzie grows up to be a famous singer herself, the beautiful gambling queen known as Vanity Blade. Leaving her home in Mississippi, Vanity travels a wayward path to Sacramento, where she rules her own gambling boat. Gamblers and con men barter in high stakes around her, but Vanity's heart remains back east, with her once carefree life and former love, Trance Holloway, a preacher's son.

Trying to reclaim a happiness she'd left behind long ago, Vanity returns to Mississippi to discover—and fight for—the love she thought she'd lost forever.